You'll Hear From Us

To my darling K.C.,
With love,
Mother

James Edward Hall

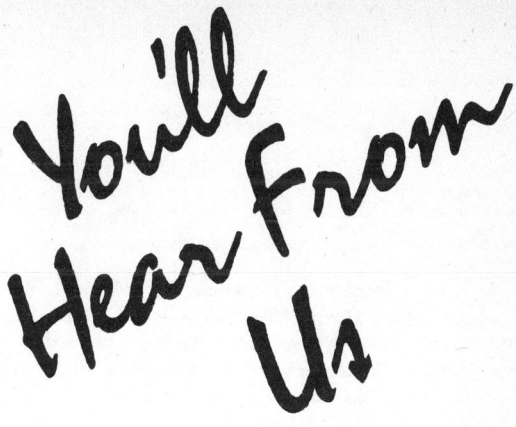

You'll Hear From Us

MARILYN COOLEY AND
JAMES EDWARD GUNN

St. Martin's Press
New York

DESIGN BY CLAUDIA CARLSON

Library of Congress Cataloging-in-Publication Data

Cooley, Marilyn H.
     You'll hear from us / Marilyn Cooley and James Edward Gunn.
        p.   cm.
     ISBN 0-312-03011-8
     I. Gunn, James Edward. II. Title.
PS3553.05645Y6   1989   813'.54—dc19   89-30083

First Edition

10 9 8 7 6 5 4 3 2 1

To Henri,
A most special person
and
Meredith Anne,
As beautiful inside as on the outside

ACKNOWLEDGMENT

Very special thanks to William H. Tyler, friend and colleague, who helped plan and plot the original story, who hewed to realism in the face of fantasy, and who proved himself a good critic. The trailblazing sessions when the three of us worked together were productive, stimulating, and even, upon occasion, great fun.

You'll
Hear From
Us

PROLOGUE

This was the third day of waiting. They were as idle, Hicks said, as a couple of department store dummies. They whiled away the time in or around the lobby of the hotel, trying to look inconspicuous, which was difficult because they were both well-built six-footers and good-looking enough to turn the heads of women and men alike. They dressed casually in slacks and open-necked T-shirts.

Braden, the blond one, checked his watch for the twelfth time since 4:45 P.M. "This is her last day in town. It's tonight or forget it."

Hicks slid far down in his chair, long legs stretched in front of him, and surveyed his Bally loafers. His skin was the color of light chocolate and his dark, curly hair was short, emphasizing the well-shaped skull. "Maybe she don't drink. Anybody think to check that out?"

"Sure she drinks. We saw her that first night."

"Yeah, I forgot. But all those people were with her. Maybe she don't drink by herself."

"She's got to eat, doesn't she? She'll come down to the dining room."

"What if she orders room service?"

"What if she goes out? What if she fasts? Don't start with the *ifs*, dammit."

"Okay, so she comes down to the dining room. What're we gonna do then? Put the stuff in her ice tea?"

"If we have to. Whatever's necessary. Three months we've been getting ready. We're not going to blow it now." Braden looked up as the elevator door opened. A man and a woman emerged. He slumped back. "There's no way I'm going back and say we blew it."

Hicks sat up abruptly, and his nostrils flared. "The boss wouldn't like that."

"You know what happened to Dooley."

Hicks squirmed in his chair. "I told you I didn't want to think about that."

The elevator opened again. He glanced up and then at Braden. They grinned at each other. "Bingo!"

She was taller than average, her chestnut-colored hair worn in a chignon. She had changed from the business suit she'd worn in the morning to off-duty slacks and a blouse. She was less curvaceous than the women Braden and Hicks were used to, and older. "Flat-assed old mama," Hicks complained. "Must be forty if she's a day."

Braden leered. "What you got against older women?"

To their relief she went to the bar instead of the dining room. They gave her time to order a drink before sauntering in. The cocktail hour wasn't in full swing yet, and they were able to sit at a table next to hers. She seemed engrossed in handwritten notes on a clipboard.

They had trouble attracting her attention. They mentioned Houston (where she lived) and an ad campaign (her profession) and even her high school (Lamar) without producing the flicker of an eyelash. Finally they had to resort to a direct approach.

Braden leaned over and put his hand on her table. "Excuse me, ma'am. My friend and I are having an argument and maybe you can settle it."

She looked up and blinked as her mind made the transition from her notes to the two young men next to her. Her eyes were a tawny brown with flecks of green.

"He says Continental is the only airline that flies from Kansas City direct to Houston. I say Delta does, too."

"You're correct." She smiled briefly and returned to her notes.

Hicks said, "But how can I be sure that *she* knows?"

She looked up. "I have a ticket for tomorrow on Delta nonstop to Houston."

2

"No kidding!" Braden sounded excited. "Do you live there or are you just going on a trip?"

"I live there."

"I've got a friend there. He's in an area called River Oaks."

"Then he must be well-off. That's the poshest part of town."

"He lives with his folks, and yeah, I guess they're well-off. We were fraternity brothers at Vanderbilt." He gave a fictitious name for his fictitious friend. "He's been wanting me to come down and visit but—" The barmaid passed between the two tables, forcing him to lean back. "Look, would you mind if we joined you? I mean, I don't want to intrude. You seem to be busy. But I'd like to hear something about Houston."

She looked at her notes. She had almost finished reviewing them and writing instructions to herself. "I don't mind. Please—" She didn't finish because the young men already were taking chairs at her table.

They introduced themselves as Ken Lane and Bob Power. She was Suzanne Hilbourne. They queried her about Houston and about herself, being careful to maintain a frank, open, youthful manner. When she finished her drink and prepared to move to the dining room, they pleaded with her to stay for one more drink, their treat. They said they were enjoying this too much for her to leave.

Finally she agreed. Somehow or other, Ken and Bob had gotten into an arm wrestling contest. Ken won and insisted that she wrestle the winner. Laughing at their silliness, she went along with it. She was facing Ken. Bob moved her drink in front of him, ostensibly to keep it from being knocked over.

Fifteen minutes later she began to feel ill. The room whirled and Suzanne leaned back, clutching the table.

They were immediately solicitous. Wasn't she well? What could they do?

Suzanne, leaning over the table now, said, "I'd better go to my room."

"We'll walk with you. You don't look too good."

That was her last memory of the evening.

Two hours later Braden telephoned a number in Houston. A man's voice answered. "Where you calling from?"

"The hotel. Room four-four-three."

"All over?"

"Done. Everything just like the boss said."

"You remembered the bottle?"

"It's where he said to put it."

"The note on the mirror?"

"Hicks is doing it now."

"Okay. Leave in a normal manner. Don't attract attention to yourselves."

"The stuff gives us plenty of time. She's not going to wake up till late tomorrow."

"Check in when you get here." The line went dead.

Braden and Hicks took a final look around the room and left. They hung a Do Not Disturb sign on the door.

She came to consciousness slowly, ache by ache, the sound of her own groaning loud in her ears. She didn't know where she was and for a moment felt completely lost, disoriented. Then she remembered. Kansas City. She was going home this morning. She half sat up to look at her wristwatch and fell back with a cry as pain slashed through her lower body.

Her fingers searched for the source of the pain, traveling across her body. Automatically she tried to push her gown out of the way, and found she was not wearing one. Why hadn't she put on her gown? Her hands moved across her navel, lower. She realized now that there was a fullness stretching her insides.

At the lips of her vagina she touched something hard and round. She tried to withdraw it, shoving her fingers far up inside herself to purchase a hold. It wouldn't move. For a moment she panicked. Twisting herself into an acrobat's position in spite of the pain, she tugged at the object. Then she fell back panting.

Mustn't panic. She took deep, slow breaths and forced herself to think although her brain flickered like a blinking television. She needed a doctor. The hotel would have one on call. Shifting her body gingerly, she inched toward the telephone on the nightstand.

She hadn't realized her mouth felt cottony until she tried to speak. Finally she summoned enough saliva to make herself understood. She told the operator she was ill and asked her to send a doctor up as soon as possible.

Suzanne went back to sleep after that and woke with a jerk. Raising her arm to look at her wristwatch, she found that she wasn't wearing it. She didn't usually take it off when she went to bed. Maybe one of the men—it was a measure of her confusion that only then did she realize the implication of the object in her body. She hadn't been alone last night. Somebody had done this to her. One of the young men? Good God, what had happened here?

The doctor was brisk, middle-aged, and reassuring. "I'm Dr. Hooks, Mrs. Hilbourne. You look as if you'd had a little trouble."

"I've been trying to remember what happened. I think I must have been drugged. There were two men—" She glanced self-consciously at the hotel security guard who had accompanied the doctor to her room.

The guard said, "That's all I need to know at this point. I'll be outside, Doctor."

As soon as he was gone, Suzanne said, "There's something inside my vagina. I can't get it out. I think it's glass."

"All right, let's have a look." He lowered the sheet by stages. "Bend your knees. Um, yes, they did a thorough job on this one."

"I tried to get it out but—"

"A suction is formed so it can't be withdrawn manually. I wish I'd known about this before I came, but we can handle it." He went to the phone, called the desk and identified himself. "I'm going to need a drill and a prismatic one-thirty-second of an inch bit. I expect your maintenance people will have one. Send it up as soon as possible." He gave the room number, hung up, and returned to the examination.

"You say you think you were drugged?" He turned on a small flashlight. "Look at the light, please."

"I think I must have been. I can't remember anything

after leaving the bar and that was early, about five-thirty. By the way, what time is it? I couldn't find my watch."

"Three-thirty."

"In the afternoon? I've missed my plane."

"That's the least of your worries just now. Put out your tongue."

She fretted about the missed plane as he tested the glands below her ears. She had been scheduled to be back in Houston by 10 A.M. She'd had a business lunch. Never in the five years she had been at the agency had she missed an appointment.

There was a knock and the doctor went to the door. He returned with a drill and bit. "Now we're in business. Just bend your knees again, please. I'm going to drill a little hole in the bottom of the bottle to release the suction."

She held her breath as he positioned the drill. There was a grinding sound. A moment later she felt the object sliding out of her body, and the subsequent blessed release of pressure. She lay back, breathing deeply, as the doctor held up a Coke bottle. He replaced the sheet and dropped the bottle on the floor.

"Do you know who did this to you?"

"No. Well, yes, I suppose it must have been . . ." She told him about the two men, her sudden dizziness and the void in her memory.

He said, "The second drink must have held a drug, and a potent one to act so quickly. You're lucky you don't feel worse than you do. I'm going to give you some tablets that should help." He brought a glass of water. "Drink the whole glass." As she drank, he asked, "Were you robbed?"

She followed his glance around the room. Her suitcase had been turned upside down and her clothing flung around the room. Her purse lay on the floor. The clothes in the closet had been ripped off the hangers. Tears suddenly blurred her eyes.

"I don't know. It looks like it."

He picked up her purse and held up an empty billfold. "Did you have credit cards?"

She nodded. He said, "I don't see them here. You'll want to report this to the police. And when you feel like it, say in the morning, you'd better come down to my office for a pelvic examination."

"But I've got to go home."

"Then have one there. Please have your doctor call me after he's examined you. I suspect that you've been raped and I want to be assured that all precautions have been taken to prevent your contracting a venereal disease."

"Venereal disease. My God, you don't think—"

"I don't think anything. I just want to take precautionary measures. And unless you've had a hysterectomy, I'd suggest a D and C to avoid the possibility of a pregnancy."

When he had gone, the guard returned. She repeated her story to him.

"We're going to have to get the police in, Mrs. Hilbourne."

She was so weary. "Can't it wait till tomorrow?"

"No, ma'am." He dialed, and waited with her until two officers arrived. Again she went through the story, with the officers taping it. Finally it was over and they were gone.

She lay still, thinking of what the doctor had said. My God, there was a possibility that she had contracted AIDS. It was too much for her to cope with at the moment. She dragged herself out of bed and went to the bathroom. Scrawled on the mirror with lipstick was the message "You'll hear from us."

1 Lt. Anthony MacIver, Homicide Division, Houston Police Department, was surprised and not particularly pleased on Monday morning to find Suzanne Hilbourne's name on his callback list. Surprised because he hadn't seen Suzanne in years. Not particularly pleased because it was his experience that when an old friend called it meant that something unpleasant had happened to him or her and he or she needed police help. He made two quick, urgent calls and then dialed Suzanne's office.

He went through a receptionist and a secretary before he got her on the line. Then he said, "Is this little Suzanne Smith who was captain of the debate team at Lamar High?"

"And is this Tony MacIver who was captain of the football team at Lamar High? How are you, Tony? It's good to hear your voice."

"I'm fine. How about you?" That was the opening for her to explain her problem. He'd bet that either some officer had been impolite to her while writing a ticket or she had a child on drugs.

She answered slowly, and the lilt had gone out of her voice. "I had some problems last week. I was in Kansas City—it's a long story. I wondered if I could talk with you about it."

"Sure. Anytime."

"How about lunch?"

He checked his calendar. "That's good. I've got to be at the courthouse by two, but anytime before that."

They made an appointment to meet at 11:45 at the Four

Seasons Hotel. Tony hung up and leaned back in his chair. Suzanne Smith: tallish, good legs, coppery hair, not too quick to smile, a definite mind of her own, an A student. He had been in love with her during his senior year, painfully in love, because she was going steady with somebody else. In spite of her intelligence, she'd had trouble in chemistry, one of Tony's stronger subjects. He had coached her, and she had returned the favor in English class, where he'd had trouble with grammar.

"No, Tony, that's a prepositional phrase. 'By' is a preposition," she used to say. And then, with exasperation, "There are only ninety-some prepositions in the whole language. Why don't you just memorize them?"

"I don't want a bunch of tiny little words messing up my brain."

"Your brain's already messed up. Look, I'll show you how to diagram a prepositional phrase."

After high school they had slowly drifted apart. MacIver tried to remember when he had last seen Suzanne. It must have been at their fifteenth high school reunion ten years ago. She had been married, with a child of five; he remembered because his son had been a year younger. He wondered what had happened to her in Kansas City that she needed to talk to a police officer about.

When he walked into the hotel lobby she was sitting on a couch and watching the door. He felt a slight twinge in the pit of his stomach, like a moment of anxiety before a first date. He smiled to himself, thinking it had been a long time since he had felt that way. She stood quickly and came to greet him. Better-looking now than she had been in high school, she moved with an air of poise and assurance. She wore a gray-green silk suit, gray pumps, and sunglasses. When she got closer, he noted the purplish, swollen bruise on her left jaw. They embraced, and he held her close for a couple of extra seconds. Then he stepped back for a second look.

"Hey, you're not skinny anymore."

"That's the truth." She patted one hip ruefully.

"You look great," he said, meaning it.

"So do you." She reached up and brushed the hair at his temple. "But your lovely black hair has a gray streak."

MacIver touched the offending strip, which ran from his temple to the crown of his head. "It happened right after I made lieutenant. I guess it was all that studying."

"I like it. Your eyes are as blue as ever. How did a guy named Anthony get Siamese cat blue eyes, anyway?"

"From me Scots father." He put one finger on the bruise on her jaw. "That looks painful."

Her smile vanished, and she shrank ever so slightly from his touch. "You should see my eyes."

So that's why she was wearing the sunglasses. "What happened, you get mugged?"

"Not exactly. I'll tell you about it when we sit down." There was the hint of a quaver in her voice.

"Right." He took her arm, and held it as they moved toward the cocktail lounge. To help her relax, he asked, "What kind of agency are you with? I didn't get the name when I called."

"Dutton and Grimes Advertising. I'm an account executive."

"That sounds important."

"I don't know about important. It's hectic and stimulating and challenging. I like it."

MacIver asked for a booth in the corner, where they would have some privacy. They placed drink orders, white wine for her, iced tea for him, and he said, "What were you doing in Kansas City?"

"I was there on business, working on one of our accounts. Three days." The fingers of her right hand drummed on the edge of the table as she talked. "I was busy with clients practically twenty-four hours a day until the last night. Finally everything was done and I wanted to unwind."

He nodded. The drinks came and she sipped the wine. "It isn't an easy story to tell, Tony. The whole thing sounds so bad."

"I hear a lot of bad stories."

"But a stranger would have thought I led them on, the boys, I mean." Her fingers were drumming again. "It wasn't that way at all."

He put his hand over the drumming fingers. "Try to relax, Suzanne. This is just old Tony you're talking to."

She withdrew her hand, took a tissue out of her purse, and dabbed her eyes beneath the glasses. "Sorry. I can't seem to handle sympathy."

"Tell you what." MacIver took a notebook and pen out of his coat. "You write down what happened. I'll go off and make a couple of phone calls." It was standard police procedure for situations where details of the crime were embarrassing to the victim. He had thought she might prefer to talk since they were old friends, but maybe that was making it harder.

He spent ten minutes on the telephone, long enough for her to get something down on paper. When he returned she was still writing, but she stopped almost immediately. "That's mostly it. I can tell you the rest."

Her anger showed in her writing, in the slash of the *t* crossings and the heaviness of the down-slanting letters. She had used the ballpoint pen like a sword, jabbing it so hard in places that it had torn through two sheets. As MacIver read, he understood her rage, and he felt angry, too, by the time he finished the account. He resisted an urge to reach out to her, to sympathize. What she needed now was MacIver the police lieutenant, not Tony the friend.

He couldn't resist venting some of his own wrath. "Goddam animals! I hope I'm the one who arrests those two." He took a deep breath, striving for control. "You reported this to the police in Kansas City?"

"Yes, but I haven't heard from them. I thought maybe I should check to see if something is being done."

"If they'd found the guys they would have contacted you, but we can get hold of them and see what's happening. Have you canceled your credit cards?"

"I did that before I left Kansas City."

"Good. And you can give a good description of the guys?"

Suzanne said grimly, "Down to the mole on the blond one's chin."

"That will help. We may pick them up fast. If we don't—"

"They could do this to somebody else, couldn't they? That's one reason I thought I should pursue it."

That hadn't been what MacIver was going to say, but he decided to leave it for the moment. Instead he signaled the waiter and they placed their orders. He got the special, blackened red snapper. Suzanne ordered veal picata. When the waiter left, she said, "You know everything now, so let's talk about something else. You have a child, as I recall." Her voice was falsely bright, but MacIver went along with the effort.

"Yes, Jarratt. He's fourteen. Constance and I divorced eight months ago."

"It's still raw then."

"Not really," MacIver said, believing he meant it. "I'm getting along all right and she seems to be, too."

"The boy is with her?"

He frowned as he nodded. He had wanted custody but so had Constance, and the judge had decided in her favor. He said, "You have a daughter, don't you?"

She nodded. "Carol. She's fifteen. It's not the best age in the world, but I hear it gets better. Actually she's a joy, even at fifteen. I'm divorced, too, but it's been three years."

Their salads came, and MacIver worked in a question he'd been wanting to ask. "You've seen a doctor since you were attacked?"

Her salad fork waved in midair. "Yes. Yes, I have. He did a D and C."

He said carefully, "They tested for—everything?"

She turned her face away from him. "Everything they could. I have to go back in six weeks for the last test."

MacIver knew that would be the test for AIDS. The virus couldn't be traced until six weeks after contraction. He said, "I'm sorry to bring all that up. I just wanted to make sure the doctors had taken care of everything." She had laid down her fork and he took her hand. "I'm sure you're all right. The way you describe those guys, they shouldn't be sick."

She turned to him eagerly. "That's what I thought, too. They looked the picture of health."

"I wouldn't worry about it, then." He knew that was worthless advice, but he had to say something.

She squeezed his hand, released her own, and picked up her fork again. "I'm supposed to go to a therapy group, too."

"Do it. It will help."

"Oh, Tony, one thing I forgot. They left a message on the mirror in the bathroom. It said, 'You'll hear from us.'"

"Yeah," he said flatly. "I was afraid of that. You'd better prepare yourself for an extortion attempt."

Indignant, she exclaimed, "How can they extort anything from me? I'm the victim."

He hesitated before answering. She had enough problems, and he hated to add another one. On the other hand, he didn't want her to be shocked and horrified if it did happen. He said, "You don't know what happened while you were unconscious, at least not all of it." She frowned, obviously uncomprehending. He explained: "They may have taken photographs."

"Oh." She stared past him into the distance, seeing a back alley full of obscene possibilities.

2 At the courthouse, MacIver ran up the stairs to the second floor. A junior lawyer from the district attorney's office was waiting outside the double doors to the courtroom. "Jesus, Lieutenant, where've you been? The trial starts in three minutes."

"Yeah, I know. I decided to come early."

The attorney gave him a sour look. "Go on in. They're waiting for you."

Inside, MacIver nodded to Jay Hudson, the assistant district attorney leading the state's case, and took a seat two rows behind him. Leonard Odetts, the defendant, looked around and gave MacIver a cocky grin. MacIver lifted a negligent index finger in return.

He had arrested Odetts so many times that they had developed a strange sort of relationship, a kind of competitiveness. The last time MacIver picked him up, Odetts had exclaimed, "Dammit, Loot, no matter what I do, you're a step ahead." He had even adopted the police officers' way of abbreviating *lieutenant*.

MacIver had said, "That's because I'm the good guy."

"The hell it is. I didn't make any mistakes on this last job. I've learned a thing or two the past few years. There's no way you could tie this job to me."

"What job is that, Lennie?"

"Killing that woman and her kid in the Seven-Eleven. That's what you're taking me in for, ain't it?"

Odetts wasn't the smartest guy in the world. MacIver said, "You got it."

15

"I didn't do it."

"Then what job are *you* talking about?"

Odetts clammed up at that point. He was right, as a matter of fact. He hadn't made any mistakes on the job unless it was a mistake to have a brother-in-law who hated his guts and had tipped the police.

Leonard had been in trouble continually since he was eleven, in reform schools three times and prison twice. Now, at thirty-three, he had fulfilled his youthful promise by killing. MacIver thought it would be a favor to the public to get him off the streets before he slaughtered more citizens.

At two the judge entered and the trial resumed. MacIver was scheduled to testify about the tape he had recorded the day he arrested the defendant. It was the state's primary evidence, and MacIver felt confident about it. He had been careful to do everything he was legally supposed to do, including requesting Odetts's permission before turning on the recorder. The man had then made admissions that should result in a death sentence.

The tape was introduced into evidence, and the jury was ordered from the room while it played. About three quarters of the way through, just after Odetts had identified himself as the killer, MacIver realized that something was wrong. Both the defense and state attorneys were sitting as straight as hound dogs who'd just picked up the scent of rabbit. The judge interrupted the tape. "Bailiff, replay the tape from the place where the defendant asks if he can make a phone call."

MacIver had been questioning Odetts. His own voice, extra gravelly on the tape, said, "What time did you get to the Seven-Eleven store, Leonard?"

Odetts said, whining, "I don't remember. I need time to think. Look, can I call my wife?"

After a hesitation, MacIver's voice said, "Yeah, I guess so. Dial nine for outside. Don't take too long."

The tape recorded the door closing as MacIver went outside to give Odetts privacy. The judge said, "Stop there. Lieutenant MacIver."

MacIver stood up. "Yessir."

"Did you leave the room at that time?"

"Yessir."

"But you left the tape recorder running?"

"Yessir. I'd already asked Odetts's permission to make the recording."

"Yes, yes, we heard that at the beginning of the tape." He scowled at MacIver a moment. "All right, play the rest."

Odetts's voice lowered as he talked to his wife, but the tape still picked up the conversation. "Listen close. I don't have much time." Her response could not be heard. Odetts said, "Go outside to the chimley to that door you open to take out the ashes. Inside there you'll find my gun. It's wrapped up in plastic. Take it out, and after dark, drive down to the bayou and toss it. Make sure it goes into the water." After a pause, he said harshly, "If you gotta know, that's the piece I killed the gook and her kid with. It could get me dead. You got that? Okay then, just do what I tell you." He hung up. There was a minute of silence. The defense attorney wore the edge of a smile. Hudson turned to MacIver and seemed about to speak. Then the tape resumed with a knock on the door. MacIver said, "Finished your call? Okay, Leonard, back to the Seven-Eleven."

Odetts began again to deny that he had been anywhere near the convenience store the night of the robbery and killings. The tape ended, and the judge said, "That's all?"

Hudson said, "Yessir. After listening to the tape, Lieutenant MacIver drove to Odetts's house and found the thirty-eight taped under the car. Mrs. Odetts was preparing to drive away and dispose of it."

"Mr. Hudson, you know this confession is inadmissible."

"Sir, we have the gun. Odetts's fingerprints are on it. The bullets fit those in the bodies of the victims."

"That's irrelevant, Mr. Hudson. The taped information that led to finding the gun was acquired while the interrogating officer was out of the room. It is illegal to leave a tape recorder running while the suspect makes a private telephone call unless his permission is specifically requested and granted."

MacIver mumbled "Oh shit!" and slid down in his seat. There went the case and there went Odetts. Just when the hell had the Supreme Court ruled on that law?

The proceedings were over within minutes. Case dismissed. Odetts walked. He waved cheerily to MacIver as he left. MacIver muttered "Asshole," and waved back.

MacIver joined the state's attorney outside the courtroom. "Sorry, Hudson. I never heard of that ruling."

"It's about six months old. Probably up on your bulletin board."

"Hell, some of those bulletins are so old they look like the Dead Sea Scrolls."

Hudson said, "I don't know how the hell I missed that. I listened to the whole tape. At least, I thought I did. Dammit, we had a good case, Mac, except for that one little detail."

MacIver nodded, thinking that would be cold comfort for the family of the next person Odetts killed. He didn't bother saying it. Hudson knew it, too. "I guess I'd better go back and read the bulletin board."

"And I'd better try to squeeze some more time out of the day so I get all my work done." Hudson slapped him on the back. "Don't take it too hard, Mac. When people stop making mistakes, they stop being people."

"I don't think I've got to worry about that." MacIver drove back to the station and wondered how long it would be before he arrested Odetts again. He had no doubt that Leonard would be out robbing and pillaging within the month, maybe the week.

In his office he found the report from Kansas City on Suzanne's attack on the desk of Joe (Rod) Rodriguez, Homicide sergeant. There wasn't much in the report that Suzanne hadn't already told him. "Anything new on this, Sarge?"

"Nosir, nothing's come in. I can check."

"Yeah, do that. We're going to track the case from here. Have you had any other reports of this kind of thing?"

"Haven't had one in six or seven months, and that was a guy from Michigan staying out at a hotel on the Loop. Never had one where a lady was the mark."

"Let's hope it doesn't catch on. You're contacting Kansas City again?"

"As soon as I can get the computer."

"Let me know when you hear."

Before he went home that evening, MacIver made the

trek out to Sharpstown to pick up his cat. Constance had gotten sole custody of their son (he could visit his father every other weekend), but the judge had awarded joint custody of the Burmese. MacIver rang the front doorbell and waited. Constance was a long time coming to the door. He must have gotten her out of the tub, because she was wearing a pink terry cloth robe and had a towel around her head. He imagined the body under the robe, and felt a sudden urge to take her in his arms, slip the robe back, and—their eyes met. He could see that she knew what he was thinking. They had always read each other's moods well. A year ago, he would have done it. Now there was an invisible barrier between them. He forced himself to turn away.

She asked, "Why didn't you use your key?"

"I put it someplace and I can't find it."

"I waited an hour for you and finally gave up and got in the bath and the next minute ri-ing!"

"Sorry." MacIver kept his head turned away from her. He didn't want to look at her in the pink robe and have his imagination start up again. "Where's Jarratt?"

"Still at school."

"Football practice?"

"No, not this evening."

A certain nuance in her voice caught his attention. "What's he doing, then?"

"He had an appointment."

"With whom?"

"Ms. Sandos."

"And who's—" Suddenly MacIver felt the familiar annoyance that Constance was able to raise in him. He was almost relieved. Better annoyance than yearning. He snapped, "For God's sake, Constance, do I have to drag every word out of you? This sounds like an interrogation."

She lit a cigarette with quick, angry movements. "I'd just as soon you didn't know about it, frankly. You're just going to get upset and make a big stink."

He took a deep breath and tried to keep his temper in check. "If it's something that deserves what you call a big stink, I may choose to make one. I'm sure as hell going to make one if you don't tell me what's going on."

"I love it when you use that tone. It makes me remember why I left you."

MacIver clenched his teeth to keep from returning the insult.

"Okay, if you must know, Ms. Sandos is a counselor. The school thinks Jarratt should see a counselor."

"Why?"

"Oh, the usual things. His grades have dropped, he's got a bad attitude. It's not unusual for a fourteen-year-old whose parents have split up."

"How could his grades drop? School has just started."

"Apparently he's not turning in his papers. I guess he's not bothering to do anything. One of the teachers said he spent his time in class either drawing or staring out the window."

MacIver paced across the room and back. "I guess I'd better have a talk with him."

"Oh hell, I knew you were going to say that. Would you just leave him alone? Every time you have one of your talks with him, everything gets worse."

"What's that supposed to mean?"

"Just what I said."

They glared at each other and the back door opened. A moment later Jarratt walked in. He saw his father and his eyes flew wide, only for an instant, but a telltale one. "Oh, hi." He dropped his books on the table and went back to the kitchen.

"Hello, son. Your mother tells me you've been to see a counselor."

"I didn't go." Jarratt snapped on the television in the kitchen and yelled over it, "Hey, are we out of peanut butter?"

Constance called, "That's possible. If you don't tell me when you finish something, I don't know to replace it."

The refrigerator door banged and he mumbled something. MacIver went to the kitchen. "You didn't go see the counselor?"

"Nope. Shit! We've got half a glass of milk." He shouted, "We're out of milk, Mom."

MacIver said, "Jarratt, I'm trying to talk to you."

20

"Yeah. Yessir. It's just that I'm hungry." Avoiding his father's eyes, he opened the refrigerator again, got out margarine, and began spreading it on a piece of wheat bread.

MacIver's control was beginning to slip. "When you've eaten that bread, I'd like to talk with you."

Jarratt took a bite and threw the bread onto the kitchen counter. "I can't eat with somebody staring at me."

"Good. You can eat later. Why didn't you see the counselor?"

Jarratt stared at the television. The show was an old sitcom with a laugh track. "I went in and waited. I waited twenty minutes. She was busy with somebody else. So I left. I don't want to go to a shrink anyway."

"She's not a shrink." Constance stood in the doorway. "She's just the school counselor."

"Same thing."

MacIver said, "You haven't been doing your schoolwork?"

"It's all review from last year. I already know it."

"But if you don't do the work, you get Fs, right?"

"I guess so."

MacIver snapped, "Look at me when you talk to me!"

Jarratt turned and eyed him sullenly. "Yessir!"

"You know if you flunk you won't be able to play football."

"I'm not playing football anyway."

"You didn't go out for the team this year?"

"Nope."

"Why not?"

"Didn't want to."

MacIver turned to Constance. "Why didn't you tell me?"

"Because I knew you'd make a big—"

He cut her off. "Are you going out for basketball?"

"Nope."

MacIver felt anger like a heat blast. "That's it, huh? You're pissed off so you're going to sit around and do nothing all year. That's really clever, kid. Smart. You're going to flunk your courses and have to repeat the year and you think you're getting even with somebody, your mother and me, I guess. Or is it just me?"

Jarratt stared at the TV, his jaw set and unrelenting. MacIver's voice dropped to almost a whisper. "Answer me."

Jarratt looked uneasy. "I guess so. Whatever you say."

MacIver hadn't known he was going to do it until it was already done. He had snapped off the television and was holding Jarratt in front of him, grasping his shoulders. Constance shrieked something. MacIver said softly, "I don't want smartass answers and I don't want a smartass attitude. When you can carry on a decent conversation, we'll talk again." He shoved Jarratt backward into the chair, pushed past Constance, and strode out of the house.

Outside he made a tight U-turn and headed for the freeway and home. He spent the next five minutes telling himself that he had done the right thing. He would not put up with insolence from his son. The sooner Jarratt realized that, the better. He wouldn't have him behaving like some street punk. He spent the five minutes after that telling himself that he'd behaved like the bullies he despised, that he couldn't expect Jarratt to respect him when he resorted to force to show his authority. The boy was going through a difficult time and the least MacIver could do was be patient with him. He resolved to telephone and apologize as soon as he reached home. Then he remembered that in his furor he'd forgotten the cat, which meant he'd have to go back or go out again tomorrow. He decided on tomorrow. And then he realized that he was hungry and there was nothing to eat at home. Neilsen's Delicatessen was nearby, and a turkey on white sounded good. He took the next exit and headed for the deli.

He left the deli, eagerly anticipating dinner. The next second he was lying facedown on the sidewalk. A bullet had just roared past his ear and slammed into the brick building.

3 A second bullet crashed into the plate glass window, shattering it. MacIver rolled toward the nearest cover, his station wagon, which was parked facing the curb. He had his Colt .45 out by the time he reached the tire. Peering cautiously around the fender, he sighted the source of the shots, a Trans Am stopped on the street slightly ahead of and at right angles to his car. A third shot richocheted off the curb beside him.

MacIver reached out and fired three quick rounds. The first struck the right-hand door of the Trans Am. The second two went through the open window and hit the windshield glass. He ducked back behind the tire and lay flat, aiming beneath his car at the Trans Am's tires. At the exact moment he fired, the Trans Am took off with a last couple of random shots. MacIver heard glass break somewhere on his car. He sprang up, trying to stay under cover and still see the Trans Am's license plate. It was smeared with mud. The Trans Am ran the red light at the corner and roared down Drexel.

MacIver ran around his car and got in. It was the right rear window that had broken in the last volley. He got the wagon going, whipped out, and headed after the Trans Am, at the same time radioing Dispatch. "Officer fired at from Trans Am, dark blue, four or five years old. Headed south on Drexel toward Alabama. Rear license covered with mud. Request a Fox unit."

He caught a red light at Westheimer and had to stop. He had neither a top light nor a siren, and he couldn't get across the intersection in the heavy evening traffic. How the Trans Am had managed it, he didn't know.

The light turned green and he gunned forward. He couldn't see them ahead so he took a chance and turned left on Alabama. At the next light he turned right and headed for the freeway. If he were running away, that's where he'd go, try to get to the freeway to avoid traffic lights and stop signs.

Over the sound of his motor and the radio, he heard the welcome *whop whop* of a helicopter. A blue Hughes 500 police chopper pulled a tight turn over the freeway and radioed that 93 Fox was on the scene. At the same time a siren whined and a blue and white took the corner at Richmond on two wheels, also headed for the freeway. He radioed to the unit that he was following. As the two of them neared the freeway, a second blue and white approached from the opposite direction. MacIver radioed to one car to take the freeway outbound, the other inbound. He continued under the freeway, made a U-turn, and headed back the way he had come. He would cruise the side streets in case the Trans Am had gone to ground somewhere.

He drove slowly, taking time to look both right and left, paying special attention to alleyways and parking garages. The area was mostly commercial, smallish office buildings and businesses. Hot air poured into the back of the wagon through the broken window. If his shirt weren't already wet with sweat when he got in, it would be now. It pissed him off that his window had been broken. He ran into a dead end and had to turn around.

If he had been driving that Trans Am, and hadn't gotten on the freeway, he'd want to avoid traffic by heading toward town at this time of day.

The other possibility was that the Trans Am's driver had a safe location in this neighborhood. MacIver turned off the street to circle through an underground parking garage. It was empty.

The blue and whites were reporting negative contact. The Fox called ditto. The outbound unit was having a hard time getting through traffic despite its lights and siren. Two lanes were at a complete stop; the unit was progressing on the emergency shoulder. The inbound car had reached a split in the freeway and opted for the downtown route. It was making good time but hadn't spotted the Trans Am.

After half an hour MacIver gave up the search and radioed to the other vehicles to end the chase. He returned to the delicatessen, where two patrolmen were assessing the damage and trying to keep back the crowd that had quickly gathered. The Vietnamese woman who managed the deli and her teenage assistant were loudly lamenting the broken window in their own language. MacIver identified himself to the young officers and noticed them eyeing his suit. He looked down and found that he was smeared with grime from rolling on the sidewalk. Worse than that, several threads on the lapels of his jacket had snagged. Damn, this had been his only decent lightweight suit.

"Have you recovered any of the bullets?"

"We got two, but they're both smashed. The one that went through the window was inside a bag of potato chips. We dug the other one out of the brick."

MacIver looked at the bullets and agreed that they were too damaged to be of any use in identifying the weapon they had come from. There wasn't much for him to do, so he headed home. As he drove, he wondered who the hell wanted him dead.

He pulled into his parking space under the high-rise apartment building where he lived and scanned the garage. He couldn't see anything unusual. He got out of the wagon, walked rapidly to the garage elevator, and punched the button for the fourteenth floor. He didn't relax until he was inside his condo.

Actually it wasn't his. It belonged to his cousin, a hydraulic engineer who, fortunately for MacIver, had been preparing to go to South America on a project when MacIver and Constance separated. The cousin had suggested that Mac move in and keep an eye on the place for him; MacIver had accepted gratefully. It was his first experience with luxury living, and still, after almost a year, he felt that he'd wandered into the wrong place. He made full use of the amenities, however, which included a pool, exercise equipment, a sauna, and a steam room. He had lost eight pounds, and three inches around his waist, since moving in. He stripped off his sweat-soaked clothes, showered, and called

Dispatch for an update on the chase. The Trans Am had not been sighted. He mixed a drink, settled into the recliner, lit a cigarette, and closed his eyes.

He wanted to re-create the scene from the moment of the first shot. Things had happened too rapidly for him to notice everything at the time, but he had learned to relive a scene and bring to mind details that he had overlooked in the heat of battle. These "mind scenes" were always in slow motion and living color.

He remembered the rush of the bullet past his ear and his instinctive drop to the sidewalk. As his mind replayed the scene, he saw the right window of the Trans Am rolled all the way down and a figure leaning out, arm extended, holding a handgun. Flame spurted from the barrel of the weapon as MacIver ducked back under cover. He stopped the action and replayed the scene, searching for the face above the barrel. He got a vague impression of part of the head, brown hair, but he could see no features. Either they had been in shadow or his vision had concentrated so completely on the weapon that he hadn't seen the face. He went through it again, concentrating on the gun. A big one, long barrel, might have been a Colt revolver but he wasn't sure.

Continuing the replay, he reviewed everything that had happened until the Trans Am had driven off and he had felt safe enough to stand. By that time he could see nothing but the rear of the car with its mud-smeared license plate. No, wait. Something else. Something funny about the trunk. He played it through again. A dent in the trunk, a big triangular one right of center. Then the vehicle careened out of sight. He opened his eyes, said "Shit," and lit another cigarette.

So he knew something about the vehicle but nothing about the people who had been shooting at him. He tried to think of somebody who might want him out of the way. He wasn't working on any cases at the moment where he was a threat to anyone, at least not that he knew of. Somebody with a grudge from the past? He made a mental note to run a check on anybody who had gotten out of jail recently. His latest case had gone the crook's way.

Something else that bothered him was the rapidity with which the vehicle had disappeared. He'd been no more than

26

ninety seconds behind it. The Fox unit had been on the scene within five minutes, as had two patrol cars. Still, none of those guys had spotted the Trans Am. That meant, Mac-Iver guessed, that somewhere within a two-mile radius a garage door had been open and waiting for the crooks.

It had been a setup then, not a case of somebody happening to see him and cutting loose with a few rounds. It had been planned and prearranged. They had followed him; otherwise they couldn't have known he was going to be at the deli, because he hadn't known himself until minutes before. They would have had no reason to prearrange a safe place near the deli, but Neilsen's wasn't far from his condo, no more than a five-minute drive in light traffic. So the safe place could have been picked because it was near his home. MacIver went over the logic of it and decided it had to be that way.

That gave him the how, but it didn't help with the who. An image of Leonard Odetts flashed into his mind. This latest time he'd arrested the crook, MacIver had told him, "Lennie, you just won't learn, will you? You're the same punk now that you were the first time I arrested you, only this time you fucked up."

It made no sense that Odetts should want to kill him. The man should be sending him a bouquet. If it wasn't for Mac-Iver's stupid legal mistake, Odetts wouldn't be walking around free. Still, Leonard might have some fancied grievance, and he'd be cocky now after getting away literally with murder.

MacIver stood, paced to the east window, and stared at the line of buildings sparkling against the dark sky, all topped by a canopy of purple, a reflection of the lights against the smog. The beam from the Transco Tower arched across the horizon. Maybe it had been Odetts. Maybe it had been somebody else after him for some reason that he didn't know about. He wondered if they'd try again. It wasn't a cheery thought. He finished his drink and went to the kitchen to get his sandwich.

Then he realized that he didn't have it. He must have lost it when he'd dropped to the sidewalk. Hell, that left him with nothing to eat. He looked in the pantry; not even a can of tuna. Finally he thought of peanut butter. He got it out of the cabinet, and that made him think of Jarratt. He left the peanut butter on the counter and went to the telephone.

Jarratt answered. MacIver said, "Hello, son."

"Oh, hi." Jarratt sounded wary.

"I want to apologize for the way I acted this evening. I was a real jerk."

"Gee, that's okay." Jarratt sounded more embarrassed than surprised.

"Not okay. I won't do that again."

"Hey, no big deal. I was kind of a jerk myself."

"We'll work it out, buddy."

"Yessir."

MacIver wanted to say something else but he couldn't think of anything, so he said, "Well, good night, son."

"Good night." Jarratt hung up quickly.

MacIver whistled softly through his teeth as he went back to make a peanut butter sandwich.

The next morning he drove to work early, noting points of interest along the way. On his right was Archie's, a restaurant much frequented by café society. Police suspected, but could not prove, that years before in Detroit Archie had carried out a contract to gun down a prominent crime figure. His payment for the hit had enabled him to buy the restaurant. A few blocks later, MacIver passed the Corral Club, notorious for the illegal deals hatched there each night. It was a favorite of undercover officers. Next was a warehouse owned by the Baron, former pimp and murderer. MacIver sometimes speculated on just which illegalities the crook was involved with these days. Humming as he turned onto the freeway, he wondered what other people thought about as they drove to town.

In the office, he called the contract glass company used to replace the windows in undercover cars, and looked through his In box. Nothing new had come in on the people who had shot at him. He ran a check on recently released crooks; none of his had gotten out in the past two months. No help there.

He got out his file on Odetts and called the number listed in it. It had been disconnected. Next he called Odetts's brother-in-law, the one who had tipped the police about the killings. The brother-in-law didn't even know that Odetts had been freed, and wasn't happy to hear it. "Hell, you guys could've let me know. For all I know, he'll be coming after me." MacIver could see his point. He apologized and promised to relay any information he got about Odetts. Then he called a couple of other people and asked them to let him know anything they heard about Leonard. After that he went through the computer printouts looking for an update from Kansas City. It had come in early this morning.

The security people at the hotel in Kansas City remembered the two men in question and verified Suzanne's description. They had registered as Ken Lane and Bob Power three days before the assault on Suzanne. Wednesday, the night of the assault, they had checked out at eight and taken a taxi to an unknown destination. As far as security knew, they had met nobody at the hotel during their stay. A barmaid, however, reported that the pair had been talking with a woman in the bar Wednesday evening and had left with her. She had not noticed if the woman seemed ill. No phone calls had been charged to the men's bill, but a long-distance call to Houston had been placed at 7:50 P.M. Wednesday from Hilbourne's room. That surprised MacIver. Suzanne would have been in no condition at that hour to call anybody. It must have been one of the men. That, or it was the hotel's mistake. It had been placed directly, and the number was listed. MacIver went back to his office and called Suzanne.

She wished him good-morning. "I was just on my way to work."

"This will just take a minute. We got some information back from Kansas City." He told her about the phone call. "Did you call Houston that evening?"

"No. I couldn't have called anybody at seven-fifty."

"Did you call Houston at all?"

"Yes, I called my daughter every morning about seven and I called the office a couple of times in the afternoon."

"I'll ask the KCPD to verify the time with the hotel, but if this is accurate, the two guys must have made the call."

"I wonder why."

"So do I. Okay, that's all I needed. Go to work."

29

MacIver hurried back to the computer before anybody else could get on it and sent a request to Kansas City to verify the time of the telephone call with the hotel. The answer came back almost immediately. The time was correct.

MacIver called Rodriguez, and told him the information from Kansas City. "Track this number down, will you?" He read the phone number.

Back in his office, he drew a question mark beside the phone call. Suzanne would have been in a drugged sleep at 7:50. The men would have been eager to leave, yet they had taken time to make a phone call. Interesting. And why from her room? Why not from their own? That was simple malice, he guessed. They liked the thought of their victim paying for their long-distance call.

A couple of minutes later, Rod appeared in the office carrying the special directory from the telephone company that showed the location of all pay telephones. "It's a pay phone, located at the intersection of Westheimer and Voss."

"A pay phone?" MacIver frowned. "Now why would they call a pay phone?"

"To keep us from getting a phone number that would mean something?"

MacIver frowned harder. "That shows a high level of sophistication, Sarge. Maybe there's some mistake. You'd better drive out there and verify that number."

When the sergeant had gone, MacIver telephoned Constance. She was preparing to leave for work. "I'm rushing, Tony."

"I just wanted to know how Jarratt was this morning."

"Quiet but no more so than usual."

"Did you talk about his going to the counselor?"

"No. I thought enough had already been said about that." Meaning MacIver had given him a hard time.

"Yeah. I thought I'd come out and get the cat this evening. If Jarratt's there, maybe I can talk to him." The silence on the line was ominous, and he added, "Not have a talk with him; just talk to him."

"That's up to him, isn't it? Listen, I've got to run."

"Okay." He started to say 'bye but she hung up in the middle of it.

Rod called half an hour later. "Loot, I'm out at West-heimer and Voss. This is the number they called, all right. Looks like dead-end time."

"Hell." MacIver had held the sliver of a hope that there had been a mistake and they'd find the number belonged to a residential telephone. "Have you dusted it for prints?"

"Nosir."

"Do it. Dust the phone numbers where you punch, and the phone. Dust the whole phone booth."

"It's not a booth. It's one of those little cubicle things."

"Okay, dust the whole little cubicle thing. And if there are any numbers written by hand on the wall or anywhere, copy 'em and check 'em out."

Rod said yessir, and MacIver hung up. One of the other sergeants came to his desk carrying a computer printout. "Loot, aren't you working that drug-and-rape case from Kansas City?"

When MacIver nodded, the sergeant said, "We got another one, only this time the lady was DOA."

4   The victim's name was Lurinda Boggs Elsing. She had been sixty-two, black, a schoolteacher. A Houston resident, she had been in New Orleans attending a teachers' conference where she was being honored as Outstanding Teacher of the Year.

MacIver scanned the rundown and said, "Shit. Poor lady. She gets an award and the next thing she knows, she's dead."

The sergeant said, "Yeah, it's kind of pitiful. Been teaching all her life. She was down in the restaurant—"

MacIver, still reading the rundown, interrupted. "My God, a dildo down her throat!"

"Yeah. Gross, huh?"

MacIver read aloud. "Eight inches long, approximately six inches in circumference, inserted *after* death—" He remarked, "That's a blessing," and went back to reading. "K-Y jelly used. God, the things people do. Okay, Sarge, sorry I interrupted. You were saying?"

"We've got descriptions from at least ten people. A black man and woman, both in their twenties, nice-looking, well-mannered."

MacIver said, "Everybody assumed they were teachers at the conference, I suppose."

"Sure. They said that Mrs. Elsing had been an inspiration to them in their own teaching careers and they wanted to buy her a bottle of champagne. They wound up buying two bottles and treating everyone at the table. Then they walked Mrs. Elsing and her roommate to their room, taking one of the partially filled bottles along. The two ladies were found the next morning. Both had been drugged, but Mrs. Elsing was dead.

"The roommate said she and the couple had a second glass of champagne in the room. Mrs. Elsing didn't want a second glass, and the couple were urging her to have one when the roommate began to feel sick and went to bed. She doesn't know what happened after that."

"They probably insisted till she gave in. Were the women robbed?"

"Yeah. They didn't have a lot. You know, schoolteachers. Mrs. Robb, the roommate, said they took her credit cards and travelers' checks."

"No jewelry, watches?"

"Wedding rings are all they took. All they had besides that was costume jewelry and Timexes. The crooks didn't bother taking those."

MacIver leaned back and stared at the wall. The sergeant followed his gaze, then walked over and touched the wall. "I thought for a minute that was a real window."

MacIver said absently, "Yeah, I've got the only window in Homicide on the third floor."

When the new wing was put up, no windows had been built into the third floor. The existing building on the same site had had the normal number of windows, but these were regularly shot out by people driving by on the freeway, which was adjacent to and level with the third floor. MacIver had been glad he could stop worrying about unexpected bullets and shattered glass, but the unbroken expanses of off-white walls were depressing, so he'd had a window painted on his east wall. It was large, with four panes. In one of them, the painter had added a bird that seemed to be flying in the distance. Sometimes when MacIver looked out his window, he thought he saw other things, but that was mostly when he'd been working too hard. He said, "They went to a hell of a lot of trouble to rob two women. They couldn't have expected those two to have anything of much value."

"Maybe they thought the award included some money."

"Maybe." It didn't make much sense, but he'd known of people killed for half a bottle of cheap wine.

The sergeant said, "A phone call was placed from that

room at ten-fifty-two, about half an hour after the four of them went upstairs."

MacIver's glance sharpened. "Where to?"

"Houston."

"To a pay phone at Westheimer and Voss?"

The sergeant blinked as if MacIver had pulled a rabbit out of his hat. "Nosir. It was a pay phone, but it was at 6200 Main."

"No shit." MacIver rubbed his chin thoughtfully. "Why different phones?" And answered his own question. "Because they'd know we had the number of the one they called from Kansas City, so they go to another one miles away. That's damned clever for two-bit crooks, Sarge. Which means maybe they're not two-bit crooks. What else have you got?"

"There was a message printed on the mirror in the bathroom with lipstick."

MacIver stopped rubbing his chin. "What did it say?"

"You heard from us."

Rodriguez returned an hour later, streaming with sweat and looking disgruntled. "Loot, there must've been fifty jillion partials in that cubicle. Not many names though. Not much of any place for people to write. I took it all to the crime lab."

"Okay, good." MacIver told him about the new case. As the lieutenant talked, Rodriguez combed his mustache with his fingers. It was luxuriant and well on the way to a Pancho Villa droop. He was tall for a Mexican, almost six feet. He had been in Golden Gloves in high school, and his high arched, Spanish nose had been broken, set, rebroken, and reset. The end result was slightly askew, with an unfinished look as if it were substituting for the real thing. A sergeant for two years, Rodriguez had a reputation for thoroughness and following through.

MacIver summed up. "Both cases have the same MO. The pickup is similar, the quick drugging is the same, the message left behind is word-for-word except for the change in verb tense. *And* the phone call to Houston is the same. But the participants are different."

34

Rod said, "We need to try to find out more about the couple, especially if anybody saw them leave and where they went."

"Good. Listen, Sarge, why don't you put out a request on the computer for any other crimes of this sort that come in."

"You think this may be the new in-vogue crime?"

"I hope not, but it's possible."

"Okay, I'll do that."

MacIver said, "Next of kin needs to be notified. That's her husband. I guess that's mine."

The husband's name was Roscoe Washington Elsing; he was an employee of the city water department. MacIver called the water department and was told this was Mr. Elsing's day off. He thought about calling the guy at home but decided against it. He didn't want to break the news on the phone, or say that he'd be out to talk to Elsing and leave the man worrying until he got there. Instead he took a chance on finding Elsing at home.

The window had already been replaced on the wagon. MacIver circled the vehicle, looking for any other damage. The department was low on vehicles, so MacIver had been given special dispensation to use his own car. In lieu of a police radio, he used a walkie-talkie. As usual the wagon was coated with white dust from the oyster shell parking lot. One day maybe the city could find the funds to pave the lot; it would save MacIver a lot of car washing.

He could find no other damage. The wagon was its usual self—stodgy and utilitarian, empty-looking without children, groceries, and dogs, which was what it had been bought for. MacIver hadn't wanted it in the first place but Constance had insisted. Actually she'd wanted a van but that was too expensive, so she'd settled for the biggest station wagon they could afford. Somehow in the divorce settlement, he'd wound up with the six-year-old wagon and she'd gotten his three-year-old Plymouth Fury. He decided to buy a new car every time the wagon broke down and changed his mind every time he figured out how much the car payments would be.

The September sun was hot. MacIver turned on the air conditioner and let the motor idle while he looked at the map to figure out where he was going. He had broken into a sweat before the air turned cool.

He wasn't looking forward to this assignment. Most of his work he liked or at least tolerated. The endless paperwork didn't bother him too much. He had learned to handle the boredom of stakeouts and the frustration of having to let the guilty go free because of niggling legalities. He no longer got upset when he heard civilians verbally running down the police. But there were three kinds of jobs he, along with most of his comrades, hated: child abuse (the look in the kids' eyes—if they were still alive—haunted him), finding a corpse too long dead, and telling the next of kin about a death. The grief and shock and realization of loss never failed to move MacIver, and never failed to make him feel inadequate because there was nothing he could do or say that would help.

The Elsing home was a one-story white frame house, turn-of-the-century and well kept, in a predominantly black residential area. MacIver walked up a sidewalk bordered by mown and edged grass to a screened-in porch with periwinkles and mums blooming in the flower bed in front of it. An old-fashioned porch swing stood to one side. He opened the screen door, crossed the porch, and rang the bell.

A black man opened the door. He was tall with graying hair and he wore khakis. "Morning." Already there was apprehension in his eyes and wariness in his voice. When a stranger appeared at the door at this hour of the morning, something was wrong.

MacIver said, "Mr. Elsing, Roscoe Elsing?"

"Yessir, that's my name."

MacIver introduced himself and produced identification. Elsing said, "You're the law?"

"Yes. Do you mind if I come in, Mr. Elsing?"

The man stepped back. "Come on in."

The high-ceilinged living room was dim with drawn shades but well proportioned, with wall-to-wall carpeting and traditional furniture. A piano stood against one wall. Elsing turned on a lamp. "What you want with me, Lieutenant?"

"I have bad news." MacIver didn't believe in drawing it

out. "It's your wife. She was found dead early this morning in her hotel room in New Orleans."

Elsing's face went gray. His expression didn't change, but tears welled in his eyes and slowly overflowed, coursing down his cheeks. MacIver looked away. "I'm sorry, Mr. Elsing."

"What happened? Was it the pressure?"

It took MacIver a second to realize he meant blood pressure. "Well, that may have been part of it. She went very quickly. There was no pain."

"I'm glad of that, mighty glad." Elsing had been fumbling in a back pocket and now he drew out a handkerchief, wiped his eyes, and blew his nose. "I had a feeling about this trip. I had a feeling more than a week ago. I told her I didn't want her to go but she wanted to be there to get that award herself." His voice cracked.

MacIver said, "She received the award last night."

"Before she—that's good then. It meant an awful lot to her." Elsing took a sideways step and dropped onto the couch as though his knees had buckled. "I can't seem to understand it yet. She told me she'd be careful. She told me she'd get plenty of rest. She wasn't going to take any chances with the pressure."

"She did what she said, Mr. Elsing. She had one glass of champagne with well-wishers after the banquet. Then she was going to go to bed." He sat down beside the grieving man. "Can I get you anything? You have coffee?"

"There's some left but I don't want it." He roused himself. "I can pour you a cup."

"No, thanks. There're some other things I've got to tell you."

Elsing looked at him, but after a moment his eyes lost focus. MacIver told him as quickly and succinctly as possible about the couple and the drugged champagne. The creases in Elsing's forehead deepened as MacIver talked. Finally he said, "Now wait a minute. You're telling me Lurinda, Mrs. Elsing, had a second glass of champagne? She *never* had a second glass of anything. She'd barely have one, even on special occasions. She didn't hold with spirits."

"I'm sure the couple insisted." For all MacIver knew, they

could have forced it down her throat, but he wasn't going to tell Elsing that. He wasn't going to tell him about the dildo either.

"They put something in it, you say? You mean like knock-out drops?"

"Something like that."

"Why would they want to do that?"

"They wanted to rob her, probably."

"All she had was a hundred dollars in travelers' checks and her watch and wedding ring. She didn't take to fancy jewelry even when we could afford it."

"Maybe they thought she had more than she did."

"They took all that, the travelers' checks?"

"No travelers' checks were found, so I guess they must have."

"They didn't take her wedding ring?"

"I'm afraid they did."

Elsing closed his eyes a moment, then wiped them again with his handkerchief. "I can't quite get it in my mind yet, that she's passed."

"Do you have somebody you could call to be with you, any children?"

"Got two daughters and a son. My youngest daughter, she lives just over on the next street. She'll come. But I'm going to have to tell her about her mama." Tears were glistening in his eyes again.

"Better get it over with." MacIver gave Elsing his own philosophy. "They'll want to be with you. The bo—the deceased will be brought back as soon as the autopsy's done. Somebody will let you know."

Elsing said dully, "Yessir, all right."

MacIver put his business card on the coffee table. "This is my number. Call me if you have any questions." He grasped the man's shoulder. "I'm sorry, Mr. Elsing. I wish there was something I could do." He straightened. "You go call your children now. You need them with you."

"Yessir. I'll do that. I'll do it right now." Elsing got to his feet. MacIver saw him to the telephone, then left the house.

As soon as he pulled away from the curb, he got out his handkerchief and dabbed his face. He was sweating again, not entirely from the heat. Dammit, there was a couple married forty years or so, who cared for each other, who had planned to spend their old age together. Now one was dead and the other would be lonely maybe for the rest of his life. It wasn't right and it wasn't fair, and there were too many criminals for police to catch them all. MacIver wiped his forehead again, and his eyes, and put away the handkerchief.

In the office he began a memo to the captain suggesting that any officers who had been pupils of Mrs. Elsing might be notified of her funeral when it was scheduled. His telephone rang, and he answered absently.

"Is this Sergeant MacIver of Homicide?"

"Used to be Sergeant MacIver. Who's calling, please?"

"This is Willie Thomason. I'm with the medical examiner's office."

"Yeah, I've heard of you, Willie. What've you got?"

"You may or may not be interested in this, but we found an old one the other day. Dug her up underneath a sand trap. The fingerprints were confirmed today. Dr. Jack looked up the file. He said you were the primary investigator and that you should be notified."

MacIver had been a lieutenant for eighteen years so this must be a very old one. "Go on."

"It's a white female, and the body itself is in extremely good shape, hardly any decomposition. We were even able to lift prints. Not only that, but we obtained three driver's licenses out of one bra cup and three American Express cards out of the other. The names are all different but I'll give you one—"

MacIver interrupted. "I'll give *you* one: Rita McWhirter Davis."

"Yeah, that's one of them."

MacIver had always suspected that Rita had been killed. "Is Dr. Jack out there?"

"Nosir, he's not in the office."

"I need to get my mind refreshed on this thing. Let me pull the case out of Archives. What time do you plan to be there in the morning?"

"Dr. Jack and I will be here about six-thirty. He likes to

start early. You know, we've got a full house here almost every night."

"Yes, I've heard you do. Tell Dr. Jack I'll be there about nine tomorrow."

He hung up and sprang out of his chair to pace around the desk. So beautiful Rita Davis had finally surfaced, no pun intended. She had been their sole witness to a murder committed eighteen years ago. He sat down, dialed Archives, and asked them to look up the case charging Kurt Neimeyer with the murder of Ginger Falls. After all these years there seemed little likelihood of finding enough new evidence to reopen the case. Still, you never knew.

Rodriguez rang. "I'm getting ready to split, Loot. Anything you want to tell me before I go?"

"Yeah. We've got a date with the M.E. about nine in the morning. I'll pick you up here at a quarter till."

"What does the M.E. have to do with our case?"

"Nothing. This is an old one."

Rod said okay and hung up, and MacIver got back to the present. Finishing his brief on Elsing, he set up a file that, after consideration, he designated as "Drug Assault Rob." He filed it, and noticed the Odetts folder. May as will see if anybody knew anything about Lenny.

Odetts's brother-in-law hadn't heard from Leonard directly, but he had heard from a mutual acquaintance that Leonard had botched a job and decided to leave the state for a few days. MacIver wondered if he himself was the botched job. He transferred Odetts's file to the "Pending" section. He'd be arresting Lennie again one of these days.

The phone rang again. It was Suzanne. She was almost whispering into the receiver. "I've got to talk to you, but this is a bad time. In fact, the whole day is bad. Could we get together after work? Why don't you come to my house for a drink?"

MacIver hesitated a moment. He had spent two years in Vice and he'd never quite gotten over his wariness to an invitation to meet a woman in her home. After the knee-jerk reaction, he said, "Okay. What's your address?"

She gave it to him, off San Felipe on Augusta. MacIver

said, "We're almost neighbors. That's not even five minutes from my place."

"That makes it convenient. See you about six then."

"Wait a minute, Suzanne. Have you heard something more from them?"

"I received some photos."

So they *had* taken pictures and they were going to try to blackmail her. "Okay, see you this evening."

5 At 6:15 he reached Suzanne's, a town house with a red brick facade and a Victorian lamppost at the sidewalk. She opened the door and smiled wanly. "Thanks for coming."

A small dog rushed past her, barking furiously and taking fake nips at MacIver's ankles. It was all golden brown hair and bark. MacIver looked down at the dog in amazement. "I'm being attacked by a mop."

Suzanne scooped up the little animal. "Manners, Ginnie, manners." And to MacIver, "Don't worry. The mop doesn't bite."

"Gracious sakes, ma'am, that's a relief to know. I was in mortal terror. Is that really a dog?"

"A Yorkie." She deposited it on the couch. "She'll be all right now. May I get you a drink?" Suzanne wore a rust-colored suit that brought out red highlights in her hair, but there were dark circles under her eyes and furrows in her forehead.

"Scotch and soda." MacIver put a hand on her arm. "Look, this isn't the end of the world. We'll get through it all right."

This time her smile was real. "Thanks, Tony, especially for that 'we.'"

MacIver was pleased to see her smile, and it struck him again that Suzanne was very attractive. He wondered why she hadn't remarried, if she dated anyone regularly, and how it would be to hold her in his arms. Then, realizing where his thoughts were leading, he reminded himself that he had

42

just gotten out of one relationship and didn't need to be thinking of forming another. He turned his attention to his surroundings.

The living room was mostly blue and green with an aqua couch, green patterned fabric on Queen Anne chairs, and a glass-and-chrome table. A cherry armoire dominated one wall. A second wall held a poster from the Fine Arts Museum advertising an exhibit by Houston artists.

A large first-class envelope lay on the coffee table. The postmark was Houston and it was stamped "Photos Do Not Bend."

Suzanne returned with drinks, handing one to MacIver as Ginnie sniffed at his ankles. He lifted the glass shoulder high. "Here's to getting the bad guys."

"I'll drink to that." She sipped. "I guess I should have called Sergeant Rodriguez, but I didn't even think about it till I'd already called you."

"It's okay. I told him I was coming over. He's got plenty of other things to keep him busy."

She gestured with a grimace toward the envelope. "Those are the photos. Gross. I felt slimy just looking at them."

He didn't ask to see them. "That's what they wanted. Otherwise you wouldn't be willing to pay for them. Have you handled them at all?"

"Just one corner. When I saw what they were, I shoved them back into the envelope."

"I'd like to take them with me and attempt to lift prints."

"As far as I'm concerned, you can keep them. I don't want them lying around. They were delivered to the office this morning. Fortunately the envelope was marked 'personal' so the receptionist didn't open it."

That had been calculated to frighten her, MacIver thought, to make her think of the reaction if the receptionist *had* opened it.

He asked, "Was there anything besides the photos?"

"Oh, yes indeed, a note. They want a quarter of a million dollars."

He whistled. "A quarter of a million is a lot of money. Can you raise it?"

"Barely. I'd have to liquidate my assets. Mr. Reevson would be fit to kill. My investment adviser," she added in explanation.

"When do they want it?"

"They didn't say. They said they'd call with further instructions."

"I'd like to see the message. Did you handle it?"

"It fell out of the envelope when I slit it open and I picked it up, so I touched the upper right-hand corner." She looked doubtful. "And I may have touched it in other places. I don't remember."

"Okay. Let me run a set of your prints so we can eliminate you. I'll get somebody out here with a fingerprint kit."

MacIver didn't expect to get prints from the envelope; nevertheless he handled it gingerly, covering his fingers with a handkerchief before lifting the envelope and shaking out the message. It was typed on stationery from the hotel in Kansas City. With the handkerchief still covering his thumb and forefinger, he picked up the message and read it silently.

"Dear Suzanne," it said. "What a party we had! Enclosed are some souvenirs of our evening but the videotapes are even better. Your friends and business associates probably would enjoy seeing them. If you want to prevent that, you can buy them for $250,000. We'll be in touch."

It was signed "Bob and Ken."

He said, "Okay, I'll want this and the whole packet for fingerprinting. If they were careful, we won't pick up any prints, but maybe they weren't and we will. I'll have a linguistics expert go over the note. That may tell us something about the person who wrote it."

Suzanne dropped down on an ottoman close to him. "I can tell you about *him*. Whichever one wrote it, he's a filthy son of a bitch."

The hurt sounded behind her anger. He squeezed her shoulder. "I know this is hard on you, Suzanne, but remember that none of it is your fault. You didn't do anything wrong. Try to think of the person in those pictures as somebody else. It isn't you. You, yourself, weren't there."

"I wish I could think that way. The photos show my eyes open so I must have been awake, but I don't remember anything."

"The drug was probably just potent enough to daze you but not to put you out."

She nodded, her eyes distant, her mind already on something else. It happened with people who had been victimized or too close to disasters. "It just makes me so damned mad! All this upset and worry because two creeps are too lazy to make a decent living and want to leech off me." She turned to face MacIver, her jaw set and eyes narrowed. "Well, they're not going to succeed, not with me they're not. I'm not going to pay them a penny."

MacIver was glad to see anger instead of dejection. He said, "Good for you."

"They can do whatever they like with their videotapes, put them on the five o'clock news if they like, but I'm not paying them!"

MacIver nodded, but he didn't believe it. She'd change her mind when she saw the tapes. "They'll probably contact you in the next couple of days."

"How?" She looked alarmed. "I don't want to see them."

"Probably not in person. By letter or phone, I'd guess. Do you have a tape recorder on your phone?"

"Yes, at the office. Well, at home, too. I have an answering machine."

"I've never heard of an extortionist leaving a message on an answering machine, but you *could* tape with it. It's legal to tape if one party to the conversation agrees. If you can tape the call, I can take it to a voice expert. He might be able to tell us something useful."

Suzanne's daughter arrived home then. She had hair like her mother's, a precocious figure, and braces on her teeth. When Suzanne introduced them, her daughter said, "A police lieutenant, wow," and to her mother, "Does this have something to do with—you know—Kansas City?"

Suzanne nodded. "I'll explain later."

"Okay. Nice meeting you, Lieutenant." As she disappeared down the hall, MacIver heard another breathy "Wow."

"You told her about the attack?"

"Only that there was one. Not the details. There was no way to avoid it, even if I'd wanted to. We're very close and she knew something was wrong when I came home from Kansas City."

"She seems to be handling it all right."

"I think so. She's a levelheaded girl."

"Okay, I'm going to call Rod and ask him to bring out a portable fingerprint kit."

After the phone call, he finished his drink and took Suzanne's hand. "Try not to worry. We're going to handle this, okay?"

"Okay." She leaned forward and kissed him on the cheek. "Thanks, Tony."

He had to force himself to step away from her.

As he went down the sidewalk, he felt a spring in his step and an excitement in his heart that he hadn't felt for a long time, hadn't expected ever to feel again. At least this particular ill wind had brought Suzanne and him back together, and this time she wasn't going steady. He hummed as he got into the car and headed to Sharpstown to pick up the cat.

Jarratt was watching television in the kitchen and eating a sandwich when MacIver arrived. Priscilla, the Burmese, sat on the floor watching every bite the boy took, which meant Jarratt had been giving her nibbles again. MacIver said, "Evening, son."

Jarratt's eyes swiveled toward him, but he didn't move his head. "Hi."

It wasn't the most enthusiastic greeting in the world but at least he hadn't retreated to his bedroom. MacIver went back into the living room to talk to Constance.

He kept his voice low. "Anything new on the counselor?"

"She called me this morning. Wanted to know why Jarratt hadn't shown up."

"You told her he got tired of waiting?"

"Yes, and that he didn't want to come anyway. She said that was SOP."

"Did you make another appointment for him?"

"No, she said she'd talk to him."

"And did she?"

"I don't know. I haven't asked." With a touch of exasperation, she added, "I just got in half an hour ago."

MacIver held up both hands in an okay-okay gesture. "I'm not trying to bug you; I just wanted to know how things stood."

"Well, that's how they stand." She looked at her watch. "I've got to be ready to go out in forty-five minutes."

In spite of himself, MacIver felt a twinge of jealousy. He wanted to ask if she was going out with a man, but wouldn't. "I won't take up any more of your time." He went back to the kitchen and took the other chair at the small table. "Everything go okay today?"

"I guess so." Jarratt kept his eyes on the TV screen, apparently absorbed in some rapid-moving and very noisy variety show. MacIver yearned to turn down the volume.

"I guess you know that the counselor—what's her name?"

"Ms. Sandos."

"Yeah. Ms. Sandos called your mother this morning. She said she'd get in touch with you today." He waited. Jarratt finished his sandwich. Priscilla, the possibility of food now gone, came out of her trance and moved over to greet MacIver.

"Hello, baby. You decided to say hello." MacIver petted the cat. "Did she? Did Ms. Sandos get in touch with you?"

"Yep." Jarratt refilled his glass of milk.

MacIver's patience was wearing thin. He hated having to pry every word out of the boy. He wondered if Jarratt had learned that technique from his mother or if it just came naturally. He said softly, "You're not helping, son."

Jarratt turned his head away. "She wasn't steamed because I didn't show up yesterday. She said she'd like me to come in tomorrow after school."

"Good. So you're going to do that?"

"I guess so. She said she'd probably want to talk to you and Mom soon." He looked at MacIver, satisfaction showing in his eyes.

MacIver knew intuitively that Jarratt expected a negative response. He said, "Fine. The sooner the better. We've got to get this cleared up so you can make your nine-weeks grades."

Jarratt's gaze returned to the television. MacIver said, "We're supposed to get together this weekend, you and I. Anything special you'd like to do?"

The boy shrugged. "Not much to do where you live."

"You can swim."

Jarratt made a retching sound. "I'm tired of swimming."

MacIver forced cheerfulness into his voice. "We'll think of something. Come on, Prissie, time to go."

He got the cat's carrier from the utility room and nudged Priscilla toward it. The cat entered, purring. Her docility always amazed MacIver. "Only cat I've ever known who liked her carrier."

Jarratt looked at the cat. "She's kind of a dope sometimes."

"See you this weekend, son."

"Yeah. So long." Jarratt had turned back to the television.

MacIver called good-bye to Constance as he walked through the living room. She appeared in the hall doorway.

"Good-bye, Prissie. Be a sweet kitty." Her tone changed when she addressed MacIver. "Just make sure she doesn't come home with fleas."

MacIver had kept a friend's Siamese for a week, and the animal had turned out to have fleas, leaving behind a supply of the parasites that took up residence on Priscilla. Constance had been convinced ever since that MacIver's apartment was a den of fleas.

He thought of trying to explain to her one more time that all the fleas were gone but decided he'd be wasting his breath.

Outside, he took a deep breath. He had exerted so much self-control in the past fifteen minutes that he felt as though he might explode, but he had accomplished his goal: kept cool and left on a good note.

He put cat and carrier in the passenger seat. "How about a little music, Pris? What are you in the mood for, the barber?" He sang, "Figaro, Figaro, Figaro." A passing jogger, without looking at him, made a thumbs-down gesture. MacIver said, "So I'm not Domingo." He put in the tape of *The Barber of Seville* and sang along as he drove home.

6 He parked under the building in his appointed space, extracted the cat from the carrier, and put her into the paper sack with the cans of food. It was time for covert action. "If all goes well, this will take only two minutes. It would help if you wouldn't meow." Priscilla mewed softly in response. MacIver said, "I won't talk to you if you don't talk to me."

He moved rapidly toward the elevator, hoping that it would not be occupied. Priscilla lost her docility on the elevator and carried on as if she were going to be flung into a cage full of pit bulls. The Towers prohibited animals, a rule MacIver ignored. He had argued long and hard to acquire joint custody of the cat, and he wasn't going to have his time with her nullified by a silly regulation. Nevertheless the ride was traumatic for both of them.

The first time MacIver had tried to carry her in his arms, she had torn herself free at about the sixth floor, ricocheted around the walls like a racquet ball and wound up on the floor, back arched, eyes maniacal and a tiger growl rumbling from her chest as she stalked around him. He had actually wondered if she were going to attack. Fortunately they had reached the fourteenth floor and the doors opened. She leapt out with the speed of a pilot ejecting from a crashing plane.

The elevator arrived and MacIver started to step on, then backed up as he noticed a boy standing in the corner. When the child didn't move, MacIver asked, "You getting off, son?"

The boy's eyes, wary and watchful, widened at being addressed. He shook his head.

"Okay, then. We'll both go up." MacIver guessed the youngster had been riding up and down for fun. He stepped onto the elevator and punched fourteen. "What floor do you want?"

Without answering, the boy sidled forward and punched five. MacIver adopted the hearty manner he used with children when he was trying to convince them that cops were good guys. "Been told not to talk to strangers, eh? That's a good rule to follow."

The elevator began to move. So did Priscilla. MacIver tightened his hold on the top of the sack. At the third floor the cat let out a yowl and began to thrash. MacIver clasped the sack against his chest. "It's all right, Pris. It's okay."

The boy was watching with interest. "What you got in there?"

"A cat. She doesn't like elevators."

Priscilla made a lunge, almost catapulting the sack out of MacIver's grasp. When he had it secure again, he saw the child staring at his belt. His coat had fallen back, revealing his Colt .45 automatic. Without taking his eyes off the weapon, the boy asked, "You a gangster or something?"

"Police officer."

"You gonna arrest somebody here?" His voice was shrill with hope.

"No, I live here."

"Oh." Disappointment was evident. The elevator began to slow for the fifth floor.

MacIver said, "Look, son, I haven't told anybody in the building that I'm an officer. I'd just as soon you didn't mention it."

"Okay." The elevator stopped, the doors opened, and the boy got off without a backward glance. MacIver concentrated on keeping Priscilla from ripping the sack apart until he reached the fourteenth floor.

The apartment was a corner one, southeast, which gave him a view of both downtown and the Galleria area. The furniture, his cousin's, was predominantly blue and brown with lots of glass and chrome. Even after almost a year, MacIver didn't feel really at home. He always had the feeling that he was walking into a designer's set labeled "bachelor pad." He set the sack and Priscilla down, and the cat freed herself and sped to the sanctuary of her litter box.

MacIver opened a can of food for her and went off to change into a swimsuit and robe. He walked to the long east windows. It was a clear night and the skyline showed dark against pink and magenta. Off to the right, the Galleria glowed more brightly.

MacIver decided to head down to the pool. At the door, he wedged a matchbook at the top, a precaution that had become automatic. If it wasn't there when he came back, he would enter his apartment very cautiously.

Downstairs, he took a brisk swim and then did easy laps for half an hour. Then he hoisted himself out of the water and signaled Ravi, the waiter, to bring a dry vodka martini. MacIver settled on a lounge chair and toweled his face. When he looked up, he saw the boy from the elevator sitting at the shallow end of the pool. He was a skinny little kid, all ribs and knobby shoulders. Probably ten or eleven, MacIver guessed. The boy kicked his feet desultorily in the water and stared at nothing. Must be boring for him here, MacIver thought, with so few children around.

The boy looked up and saw him, and MacIver raised a hand in greeting. After glancing over his shoulder, the child scrambled up and came toward him. "What happened to your"—he lowered his voice to a whisper—"cat?"

"I got her into my apartment before she ripped the sack apart. She's okay now."

The child lingered and MacIver's martini arrived. He asked, "You want a Coke?"

"No, thanks." When the waiter had gone, he asked, "Why don't you want anybody to know you're a"—he glanced around to check on possible listeners—"a you-know-what?"

"People are funny about it. They get the idea you're watching them. All I want to do when I get home is relax. I don't want people getting nervous around me."

"Oh." The boy dropped down to sit on the concrete. "You ever shoot anybody?"

"Yes."

"Kill 'em?"

"Sometimes."

"You must be a good shot."

"Ninety-eight point five percent accuracy." MacIver grinned. "That's with my eyes closed."

"My Dad had a gun." The boy looked up and his eyes rounded. "I gotta go." He ran around the pool to meet a man whom MacIver hadn't seen before. He wore a pale yellow silk shirt and light blue denims. He was slim, but he had the well-developed shoulders of a longtime pumper of iron. He said something to the boy and glanced fleetingly at MacIver. Then the pair headed out of the pool area. New residents, MacIver thought. From the North, judging by the youngster's accent; Michigan or maybe Ohio.

MacIver finished his martini and stood up. He wanted to make it an early evening. He had a date with the medical examiner in the morning.

7   MacIver filled Rod in on the old case on the way
    to the medical examiner's office. It was fresh in his
    mind because he had reviewed it in Archives yes-
terday afternoon. "Rita and Ginger Falls were a couple of
prostitutes working for Kurt Neimeyer, a.k.a. the Baron."

"I've heard of him. He's kind of a big man in the commu-
nity now."

"That's his story. He's as crooked as ever. He just hides
it better. Anyway, he and Ginger had some kind of argument. It happened out on Bering. We had an eyewitness
across the street, a senior citizen who'd gone out to pick up
his newspaper. He said two men were throwing clothes in
a car. Then two women came out. They were yelling and
cursing, our witness said. Then one of the men hit Ginger.
The problem was that he was holding a pistol in his hand
when he hit her and the gun went off. The slug went
through her cheek and up through her brain, killing her instantly."

The men had jumped into the car and driven away.
The senior citizen had gone inside and phoned the police.
MacIver and his partner took the call. They got there
just as the other girl, Rita Davis, was trying to drive
away.

She had been held as a material witness, and she finally
told them what had happened. It was the Baron who
had killed Ginger. He didn't intend to—she was bringing
in too much money for him to kill her intentionally—but
she was dead, just the same. So they had a case against the
Baron.

54

MacIver opened his coat and turned around. "Get a lot of robberies in here, do you?"

"Nosir. None. Follow the green line on the floor."

MacIver and Rod followed the green line, which eventually led to Dr. Jack's office. The medical examiner waved. "Would you like a cup of coffee and a Danish?"

Both MacIver and Rodriguez accepted. "How've you been, Dr. Jack?"

"Can't complain. Got a popular place here. People are dying to get in."

MacIver groaned. The medical examiner had made the same remark the first time MacIver met him. Dr. Jack beamed at him. "Let's go on into the morgue. This one you're going to see is in a remarkably preserved state. I attribute it to the fact that no oxygen reached the body and it was in a cool spot. Eight feet underground in a well-drained area."

"How did they happen to be digging in a sand trap?"

"Renovating the course. That one out on Jack Rabbit Road. If you're ready, we can go on in. I'll do my orals while you're here."

MacIver hastily finished his Danish and coffee before following the medical examiner inside.

It was chilly in the room, about sixty-five degrees. Dr. Jack asked for number eight-nine, and an attendant wheeled a gurney forward. The body remained the way it had been found, covered with a triple plastic bag. The medical examiner pulled the bag back and MacIver stared at Rita Davis.

He realized that, without thinking, he had been holding his breath. Now he let it out slowly. She was still pretty— still looked nineteen years old. The only difference he could see between now and the last time he had seen her was a slight shriveling of the features. She wore a red blouse and a bra. The lower body was nude. He was relieved to find that there was no smell of decay.

Dr. Jack spoke into a microphone. "Before us we have the body of a white Caucasian female, well nourished, about five feet four inches, approximately 110 pounds. Very little swelling. Subhematoma left rear of the head. Nothing remarkable

Then Rita talked the police into letting her go to Wichita to visit her mother. She was there for a couple of weeks. When they tried to reach her before the trial, she was gone. Her mother said she'd left a month before to return to Houston.

"That was the last we heard of Rita Davis, until now."

"What about the senior citizen?"

"He hadn't been wearing his glasses. He couldn't identify either of the men."

Rod said, "But there was a case back there sometime against the Baron, wasn't there?"

"Yeah, three years later he was arrested for violating the Mann Act. We got him that time. He spent a couple of years in prison before he walked."

"So what are we expecting to find out with this body?"

"Best case: there'll be enough evidence to reopen the case against the Baron. Worst case: we'll find out how Rita died and that's about all."

They parked outside the medical examiner's building in the officers' restricted zone, and rang the bell at the door, where they were scrutinized by closed-circuit TV and asked for identification. Dr. D.G. "Jack" Jackacheck ran a tight ship.

MacIver announced, "We're here to meet with Dr. Jackacheck."

"Are you armed?"

"Yes, we are."

"Dr. Jack has asked that people leave their weapons in their cars."

MacIver and Rodriguez exchanged glances. The voice added defensively, "He's tired of bullet holes in the ceiling All the holes in the ceiling have been caused by Housto police officers moving around inside with weapons whil they look through private effects."

"Okay, we'll be right back."

Locking their automatics in the spare tire compartment the wagon, they returned to the door. This time they we admitted. The sandy-haired man at the door said, "Wo you please open your coats and turn around?"

about the head. Hair sandy blond, pulled back into a pony-tail; teeth exposed, no dentures—"

MacIver interrupted. "Can we get on to the wounds, Dr. Jack?"

The medical examiner turned a frosty gaze on him. "This is the way we do it here. We start at the head and proceed in a logical manner. I'm in the medical examiner business here, not the let's-get-on-to-the-wounds business."

"Yessir." MacIver shoved his hands into his pockets and listened to the physician drone on. He perked up when the medical examiner described the wound behind the left ear. It was a contact wound with heavily pitted nitrate particles. In Dr. Jack's opinion, the bullet did not exit the brain.

It took another fifteen minutes for the physician to work his way across the torso and abdomen. "Judging from the gaping of the vagina, I think there was intercourse after death. Ralph, I want you to do a scraping of the walls of the vagina and rectum to attempt to recover male sperm that may be in a dried state."

He told MacIver. "The criminalistic techniques that we have now can give us a DNA reading of the man who had intercourse with her that is as unique to that person as fingerprints. I don't know how much help that will be because we don't have DNA records on the population at large."

"That's all right, Doc. In this case, I think I know where I can find a matching DNA."

The medical examiner instructed Ralph to do a comb-out of the pubic hairs to determine if there were any foreign hairs, to get scrapings of both fingernails and toenails, and to take an earth sampling from the soles of her shoes. Her missing garments and shoes, he explained to MacIver, had been dumped into the bag along with the body.

Finally the physician was finished with the oral and preparing for the opening. "I don't suppose you gentlemen want to remain for this."

MacIver definitely did not want to remain. "I would like to have the slug, if you find it."

Dr. Jack nodded and prepared for the layback of the scalp. "It should take about thirty minutes."

MacIver and Rodriguez escaped to the lobby.

Thirty-five minutes later Ralph appeared. "Do you have any use for fragments that, when weighed, are going to equate to a twenty-five-caliber automatic copper jacket slug?"

"Just give it to us in a sealed bag."

At the office, the captain glanced at his watch. "You finally decide to join us?"

"We've been out at the medical examiner's, Cap." MacIver told the captain about the newly unearthed body. "Dr. Jack is making some further tests. I don't know how much evidence we're going to have. Could I get some help from Criminal Intelligence Division surveillance teams, get Neimeyer located, in the event that we have something to go with?"

After consideration, the captain said he would talk to CID and see if they could commit for that.

MacIver sent the material he'd picked up from Suzanne— photos, envelope, and message—to the crime lab. Next he got an update from the New Orleans police on their investigation of the Elsing homicide. Nobody admitted knowing the couple who had gone with Mrs. Elsing to her room, and no fingerprints or other identifying evidence had been found. The lipstick used to write the message on the bathroom mirror was Mrs. Elsing's. A bellhop claimed he had seen a young man, who fit the description of the man who had accompanied Mrs. Elsing, carrying two large bags into her room. The time given by the bellhop was within ten minutes of the time the two schoolteachers and their escorts must have arrived at the room. The New Orleans police had no explanation for the bags, but MacIver thought they could have carried a video camera and floodlights. The pair might have intended to film Mrs. Elsing. Probably her death had prevented it. It also must have prevented their attacking the roommate. He sent a message back about the photographs and the alleged tapes.

Looking back over the printouts that had come in during

the night, MacIver found a query from Minneapolis. A Mrs. Betsy Craddock had reported to police that she had been drugged, assaulted, and robbed while staying in a Houston hotel. She identified her attackers as two men in their twenties, one blond, one black. They had called themselves Ken and Bob.

8 Betsy Craddock had a clear, high voice with an old Houston accent, and she was a talker. "There was just no way I was going to go to the police while I was in Houston. I was feeling like death warmed over. I didn't what to talk to *anybody*, but even if I had—my daddy was a lawyer and my husband was a lawyer, and I was just afraid if I reported it I'd be stuck in Houston for God knows how long as a witness. I'd already been there ten days visiting friends. I'm a Houston girl. Lived there all my life till my husband died ten years ago and I moved up here to be with my sister.

"And anyway, I didn't want to go through all that with the police. It's not something you want to talk about with anybody, but the police are worse. They *always* think it's the woman's fault. A woman can be raped and beaten up till she's half dead and the police will say it's her fault 'cause she lured him. Lured, hah! You'd probably deny that, Lieutenant, but I know it for a fact. But when I got home, my sister landed on me with all four feet, said I hadn't done my civic duty. We were brought up on civic duty. So finally I went down and reported it."

MacIver managed to get a word in. "I'm glad you did. Do you mind going over it one more time? I'd like to know what happened from the beginning."

The story sounded much like Suzanne's. It was Mrs. Craddock's last night in Houston. She checked into a hotel near the airport because she had an early morning flight. She went into the bar early in the evening and fell into conversation with two young men, Ken and Bob. "Nice-looking

60

young men. One of them was black, but I didn't mind that. I like to see young black people getting ahead."

"That's damned white of you." The remark slipped out of its own volition and hung between them like a challenge.

There was a silence. Then Mrs. Craddock laughed. "I can tell you have a sense of humor, Lieutenant—what was your name again?"

"MacIver. Anthony MacIver."

"Are you related to Lamar MacIver?" It was a famous name in Houston—old family, old money.

"No, we're not related."

"Oh." The inflection dropped MacIver into the gutter with the rest of the hoi polloi. She picked up her narrative. "Anyway, we talked and they bought me another drink." Halfway through she had begun feeling sick to her stomach: "I thought I was going to upchuck right there in front of God and everybody." When she woke around noon the next day she was bruised, battered, and nauseated. "I knew without looking that I'd been robbed."

"Did they leave any kind of message?"

"How'd you know about that?"

"We've had a couple of similar cases."

"Have you! Thank God nothing like that's going on up here. Yes, the message was written in lipstick on the bathroom mirror. It said 'You'll hear from us.'"

"And have they contacted you?"

"Good Lord, no. You mean that message was real? Oh, I see. Next comes blackmail. Is that their game?"

"We think so. One woman has received photos of herself, taken while she was unconscious."

"I can imagine what kind of photos. Well, it'll be a cold day in hell when they get any money out of me. I know better than to pay off blackmailers."

"One more thing, Mrs. Craddock." MacIver had been trying to think how to ask the next question. "Was any kind of foreign object introduced into any of your body cavities?"

There was a short silence. Then she said, "Did that happen to the others?"

"Yes, ma'am, it did."

"Well, it happened to me, too."

61

"Would you mind telling me—"

"It's not something I enjoy talking about but—it sounds sort of funny when you just hear about it, but I can tell you it was no laughing matter. They pushed a whole banana with the peeling on up my rectum."

MacIver winced. "I'm sorry, and sorry I had to ask that question. If you hear anything more from them, will you please let me know?" He left his number, thanked her, and turned to Rod, who had been listening on another phone. "That's three, Sarge. One last Wednesday in Kansas City, one Monday in New Orleans, one Saturday in Houston. The same two guys were in Kansas City and Houston. A different team worked New Orleans. And all Houston women." Mac-Iver stared out the window that wasn't a window. "Put the word out to all major hotels to watch for men answering the description of our two assholes. Call the hotel where Craddock stayed and find out if any telephone calls were placed from her room. And then put out another query on the computer. Let's see if this is a local epidemic or if it's spreading around."

The woman's voice on the telephone was so choked that MacIver didn't recognize it. She said, "They called."

"Who called? Who is this?"

"Suzanne. Suzanne Hilbourne."

"Suzanne, I'm sorry. You didn't sound like yourself." Now he understood. "You mean the two guys called?"

"Yes. I'm going to have to pay them after all. They say they'll send a tape to Carol's school if I don't. I can't risk that." Her voice was close to breaking.

"When and where are you supposed to turn the money over to them?"

"Tomorrow, in Galveston. I'm supposed to go to—wait, I have the name of the hotel here."

"Did you get this on tape?" When she said yes, he said, "Why don't you just play the tape for me?"

"All right. Wait till I rewind." Seconds passed. She said, "Okay, here it is."

MacIver heard Suzanne's voice. "This is Mrs. Hilbourne."

"Mrs. Hilbourne! Come on, don't we know each other intimately enough for me to call you Suzanne?" His voice was boyish, smug, cruel. MacIver could imagine him smiling, enjoying the hold he had on his victim. The voice continued. "Ready for your instructions, Suzie? Got paper and pen?"

She said shortly, "Yes."

"You will get two hundred and fifty thousand dollars in tens, twenties, and fifties—no hundreds. Get the money today. Put it in a bag. Tomorrow, you will drive from your home to Hobby Airport. Rent a Lincoln Towncar there. As soon as I hang up, you should call the airport and reserve the car. When you pick it up, transfer the money into the trunk of the Lincoln.

"Drive directly to Galveston. Check into the Key Largo Hotel. A room will be reserved for you. When you arrive at the hotel, turn your car over to the valet parker. Tell him to lock the car and bring the keys to you. Check in and wait for the car keys, then go to the piano bar in the main lobby on your right as you enter. Take a table with an empty table nearby. A man will come in and sit at the empty table. You order a drink. Then get up and go to the john but leave the keys on the table beside the ashtray. When you come back, they'll be gone."

So that's how they'd get into the car, MacIver thought. He was familiar with the Key Largo, and he could visualize the parking lot where the car would be parked. There was no cover there for a stakeout.

The voice continued. "When you leave the hotel, you'll find your keys on the left front tire of the Lincoln. In the trunk you'll find the videotapes, one original and three copies. If you do not comply with these instructions, one tape will be mailed to your daughter's school, a second to your office, and the remainder to some of your clients. Do you understand?"

Suzanne had to clear her throat before she could speak. "Yes. How can I be sure you don't have other copies?"

"Would we do a thing like that to you?" He laughed.

MacIver growled deep in his throat. One of these days he'd be face-to-face with this asshole. They'd see who was laughing then.

"You're just going to have to trust us, doll. Incidentally,

we thought you might like to have a private viewing. We're installing a VCR in your room along with a copy of the tape. It makes *Behind the Green Door* look like Sunday school stuff. Definitely a triple-X rating."

MacIver could imagine Suzanne's humiliation. He wished he'd waited until he was with her to hear the tape. The man's voice went on. "You've got all the instructions?" She said she did and he asked, "You're not going to disappoint us, are you, Suzie?"

Her voice was steely. "I'll follow your instructions."

"Wise decision. 'Bye now." The telephone clicked. There was a second click as Suzanne turned off the tape recorder. She said, "You heard?"

"Yeah. Can you get the money by tomorrow?"

"Yes, I—it won't be easy, but yes, I can manage."

"Good. We can handle the drop." He already knew what kind of vehicle he wanted for the stakeout. He'd have to have a homing device so the vehicle could park out of sight of the hotel parking lot. "We'll put a tail on them and pick 'em up after they take the money."

"But I can't risk—"

"I know. I don't want you to risk anything either, but we've got ways of dealing with drops like this. Let me see what I can come up with." He started to ring off, then added, "And listen, Suzanne, I know you feel rotten about this, but hold a good thought, okay? We'll take care of it." When she didn't answer, he said, "Okay? You there?"

"I'm here." He could hear tears in her voice. "I hope you can—take care of it, I mean."

"We'll do it, don't worry. Try not to, anyway. I'll call you later." He rang off and thought about it. Then he called the Criminal Intelligence Division. He would need help from the technical equipment detail. After that, he called Sergeant Rodriguez. "Bring us some coffee. We've got some planning to do."

Rod's mustache looked longer than it had the day before. MacIver wondered if it grew in spurts; it was tending toward a villainous look. "Tell me, Sarge, what are your plans for that mustache?"

Rod reddened, and stroked the object with both index fingers. "I guess I'll just go on growing it. I don't really have any plans."

"If it gets much longer, you're going to have to braid it."

"It's Rosa, see. She's my girl. She's got a thing about mustaches, so I said 'Okay, I'll grow one.'"

"Well, you did that, all right." MacIver sipped his coffee and spluttered. Rod hadn't put in sugar. The sergeant pulled three packets out of his pocket. "Sorry, Loot, I forgot. I didn't want to put it in because I didn't know how much you used." MacIver dumped in two packets and explained the instructions Suzanne had received.

Rod said, "They sure have got themselves an involved plan here for a couple of gigolos."

"The same thought occurred to me." MacIver loosened the ties on his shoes and worked his feet free. He wiggled his toes and breathed a little sigh of comfort. "Of course, a quarter of a million ain't peanuts. Now this is what I want to do." He outlined his plan.

When he'd finished, Rod said, "Your plan is as complicated as theirs."

"Got to be if we're going to catch them."

"I guess so." The sergeant still looked doubtful. "I've worked a lot of extortions and I've never come across one that was this involved."

"Maybe they've been watching too many TV shows. Or maybe we're not dealing with just a couple of hot dogs. This may be a bigger operation than we realize."

"I put the query out on the computer nationwide. We should start getting some answers this afternoon." Rod started to leave, and paused. "Loot, you think my mustache looks bad?"

"No, hell no. It's great, Sarge."

Rodriguez looked relieved. "Good. That's what Rosa says, but sometimes women . . ." He left the room with the sentence unfinished.

At two, Rod returned to MacIver's office. "You hit it, Loot. We got one on Hilton Head Island, two in Miami. The MO's the same on all of them. All women. All drugged, assaulted, and robbed."

"Any more foreign objects?"

"None mentioned."

"Call the lead officer on each case and determine if a foreign object was used on any of the complainants. And find out if there were phone calls from the hotel rooms, assuming the attacks took place in a hotel."

"Got it, Mac."

"When did they happen?"

"The earliest was the twentieth and the latest the twenty-third."

MacIver looked at his calendar. "Suzanne was the first, then. No more from Kansas City?"

"Nope. They all come from resort-type places."

"Except for Kansas City and Houston. Interesting."

"Yessir. But what does it mean?"

"I don't know. Coincidence? It's such a bizarre crime and it's occurred in such diverse spots at approximately the same time. Group think? Possible but unlikely. I'm more inclined to think that it's an organized scam. Somebody put teams in different places and pushed the button for action. Okay, Rod, start tracking these. Get descriptions of the participants. Another thing: find out if there have been any follow-up extortion demands."

The sergeant had been gone thirty minutes when he called back in. "We got another one, Mac. She's in the hospital with a fractured skull."

9 Her name was Hermione Schultz, and she was in Ben Taub, the charity hospital. When MacIver and Rodriguez walked into the room, they found her propped up in bed sipping a Coke and wearing a pink bed jacket. She was a large woman; what might have been pretty features were hidden beneath swollen, discolored skin. Her hair was red, matted, and straggly, but she seemed undaunted by her experience.

She greeted them with, "Hi. You guys made good time and it's a good thing. I'm getting out of this dump as soon as I can." She waved a hand at the three other beds in the room. "I was unconscious when they found me and those bastards took all my identification so the hotel had no option but to bundle me off to Ben Taub. Pull that curtain so we'll have a little privacy."

Rodriguez pulled the curtain, shutting them off visibly from the other three occupants of the room. Ms. Schultz said, "Pull up some chairs."

They moved chairs closer to the bed, and Rod asked permission to tape their conversation. Hermione said, "Help yourself. I got nothing to hide."

The attack had taken place at the Carlton Hotel on Sunday afternoon. Ms. Schultz had been there on business. "I have my own jewelry business and the way I sell is by showing my stuff in places where I can get a big crowd. The Savings and Loan Association of Texas convention was going on at the Carlton so I rented one of the conference rooms, put up a few signs, and I was in business." She paused, took a sip of

Coke, and made a face. "Diet Coke, yuck. But I have to watch the calories."

She had wound up her showings at 4 P.M. "The convention was over by that time and everybody was moving out. I did a pretty good volume over the two days, close to ten thousand dollars gross. They took all the cash. At least the people at the hotel tell me they didn't find any cash, but they left me the checks and charge slips. Guess they thought they couldn't use them. Took my stock, too." She chortled. "I'd like to see their faces when they find out the jewelry's worthless."

"Your jewelry is worthless?"

"All paste. Not worthless to me, of course. It'll cost me a bundle to replace it. Good imitations are expensive. But it isn't worth shit to them. I can't risk traveling with the real stuff, fourteen and eighteen karat gold, diamonds worth up to five thou retail. I'd be stupid to carry around that kind of merchandise. I could be ripped off anytime."

"Too bad the robbers didn't know that."

"Isn't it! Maybe they would have left it. I always figured if I got held up I'd explain that the stuff was just paste, but these shitheads didn't give me a chance."

The team had followed the usual pattern, first striking up a conversation in the hotel bar. "I was pooped and ready for a drink. These two guys moved from the bar over to my table." She shrugged, then winced. "Every once in a while I feel like my head's about to come off. Anyway, it was okay with me if they wanted to buy me a drink. I don't see any point in paying if somebody else is willing to."

She had begun feeling dizzy at the end of the second drink. "I've got a stomach like cast iron so that really surprised me. I thought I might have picked up a virus and decided I better get out of there fast before I got any worse. The two guys came along with me. At the time I thought it was sweet of them."

"You went to your room?"

"The conference room, yeah. That's the only room I had booked. They got kind of excited when they saw all the jewelry. That's when I tried to tell them that it wasn't real, but I couldn't seem to get the words out. Strangest sensation. I was talking and they were just ignoring me. Then one of them said, 'She sounds funny, doesn't she, kind of like a tape running down.' The other one said, 'Yeah, I wish she'd just go on and pass out. You must not have put in enough stuff.' The black guy said, 'Shit I didn't! I put in more'n usual on account of her being such a big mama.'" She added, "Sons of bitches."

MacIver said, "So you were conscious when you got back to the conference room."

"Oh sure. I never passed out till they banged my head on the floor. I knew what was going on most of the time. I didn't remember when I first woke up, but it came back gradually. The doctor said that was normal."

MacIver lifted an eyebrow at Rod. An awake witness could be important. She sensed their interest. "Oh hell yes, I was awake. Couldn't defend myself. Couldn't talk sense. Couldn't even scream, but I knew what was going on, all right. It took me a while to figure out what they were doing when they got out the camera. Then one of them shoved me down on a table and began tearing my clothes off. There was a lot of fussing around about the camera angle, so they shoved me off the table onto the floor, and I don't remember anything else. I guess that's when I got the fracture."

They asked for descriptions of the men. Hers tallied with Suzanne's and Betsy Craddock's. MacIver said, "This has happened to some other women, but they don't remember anything after having the drugged drink, so your being partially conscious may be a big help in catching these men. I want you to think carefully. Did they say or do anything that you haven't told us?"

"They talked a lot about lights and camera angles, but I don't remember exactly what they said."

"What about the camera? It was video?"

"Yes, a portable one, but they had a stand for it, too."

"Did you notice the make?"

"No. I don't know boo about cameras."

"You said they mentioned lights?"

"They had at least two. *Bright* lights, and hot."

"What kind of accents did they have?"

"Local. They sounded like we do."

"Did they call each other by name?"

She thought about it, started to shake her head, and thought better of it. "Not that I remember."

MacIver asked the next question as tactfully as possible. "Did they rape you with anything that was unusual? I mean, did they use an object to rape you?"

She shivered. "Yeah, they did, as a matter of fact. Shoved a Pepsi bottle up my wahoozie. That's one reason I'm so sore."

"I guess your doctor's making all possible tests."

"I suppose so. Oh, you mean is he testing for AIDS? He's going to in six weeks, but I'm not *too* worried about that. Those two guys were in such great shape, they couldn't possibly be drug users, and they sure weren't gays."

"Did they leave you any kind of message?"

"Not that I know of. The hotel has my stuff stored, what was left of it."

MacIver asked for permission to go through it. She said, "Sure, help yourselves. You want me to sign something?"

He wrote out a note of authorization and Ms. Schultz signed it. They had her run through the story again, but nothing new came out. MacIver said, "We'll get your statement typed up and bring it back for you to sign. If you think of anything else, let us know."

"Okay, fine. I hope you get 'em."

"We will, sooner or later. Sooner, I hope."

In the car, MacIver reviewed his notes. "This happened on a Sunday afternoon. The Minnesota woman, Craddock, was Saturday night. Our guys have been busy. You've got the descriptions out to the hotel security people?"

"In all the major hotels both downtown and in the outlying areas. They're supposed to be checking the bars regularly. These two should stand out like a neon sign."

"If they keep working this area, we're bound to get them. Let's go by the Carlton and go through her things."

The manager of the Carlton was helpful, making sure that all of Ms. Schultz's remaining possessions were available for investigation. He also summoned hotel employees who had been on duty on Sunday for questioning. The bartender remembered the two men, as did a bellhop, but nobody had seen them leave the hotel. The bellhop said they were not guests in the hotel. He assumed they were convention members.

MacIver asked, "Were any phone calls placed from Ms. Schultz's conference room?"

The associate manager said, "I'll find out, Lieutenant." She was back in a couple of minutes. "Yessir. One call was placed at five-thirty P.M."

MacIver said, "Find out which pay phone this one went to, Sarge."

When they went through Schultz's possessions, they found the message scrawled on her white silk blouse, with lipstick, as usual. "You'll hear from us."

They took that with them, signing a receipt for it, and returned to the office. They had to get ready for the drop in Galveston.

MacIver explained the plan to Suzanne that evening at a cocktail lounge close to her office. Her face seemed to have shrunk since last night. The area under her eyes was dark and the skin looked translucent; blue veins seemed too close to the surface.

MacIver had been preoccupied with plans for the drop much of the afternoon. Just as there were a few things he hated about his work, there were a few things he loved, and planning how to get the bad guys was one of the best. But now, looking at Suzanne and remembering what she was going through, he felt pity and a surge of protectiveness. He had met her at the door, put an arm around her, and said, "Lady, you look like you've been going through hell. What you need is a drink. That will relax you. Then I'm going to tell you what we're going to do to those SOBs, and that will make you feel downright happy."

"You do have a plan, then?"

"Of course I've got a plan." He had been leading her toward a booth as they talked, and now he set her down and waved at the barmaid. "What do you want to drink?"

"A big glass of water first. Then—I don't know."

"Scotch," he decided for her. He ordered two Chivas doubles with soda. "And two glasses of water. Now then—" He was eager to tell her the plan, but when he looked at her across the table and saw her unhappiness, he interrupted himself. "Give me your hand."

She looked at him, at the hand he had stretched across the table, and finally held out her own. He said, "Now then. Listen to me. We're going to get the tapes back. We're going to get the bad guys. By this time next week, all of this will be nothing but a bad memory."

She stared at him for a long moment, tears filling her eyes. "God, Tony, I hope you're right."

"I'm right. Everything's going to be okay."

She squeezed his hand, released it, and reached for a tissue. "Sorry, but this has been a bitch of a day. Mr. Reevson at the bank almost went into cardiac arrest. He kept telling me I should keep the fund intact for my heirs, and of course he wanted to know what I was going to do with such a large sum. The only thing I could think to tell him was that I had come across a good investment. That really set him off."

The drinks came and MacIver lifted his glass. "Here's to getting the tapes, arresting the bad guys, and keeping your money."

She stared at him over the glass as she took a ritual sip. "You think we can do that?"

"If the plan goes right. Are you ready to hear what we're going to do?"

Spots of color had come into her cheeks. "Ready."

"Okay. These guys are supposed to leave the tapes in the trunk of your car, right?" She nodded. "The logical thing for them to do would be to put the tapes in the trunk when they take the money out. So, first hurdle, we've got the tapes.

"In the bag of money, we've got a tracking device. We follow the people who make the drop. We're in a disguised vehicle. We stay with them till they get to wherever they're going, and we take 'em. End of scenario."

"Why don't you just arrest them when they leave the tapes?"

"Because we don't know who will leave the tapes. It may be the guys we want. It may not."

"Yes, of course. They may just send a messenger."

"Another thing we're going to do is take your money and

spend a little time cutting out paper dolls. We're going to make a boodle."

A boodle, he explained, was a package the same size as a bundle of money but only the bills on the top and bottom were genuine. In between was newspaper cut to bill size. "I haven't figured it out because it gets complicated with the fifties, twenties, and tens, but if they should, by any chance, get away with the money, you'd lose a lot less than the whole quarter million."

"Tony, that's wonderful. I thank you. Mr. Reevson thanks you." She came close to smiling.

"Hey, you don't have to thank me. It's my job." He reached across the table again. This time she put her hand in his without hesitation. "I know I was overbearing when you first came in. My wife, former wife, used to say that I forgot to change hats when I got home, and I guess she was right. I'm in the habit of taking charge and sometimes I take charge when I shouldn't. But you looked terrible when you came in, like you'd lost your last friend and the homestead, too. I don't like seeing you look like that, so maybe I was a little too bossy, but I was just trying to help."

She smiled. "I did feel as if I'd been caught up by a whirlwind for a couple of minutes, but at least it was diverting. And you did help. You were right about the drink, too. It relaxed me. I think I'll go home and go to bed."

He walked with her to the car, and watched her lock the doors. "See you tomorrow, then. Get a good night's sleep." Then he added the usual, "And try not to worry."

He hoped by this time tomorrow she'd have nothing to worry about.

10 MacIver reached home at 7:30, but he was still mentally on duty. He gave Priscilla food, changed into his swimsuit, wedged the matchbook above the door, and went down to swim. After thirty minutes in the pool, he relaxed in a lounge chair and reviewed his plans for the drop.

The transfer of extortion money was a situation where the police had everything on their side. They knew where the crooks would be and when they were scheduled to be there. Even so, this kind of operation occasionally went sour, and MacIver wanted to make sure that didn't happen.

He would have a bug in the money bag; a technician would install it tomorrow after Suzanne picked up the bills at the bank. The vehicle, seemingly a dilapidated van, actually would be capable of making a high-speed chase. A male and female officer in the front would seem to be a husband and wife. To complete the masquerade, they would have a baby-size doll in a carrier between them. Rod and MacIver would be in the back of the van watching from the one-way glass windows. The same technician who installed the tracking device would be present to monitor it.

The device would tell them when the money was transferred from Suzanne's car to the crooks' vehicle, and when it began to move. They would then trail it. If they were lucky, MacIver thought, the trail would lead to the brains behind the operation. He strongly suspected that the teams around the country were fielded by an organized gang, and the phone calls after the attacks suggested that the headquarters were in Houston.

He closed his eyes and considered possible glitches. Traffic was always a hazard. The police van could get hung up in a traffic jam, but that was unlikely in Galveston in the early afternoon on a Thursday. The van could break down: he made a mental note to have mechanics go over the vehicle thoroughly tomorrow.

The most likely glitch was that the tracking device could malfunction, but again he would have it checked carefully, and Gene, the top technician in the department, would be with them to deal with any difficulties. Or they could be spotted by the extortionists, but that wasn't likely, considering their cover and the distance they would stay behind the others' vehicle.

He couldn't foresee any other glitches. Still, if something strange happened and both plans A and B failed, there was always plan C: lose the crooks but, he hoped, save the boodle. And of course there was plan D. God, he hoped they didn't have to go to that one: lose both the money and the crooks. He didn't even want to think about that.

He went over it all again, and decided that he had covered every possibility, both negative and positive, barring an act of God over which he had no control. Satisfied, he waved at Ravi and ordered a scotch and soda.

He had been immersed in his thoughts, oblivious to everything around him. Now he saw the boy from the fifth floor and realized that he had unconsciously noted the youngster's presence minutes before. The boy was moving toward him, not directly but in stages, stopping at a table to look at an open magazine, moving back to poolside and testing the water. The boy picked up an abandoned towel nearby, moved back to the water, and finally turned to look at MacIver. "Hi."

"Evening, *Que paso?*"

"How's your cat?"

"She's all right."

The youngster glanced around and then came over to MacIver. "You ever arrested anybody?"

"Quite a few people."

"What for?"

"Murder, armed robbery, theft, extortion."

The boy sat down on the concrete. "Is that all?"

"No. I've arrested people for breaking and entering, being a public nuisance, rude and disorderly conduct."

"Oh." The boy seemed to lose interest. His glance darted repeatedly to the entrance to the pool area. MacIver said, "My name's MacIver. What's yours?"

"Richard."

"Richard what?"

"Pierce." He stuttered a little over the name.

"Where's your father?"

"He was taking a nap when I left, but he'll probably be down in a little while."

"Where are you going to school?"

Richard ducked his head and mumbled something. MacIver said, "What was that?"

"Saint Michael's." He scrambled to his feet. "I better go."

"That's a good school. You like it?"

Without answering, the youngster made a running dive into the water. MacIver watched him surface and swim to the far end. Then he saw the father standing a few feet from the edge. MacIver wondered if he was the reason the boy had left so abruptly, or had it been the question about school? Richard climbed out of the pool and walked away with his father. MacIver finished his scotch, debated having another, and decided it was a good idea.

When Ravi brought his drink, MacIver asked, "That youngster I keep seeing around here, Richard Pierce—" Ravi nodded. "Does he have a mother?"

"Nosir. There is only the boy and his father."

"Does he go to school, do you know?"

"I do not know. I am not here during the day, but I can ask one of the men on the day shift."

"Yes, please do that, Ravi. Let me know what you find out."

The next morning, MacIver interviewed Mrs. Robb, Mrs. Elsing's roommate in New Orleans, who had not been well enough to return home until the previous day. She was propped up in her bed wearing a frilly yellow robe. She told

76

the story he had already heard about the evening of her friend's death, describing how the young couple had urged the two teachers to have a second glass of champagne. Mrs. Robb had done so, but Mrs. Elsing had refused. The couple still were trying to persuade her when Mrs. Robb had begun feeling ill.

"I said I must have gotten hold of some bad food. I lay down and that's all I remember till the next morning when they woke me up. Lurinda was lying there with that awful thing sticking out of her mouth. I'm still having nightmares about that." She wiped already red eyes. "Lieutenant, why would they do that? She never hurt anybody. Neither did I. We didn't have anything worth stealing. Why would they do it?"

"I don't know, Mrs. Robb. We may not have the answer to that until we apprehend one or both of them. By the way, I didn't tell Mr. Elsing about the thing in her mouth. I thought that was too painful for him to know."

"I'm not going to say anything about it to anybody. I don't even like to think about it."

As soon as MacIver finished the interview, he met Rodriguez and the others, and they headed for Galveston.

Suzanne checked into the Key Largo Hotel at 1 P.M. She couldn't have felt more conspicuous if she had been spotlighted on a stage. They were watching her, but who were "they"? The man who sat in the café reading a news magazine? The woman staring into the windows of the sundries shop? Or the bellhop leaning on his luggage cart by the front door?

She gave her name. It seemed to her that her voice reverberated throughout the lobby, but the clerk said, "Pardon?" and she had to repeat it.

The young woman found her reservation. "This has been prepaid, Mrs. Hilbourne. If you'll just sign the register."

Suzanne signed and was handed a key. A moment later a young man brought her car keys. Continuing to follow directions, she went to the bar and took a table with an empty table behind it. A minute later she glanced around. The table was now occupied. The man sitting there held a newspaper in front of his face.

Suzanne ordered lemonade and asked for directions to the ladies' room. She laid the keys on the table beside the ashtray and left. In the rest room she stared at her face, noting without interest that there were tight lines of tension around her eyes and mouth. She washed her hands and returned to the table. The keys were gone, as was the man who had sat behind her. She paid for the lemonade without tasting it and went to her room.

Her room had a magnificent view of the water, but the thing that caught Suzanne's attention was the VCR sitting on a credenza. She stared at it with fascination and repugnance. A blue ribbon was tied around it and a card lay on top. It read, "Congratulations! You are the first-prize winner in the Fuchham National Sweepstakes." She dropped the card in disgust. Sixth grade humor, just what she would have expected from those two.

She backed away from the machine and looked around the suite, noting without appreciation that it was tastefully decorated with Victorian pieces rather than the usual modular hotel furniture. A corner armoire and a marble-topped commode looked like genuine antiques. The colors were blue and white, and they gave the room a summery, island feel. She walked to the front windows and stared at the Gulf. It was a cloudy day, and a strong south wind whipped the water into spewing whitecaps. In spite of the weather the beach was crowded with determined vacationers. Suzanne took a deep breath and turned back to face the VCR.

She had debated all the way to Galveston whether to watch the tape. She didn't want to see it. On the other hand, she thought she should. She retained a hope that she would be unrecognizable. Or perhaps it would be obvious that she didn't know what she was doing. She found the On button and then punched Play.

The screen was blank for a moment; then the title, *A Night of Delight,* appeared. The title, like the note, seemed childishly crude. A picture came on: Carol and herself walking down the sidewalk in front of their home. Both wore tennis dresses and carried rackets. Carol was saying something and laughing. Suzanne stared in surprise. This wasn't what she had expected. Abruptly the scene changed.

She saw a woman on a bed, naked. It took her a moment to recognize the woman as herself. The camera panned her face. Her lips were parted, and her jaw slack. Her eyes were glazed, but open. The camera moved back and she saw Bob from the neck down. They would be careful not to show his face, she thought. She wrapped her arms around herself and huddled in the chair as the tape continued.

It seemed to go on a very long time, and Suzanne sank lower and lower in the chair. Then the camera closed in on a Coke bottle. She tensed and moaned softly, dreading what was to come. The view switched to the woman's crotch. She saw the bottle being worked into place. Then a hard blow jammed it deep inside her. She cried out. That was real. She remembered the agony of it. "Damn you! Goddam you to hell, you bastards!" She was crying.

The film ended. She snapped off the tape, blew her nose, and paced to the window. Cars scurried back and forth on the boulevard below. They might be down there in one of those cars. Wherever they were, she hoped Tony caught them. She hoped he caught them and they tried to run away and he killed them. She thought she'd like it better if she could kill them herself.

MacIver, his technical surveillance crew, and Lt. Gene Maxwell rolled east on a side street. All five officers in the van were intent on the steady *beep beep beep* of the tracking device. In the front Chuck and Liz were dressed in shorts and T-shirts with a baby crash seat between them. The carrier held a Cabbage Patch doll that from a few feet away looked like a live infant. MacIver, Rod, and Gene were in the back.

Less than five minutes after Suzanne's car was parked, the needle of the device began to move. MacIver said, "They'll be switching the money from her car to theirs. And putting the tapes in her trunk, if they kept their end of the bargain."

The tracking device began to show movement to the left. The vehicle with the money was rolling. Chuck turned on the ignition and signaled for a right turn. MacIver said, "Give them a lead of about three blocks."

When they turned onto Galveston Boulevard, MacIver viewed the vehicles ahead through binoculars. An old van made a left turn off the boulevard but the tracking device's signal didn't vary. They were headed toward East Beach and Stewarts Beach and rapidly approaching Eighteenth Street. Abruptly the indicator in the tracking device moved to the left. MacIver said, "Left on Fourteenth." As they turned, coming off a twenty-foot seawall on a slope, MacIver spotted what he guessed was the target vehicle, a black van, heavily ornamented with chrome, four blocks in front of them.

Chuck said, "I like the Corvette."

"Too noticeable," Rod said. "I like the black van."

At Avenue J, the signal took an abrupt left. The Corvette continued straight. The van turned. Chuck grinned. "You win, Rod."

They continued to follow west, passing the monument to veterans of the war between Texas and Mexico, and northwest onto I-45. The tracking device still emitted a strong signal, operating at top efficiency.

The black van passed Primo's Restaurant at Seventy-first Street. They were approaching the causeway that connected Galveston Island to the mainland. The outbound lanes were almost deserted. Only the van and a truck hauling hay were ahead of them. As they neared the causeway, the van's brake lights flashed on.

"Why are they slowing down?" There was nothing out here but the four-lane causeway and miles of water. The hay truck, too, was slowing. It was overloaded with bales of hay arched precariously high over the tailgate. MacIver said, "That hay looks like it's going to fall off." As he spoke, two bales plummeted to the pavement in front of them. Chuck braked and swerved. The whole stack was teetering. Chuck yelled, "Goddam!" and stood on the brakes as bales of hay cascaded over the highway.

MacIver suddenly realized what was happening. "It's a diversion." He got the back door open and jumped out. The black van had pulled to the side of the causeway and stopped four hundred and fifty feet ahead. He heard a shout from

Rod, and turned. A man in the back of the truck was kicking the last two bales onto the highway. He gave them the finger as the truck rolled away.

"Get the license number," MacIver shouted, and ran toward the black van.

Two figures had gotten out of the van and were standing at the causeway railing. MacIver clambered over broken hay bales and started toward them on foot. They were tossing something over the railing. Then he recognized the money bag. They were tossing the money into West Bay. He ran to the railing and looked down.

A shrimp boat, its nets almost at the surface of the water, was below the causeway. The bag had fallen on the boat's flat back deck and bounced into the nets. As MacIver watched, one of the crewmen gave a thumbs-up sign and the boat steamed under the causeway. The figures jumped back into the van. MacIver stopped. There was no way he was going to catch them. He watched the black van speed away.

"Shit! Okay, let's get that goddam hay off the highway."

While the others dragged hay bales to the side of the causeway, MacIver radioed for assistance from the Galveston Organized Crime Unit.

"Did you get the numbers of the boat, Lieutenant Mac-Iver?"

"No." He had been too busy thinking about the black van and the hay to think about the boat's numbers, even if he could have seen them from this distance.

The dispatcher continued. "We'll notify the Coast Guard, but without the numbers, there's not much chance of apprehending them."

"We had a bug in the bag. That should help."

"What frequency were you operating on?"

MacIver told him. "Okay, Lieutenant, we'll get back to you when we know something."

MacIver got out, took off his coat, and began hauling hay. Even though the sky was overcast, it was hot work and his shirt was soaked with sweat in minutes. The damned hay was dusty, too, and soon all of them were sneezing. But they worked silently, without kidding as they normally would about the oddball jobs police officers found themselves performing.

To make it worse, cars had lined up far behind them and impatient drivers had begun to honk. Chuck snarled "Shaddup," and Liz was muttering to herself. The only words MacIver caught were ". . . listened to what Mom told me."

Finally they had the causeway clear, and they climbed back into the van. MacIver stared glumly at the now-silent tracking device. Plan D. In spite of all his precautions, they had gone to plan D: they had lost both the crooks and the money. He just hoped the tapes were in Suzanne's car.

11 The Lincoln Towncar wasn't hard to find in the parking lot. The keys were on the left front tire, as promised. MacIver opened the trunk and breathed out a gusty "Whew!" Four video tapes were stacked in a box.

"Okay, let's get these back to the lab for testing. Liz, check the trunk lid for fingerprints. I'm going up and give Mrs. Hilbourne the bad news."

A slim, neatly dressed young man stood at the door of Suzanne's suite. MacIver was pleased to see the Galveston Organized Crime unit doing its job. He identified himself and knocked.

Suzanne's face was tight and drawn, the bones close to the skin. She said, "You don't have the tapes."

He hastened to reassure her. "We got them. The others are taking them back to the crime lab."

"Thank God! When I saw you empty-handed—" She took a step forward and for a moment MacIver thought she was going to throw her arms around him, but she stopped. "You don't know what a relief that is."

"I have some idea." He turned away from the glow in her face. He'd tried to think of a tactful way to tell her the bad news and hadn't been able to, so he made it fast. "We got the tapes but they got the money. They got away. I'm sorry, Suzanne."

After a long moment, she said "Oh." It had the sad, hollow sound of a stone falling into a deep well. She turned to the window. "Then they're loose. They could be anywhere."

He crossed the distance between them in a stride and

gripped her arms. "Don't worry about them. We'll get them. It will just take us a little longer."

"Did they know that you were following them?"

He admitted it reluctantly. "They knew."

"Then they'll know I told you. And they'll find that the money is fake. They'll blame me. No telling what they'll do. What time is it? I've got to call Carol." Her voice was climbing toward hysteria.

He held her more tightly. "Take it easy. They're not going to bother you tonight. They're going to be busy with other things." That wasn't completely the truth but he wanted to calm her.

"But they'll be angry that I told, and that they don't have the money. They may come after me. I don't want Carol there alone."

"She's in school. Besides, they're not interested in her."

"They had her picture. It's on the tape. The two of us together. Maybe it was a warning. I've got to—"

He interrupted. "On that tape? They have pictures of Carol and you?"

"Yes, at the beginning—"

"How did they get those?"

"I don't know. I guess they came to our house and took them."

"Why would they do that?" MacIver was talking as much to himself as her, and he was already on his way to the phone. "I'll get an officer out there to meet her. He'll stay with her till we get back."

"Yes, that's good."

As soon as he hung up, he went to the recorder. "I want to see that tape." He added quickly, "Just the intro, the part with Carol." He knew she would be humiliated if he looked at the tape. He would view it later.

He rewound and punched Play. As soon as mother and daughter came into sight, he stopped the tape. "You were going to play tennis?"

"Yes."

"When? Can you tell?"

"I don't know. We haven't played since school began, so it would have been in August. Oh!" She pressed her hands against her throat as she realized the significance. "They shot it before I went to Kansas City."

"You're sure you haven't played tennis since school started?"

"Positive."

MacIver had assumed that Suzanne was attacked because she was in the wrong place at the wrong time, but the intro on the tape proved that was not the case. She had been targeted at least three weeks in advance. He rewound the tape and removed it from the recorder with handkerchief-covered fingers. Somewhere out there Suzanne had a bad enemy.

Before they left the room, a call came in from the first officer on the Coast Guard cutter *Painter*. They had crisscrossed the area, monitoring the frequency that the tracking device was on. "We found your bag under eight feet of water. Scuba divers brought it up. It was empty, Lieutenant, and there's no way we can get fingerprints off of it. What do you want us to do with it?"

MacIver said he'd have it picked up. He and Suzanne went downstairs, where he questioned the desk clerk. Suzanne's room had been reserved by an L. K. Luciano. The VCR had been installed in the room by the hotel's engineer. A credit card number had been given over the phone, but this morning cash had been hand-delivered for the room. The carrier had looked Mexican and wore a heavy beard and sunglasses. MacIver copied the credit card number and took a description of the man, but he suspected both card and beard had been false.

Suzanne, frantically eager to get home, was already outside the hotel door and headed for the car. When he caught up, she said, "You drive, Tony. You'll make better time."

Once out of town, he pushed the speedometer up to an illegal eighty-five. Suzanne was leaning forward as though urging the car to go faster, and her fingers drummed against her knee.

He said, "Suzanne, is there anybody you might have harmed, or who might think you meant to harm them?"

"I've been thinking about that." She glanced at him, then turned her eyes back to the highway as though it were necessary for her to watch to keep them on the road. "It does look as if they picked me out, doesn't it?"

"I'm afraid it does, and I'm sorry. Dammit, you've had enough problems, but somebody—what about your ex-husband?"

"Tim? No, he wouldn't do a thing like that. Besides, we're on good terms. He's remarried and very happy."

"Business? Have you fired anyone or caused anyone to be fired?"

"No, never." Her fingers drummed restlessly.

MacIver reached over and took her hand. She said, "Sorry. Am I driving you crazy?"

"No, I just wish I could make you feel better." He squeezed her hand and released it. He had speeded up to ninety and needed both hands on the wheel.

"What about men friends? Have you dropped somebody who could be carrying a grudge?"

"No. I haven't been close to anybody since I divorced—not close enough to cause any bad feelings."

"Have you had trouble with household help, a maid or yardman?"

"No. There's nobody—that is, I can't think of anybody who hates me that much, or who even hates me at all! But there must be somebody—maybe it's just that I had enough money to interest them—but so many people have more."

MacIver sighed. "Well, keep thinking. Maybe you'll remember something."

They were back in town by five o'clock, in time for the rush hour traffic, which didn't help Suzanne's nerves. MacIver tried to reassure her again. "Carol's all right. She has an officer with her."

"I know that and I know that I'm behaving irrationally, but I just can't wait to get her out of the house. I'm going to call her father as soon as I get home and see if she can stay with him in Dallas until this thing is over."

"How's she going to feel about that?"

"She probably won't like it—at least, she won't like being away from her friends. Being out of school will worry her, too. She's a good student. But she can take assignments with her. I think the school will work with me on this. I just want her completely away until those men are caught."

"Tell her we'll try to catch 'em quick so she can come back home. What about you?"

"I'll call my friend Marge Stapleton. Her husband is out of town, and she won't mind company for a few days."

"Give me her number and address so I'll know where to reach you."

"Yes, I'll do that now."

As soon as they turned onto her street they could see the police unit in front of the house. A young officer was behind the wheel. MacIver went to talk to him while Suzanne hurried inside. "Any action here?"

"Nosir. The girl came home about three-thirty. She's been inside ever since."

"Nobody tried to enter?"

"Nosir."

"Okay, thanks. I'll take over from here."

Inside, Suzanne was on the phone, talking to her former husband. "I haven't told her yet . . . I'll explain as soon as I can. Thanks. I'll call you back when I've made the plane reservation." She hung up and smiled wanly at MacIver. "He's mystified but he says he's always glad to see Carol, and she gets along well with his wife. I'm going to talk to her now. Make yourself a drink."

MacIver mixed scotch and soda and waited. Suzanne was back in five minutes. "She took it well, bless her."

Carol called from the bedroom, "Just remember, Lieutenant, if you don't catch those guys fast, I'm going to flunk the semester."

In his condo, he undressed and put on his swimsuit. He didn't want to make the effort to swim, but he was damn sure going to. Maybe the exercise would get some oxygen to his brain and help him shape up. He had made some serious mistakes today and he wasn't happy with himself. He stayed in the pool for half an hour and climbed out, physically tired but less angry with himself. Dropping into a lounge chair, he argued with himself briefly and then gave in and had a cigarette.

What was the message intended by the lead-in on the tape? All he could make of it was that they wanted to show Suzanne that she had been known to them before the attack, that she had been deliberately targeted. That looked like a revenge motive. Plain extortionists wouldn't have bothered. This had been meant to terrorize her, and it had succeeded. He couldn't blame her for wanting to get Carol and herself out of the house. She didn't know what else they had planned for her. Neither did MacIver.

If the motive behind Suzanne's attack had been revenge, what about the other women who had been similarly victimized? Should he assume that they, too, had been specifically targeted, that somebody was seeking revenge against them? Suzanne, Mrs. Elsing, Mrs. Craddock, Ms. Schultz. They all were or had been Houston residents, but Craddock had been gone for ten years. Schultz had been gone seven. Hard to make a link among the four of them on that basis. Three of them were business or professional women, but not Craddock. Three had enough assets to pay the extortionists, but not Elsing. Then there were the attacks in Miami and Hilton Head. He stubbed out his cigarette. He couldn't see any way to link those with the local cases.

Maybe the tape intro had been shot simply to increase Suzanne's fear and willingness to pay. But she had already paid by the time she saw the tape. Okay, then, the person who made the tape was a sadistic son of a bitch who got his jollies by terrorizing people. It wasn't a satisfactory answer, but it was all MacIver could come up with at the moment. He decided to tuck the questions away for the time being and hope that the part of his brain that stayed on twenty-four-hour duty would come up with a reason.

Ravi appeared as MacIver got up to return to his condo, giving him a sidelong glance that was as subtle as a trumpet blast. He whispered, "I have information for you, Mr. MacIver."

Amused, MacIver followed him to one side. Ravi said, "I have questioned my friends on the day shift." He talked out of the side of his mouth like a character in an old gangster movie. "They have never seen the boy you mention go to school. They say he is here at all hours of the day."

"Okay, Ravi, thanks." MacIver passed over a ten-dollar bill.

"Thank you, Mr. MacIver. Does this mean that the authorities will come and arrest him?"

"No, nothing like that. I was just curious." MacIver patted him on the shoulder and went to the elevator.

What did the kid do all day, he wondered, hang around the building, watch television? Or maybe his father was one of those people who preferred to teach his own child. MacIver supposed he should call truancy officers, but he'd give the Pierces another few days to get settled before contacting the authorities.

The telephone was ringing when he walked in. It was Captain McNamee. "What the dingdong happened with that drop in Galveston?"

"It went sour, sir. They had a truck that blocked us off from the target vehicle."

"How'd they know you were following them?"

MacIver had wondered that, too. "I think they were just prepared for any vehicle that came behind them. It could have been us or it could have been a vehicle behind us. Of course, when we jumped out of the van, they knew."

"Botching a drop is rookie stuff, Mac."

"Yessir, I know."

"See me in my office at ten in the morning." McNamee slammed down the receiver.

MacIver said, "Yessir, I certainly will be there," and banged down his own telephone. Whatever the captain was going to say to him would be no more than he deserved, but that didn't help much. After the way he'd performed today, he'd be lucky if McNamee didn't take him off the case.

12 MacIver called Galveston the next morning as soon as he got to the office. They had nothing on the van, boat, or hay truck except that the licenses on both the van and truck were registered to vehicles reported stolen the previous week. They had questioned the hotel staff, but nobody could tell them anything about the bearded man who had delivered the money for Suzanne's room, not even what kind of vehicle he had been driving.

Next, MacIver called Records. The credit card had been mailed from Phoenix, but the intended owner had not received it. So that, too, was stolen.

He called Mrs. Craddock in Minneapolis to get an update. She said, "Did the police here call you?"

MacIver said they hadn't. She went on. "Oh, I thought that was why you were calling. I got some filthy pictures of the goings-on while I was drugged and a letter saying they have tapes they will make public if I don't pay them. They're asking for half a million."

"Whew! That's a heap of money."

"It certainly is, most of my estate. 'Course, like I told you before, there's no way I'm going to pay it. My husband, and my daddy, too, would both start spinning in their graves if I paid extortion money. They'd say 'Publish and be damned,' or whatever you call what you do with tapes."

"Did they say when they'd contact you again?"

"Two or three days."

"I'd like to know when they call. Would you mind calling me when you hear from them?" He could get the information from the Minneapolis police, but he preferred hearing it from the victim. There often were nuances that a dry police report could not convey.

"Certainly, I'll be glad to call you, but I tell you, Lieutenant, they're not getting a nickel out of me. They can show their nasty tapes to anybody they like. I'm not paying extortion and that's that."

She sounded determined enough that she just might hold to that resolve, MacIver thought. "Mrs. Craddock, do you have any enemies that you're aware of?"

"Enemies! Well, a couple of women in Houston hate my guts—although they'd tell you I was a dear friend."

MacIver got his pen ready. "May I have their names?"

"Oh, Lieutenant, I was just kidding. You're thinking somebody did this to me on purpose? Nonsense. I don't have *that* kind of enemies. The ladies I mentioned, we used to be on charity drive committees, things like that. They were just jealous, no big deal. They might say tacky things about me, but they wouldn't hire somebody to assault me. Besides, that was years ago."

"Time doesn't necessarily make a difference." He went through the questions he had asked Suzanne, had she ever fired anyone, and so forth. She answered no to all questions. Finally, he said, "Now what were the names of those two women you mentioned?"

"I told you, I was kidding. One of them is up in her eighties now and the other has inoperable cancer. I assure you, they did not put out a contract on me—or whatever you call it."

MacIver put away his pen, thanked her, and hung up. Next he called Suzanne. He had awaked thinking about her, hoping that she had gotten a good night's rest and had been able to shake off some of her despondency. He called the office, half expecting that she wouldn't be there, but the receptionist put him through to her. "Morning. I thought you'd take the day off."

"I didn't want to have time to sit around and think. Besides, there are things here I need to do."

"How are you feeling?"

"I don't know. Numb, I think." Her words came in short bursts as though her breath were bottled up and being released in little puffs. "I couldn't even think about it this morning. My mind felt like it was overloaded. It couldn't deal with this anymore. Have you heard anything?"

"Not yet. Zip from Galveston. The crime lab hasn't had a chance to go over the tapes yet. When they get something, I'll let you know. Try to take it easy today."

He decided to call Hermione Schultz. Maybe she'd have some known enemies.

She insisted, however, that she didn't. "I get along with almost everybody, Lieutenant."

"No former husbands who might want to get even for something?"

"Three former husbands, but they don't have anything to get even for. If *that's* the way it works, *they* should have been the ones attacked."

"What about business dealings? Any disgruntled customers or suppliers?"

"I have only *very pleased* customers, and I get along fine with my suppliers. I just don't have any enemies. Lieutenant, does that mean you think somebody did that to me on purpose, I mean, to *me* on purpose?"

Thinking of the intro on Suzanne's tape, MacIver said, "It's one possibility."

"Not a very good one, I don't think. That would take somebody who really hated me, and I don't know anybody like that. I think the guys were there planning to set somebody up from the convention, and I just happened to be handy."

"Maybe," MacIver said. "But think about it, please. If you do remember anybody who might want to hurt you for some reason, let me know."

He hung up, and the phone rang. "Lieutenant MacIver, this is Willie Thomason at the M.E.'s office."

"Yeah, Willie, you got something for me?"

"We've run the tests on that old body that was dug up. Foreign pubic hairs were identified. We have four. Reconstruction of the body fluids was iffy after all these years, but we did manage it."

"So you do have body fluids?"

"We've got 'em."

"Okay, I'll see what we can do about getting a comparison for them."

By this time it was almost ten, and MacIver prepared to go to the captain's office. He wasn't looking forward to this meeting. Captain McNamee would say things that MacIver already knew; he knew that MacIver knew, but he'd say them anyway because when things went wrong everybody's ass got chewed. MacIver would be chewed out by the captain, who in turn would be chewed out by the deputy chief, who would be chewed out by the assistant chief, who would be chewed out by the chief, who would be spoken to sharply by the mayor. Each one hoped the routine would spark some results, because if it didn't, nobody knew what else to do. MacIver wondered if the pressure from the top had already started or if the captain was just anticipating it.

McNamee was on the phone when MacIver went in. Sergeant Rodriguez was there, seated. He'd done something to his mustache so that it looked more tamed than usual. He shot MacIver a partners-in-misery glance and didn't look at him again. MacIver sat down. The captain hung up, looked at his desk, looked at them. "Well, gentlemen, you blew it."

MacIver and Rodriguez said, "Yessir."

"What went wrong?"

Copies of their reports lay on the desk in front of him, so he knew damn well what had gone wrong. MacIver said, "We were concentrating on the van with the money. We didn't realize until too late that the hay truck was part of the operation."

"You're certain that it *was* part of the operation? Why couldn't it just have been an overloaded truck? Happens all the time."

"Because it lost the whole load of hay. That's one reason," MacIver said. "Two, because it didn't stop to retrieve its load. Three, because at the end we could see a guy kicking the bales out. Four, the asshole shot me the finger—twice!"

"Hum." McNamee shuffled through the reports. "Now, this business with the shrimp boat. You actually *saw* them tossing the money over the causeway rail?"

MacIver and Rodriguez said yessir again.

"How do you know that bag had the money in it? Maybe it was a duplicate bag."

"It was the same bag, sir, because the Coast Guard recovered it with the bug still in it. If they'd taken the money out before they tossed the bag over, it would have drifted because it would have been lighter."

The captain said, "Yes, well," and the phone rang. The call took three minutes. MacIver and Rodriguez stared at a picture of the mayor on the wall above McNamee's head. She'd changed her hairstyle since it was taken; MacIver wondered if new photos would be issued soon. McNamee hung up.

"Mac, the way you've written this report—you, too, Sergeant—makes this thing sound more complicated than a 'Mission Impossible' plot. Do you really think the extortionists had a hay truck and a shrimp boat on the scene in addition to the primary vehicle? That would require the precision of a military operation."

MacIver said, "Yessir. But they were all there."

"And you couldn't apprehend one single vehicle or get the license numbers?"

"Sir, we got the license numbers of the hay truck and the van. Both belonged to stolen vehicles."

"This makes the department look pretty bad, you know." Then the captain, who was Southern Baptist and frowned on cursing, used one of his strongest expletives. "Cripes, if the media gets hold of this we'll be the laughingstock of the state, maybe the nation."

"Yessir." The misery in MacIver's voice wasn't feigned.

McNamee glared at the two of them, shuffled through the papers again, smoothed his reddish hair. "Now about these two men who did the assaults—first you have them in Kansas City and then in New Orleans. Is that correct?"

"Nosir. The team in New Orleans was a man and woman, both black. The Kansas City and Houston team consists of two men, one white, one black. Also we've gotten information from South Carolina and Florida that they've had similar crimes within the last week. We're waiting for descriptions of the suspects."

The captain said, "Those may be copycat crimes."

"That's possible, sir, but so far the media hasn't picked up on these. We've tried to keep it quiet for exactly that reason: to avoid copycat crimes, so the possibility of someone picking up the exact MO is very remote. We're going to separate the individual cases from each other and study them to determine both the common factors and the dissimilar ones."

"Yes, well. What are we doing to apprehend the two men working Houston?"

MacIver had just told him that, but he went through it again. Rod amplified. The captain asked, "Have there been any more extortion attempts?"

"The first woman attacked here in Houston, the one who lives in Minnesota, received a demand for half a million. The drop hasn't been set up yet."

The captain frowned at his desktop. MacIver said, "We'll be able to tell more when all the reports are in from the various cities. When they are, I'll go into a more detailed explanation."

"Um-hum. I don't know how you think you can take on another case when you can't even get a handle on this one. We've got to get an indictment on *this* case. Mac, I want your daily supplement to your original case on my desk every day when I come in. You're either going to make progress or I'll take you off the case. Anytime anything new comes up, I want to know about it immediately. Both of you got that?"

They said they had it.

"All right." He glared at them. "Let's get on it."

MacIver and Rod started to rise. The captain said, "Don't go, MacIver. I want to talk to you about a couple of things."

MacIver settled back down and made his face blank because he was suddenly apprehensive. When the door had closed behind Rodriguez, the captain hunched over his desk and became less official. "Mac, this is beginning to look bigger than the run-of-the-mill scam. If it's spread as far as Florida, we may be dealing with a good-sized organization. And all that business in Galveston means they've got manpower, big money, and somebody with brains in the driver's seat. Cripes, they could put people all over the country. And once the media gets it—and that could happen anytime now, any minute—" He looked up as if expecting a reporter to burst through the door. "Once it gets out, we'll have the copycats. No woman will feel safe alone in a hotel. And can you imagine how the mayor's going to react?" The mayor frequently traveled alone. "She'll be on us like a duck on a june bug."

"I understand, Captain."

"We've got to get those two who are operating here. I don't understand why they haven't been apprehended before now. They should be easy enough to spot, judging from their descriptions."

"I've wondered about that, too. I'm guessing that they're staying under cover for a while. Or they may have moved to get away from the heat. If they *do* surface, it will be at a busy time of evening. They'll try to blend into the crowd and stay out of sight of security people."

"I'll talk to Vice, make sure their hotel undercover people are on top of this."

"Captain, back to the organization behind these crimes. There was one peculiar thing." He described the lead-in on the tape of Suzanne. "It had to have been taken at least three weeks before the assault on her, which means that she was targeted well in advance."

"How much did they ask from her?"

"A quarter of a million, but there're a lot of people around who have more."

"You're thinking revenge. Any known enemies?"

"Not that she can think of."

"The other victims, any revenge motive there?"

"They all say the same thing: no enemies. Mr. Elsing— he's the husband of the woman who died—said everybody loved his wife; she didn't have an enemy in the world."

"Revenge for one person is believable, but four is stretching. Let's leave the personal thing for the time being and concentrate on catching these two guys. Now"—he looked closely at MacIver—"how're you feeling?"

The question caught MacIver by surprise. "Fine. I'm feeling great."

"You and your wife get things squared away?"

MacIver wasn't sure what he meant by "squared away." He guessed he could describe their relationship that way.

"The divorce has been final for several months. The stress factor has dropped off a great deal."

"Who was shooting at you the other evening?"

"Damned if I know. All I saw was the barrel of the weapon."

"Anybody you put away get out recently?"

"Not that I know of, except Odetts. He was released that day, but I don't see why he'd want to kill me."

"Anybody tried to find him?"

"I made a few calls. Nobody had seen him. I've got the word out on the street, but nobody's gotten back to me yet."

"Mac, I've been wondering if you need a vacation. It's not like you to screw up the way you did on the Odetts case. I've never known you to take illegally obtained testimony into court before. Now I know it was a new ruling and you'd missed the bulletin on it, but that's just it. It's not like you to miss bulletins. Then, the next thing I know, you've botched a drop. You know and I know that a drop is a bird's nest on the ground. Sure, they pulled some shenanigans, but you should have expected something like that. You're not working at peak efficiency these days. When a good officer starts making stupid mistakes, I have to ask myself why. You say it's not your divorce. Okay. But something sure as dingdong seems to be bothering you."

"Nosir, nothing is. I know this looks bad but—"

McNamee interrupted. "It doesn't do any good to rationalize it away. You've had two major screwups in one week and that shows something's wrong. You've got some time coming. Maybe you ought to go fishing for a couple of weeks."

MacIver liked fishing, but he had other things to do just now. "Captain, believe me, I'm feeling fine. Two mistakes in one week look bad, but they were both flukes. I don't intend to make a habit of them. I'm feeling good, physically and emotionally, and I want to stay on these DARE cases."

"DARE? You and the feds are acronym crazy. Give it to me in plain language."

"Sorry, sir. Drug, assault, rob, and extort. I don't want to walk away in the middle of the investigation."

The captain sighed. "Well, the truth of the matter is, I'd

rather have you than anybody else *if—if* you're up to par. But if you're not—like I said, it's just a matter of time until the media gets hold of this. When they do, the you-know-what's going to hit the fan. We've got to take this team, either that or make it so hot for them that they leave town. If you can't do it, I've got to get somebody who can."

MacIver used his firmest tone. "I can do it."

The captain studied him. It was so quiet in the room that MacIver heard the hand of the electric clock jump from nineteen to twenty. Finally McNamee said, "Okay, I'll give you another few days, but if you haven't produced by that time . . ." He didn't finish the statement. He picked up the reports in front of him, put them in a folder, and slapped it into the Out box. The meeting was over.

MacIver got a cup of coffee, went to his office, and stared out the painted window. The captain had never questioned his ability before. He wondered if the screwups *did* indicate that something was wrong with him and he just didn't realize it. Maybe he'd lost his touch. Maybe his career was down the drain. He finished the coffee and threw the Styrofoam cup into the wastebasket. Maybe he'd better haul ass and do something about finding the black-and-white team.

He called Rod. "The last thing we should have to do is hit the streets, but the way the captain is leaning on me, it's going to have to be the first thing we do. You and I are going to get out among the people. Shake the criminal informants down. Get physical just to the point of being rude. I don't want any grand jury investigation of violence.

"You take the downtown hotels. I'll do the Galleria area. Meet me around the Astrodome for coffee about three A.M. You got that, Rod?"

"Got it."

"The captain's going to have my ass if another one drops in Houston and we're not on top of it, so let's get to it." He hung up, threw on his jacket, and headed out the door.

13 MacIver was at a hotel near the Galleria when his beeper sounded. He recognized the number as Suzanne's, and called her home. When the answering machine switched on after four rings, he identified himself in case she was listening, but she didn't come on the line. He tried her office, but there was no answer. He hung up and thought a moment.

She had been at home, but now she didn't answer. He told the hotel's security chief that he had a problem and headed for her house.

Everything looked normal when he drove up. He went to the door and rang the bell. No answer. He tried the knob. To his surprise the door opened. He drew his .45 and entered warily. He closed the door and listened. The only sound was the hum of the air conditioner.

He moved quietly through the living room toward the kitchen. The first sign of trouble was the overturned chair. He tried the sliding door to the patio. It was unlocked. He opened it and looked outside. Nothing there. He went on through the kitchen, looked in the garage, and headed back toward the master bedroom. He recognized the sickish-sweet smell of blood before he reached the dressing area and felt a stab of fear at what he might find. Holding his breath, he edged through the door. The area was dim, without natural light. He saw something on the floor. It took him a moment to realize it was Suzanne's little dog, Ginnie. He knew by the angle of the body that the dog was dead. When he had checked to make sure the closets were empty, he returned to the animal. Its throat had been cut. Whoever had done it must have twirled the body around, because there was blood everywhere. MacIver scanned the room again, moving only his eyes. So much for the dog, but where was Suzanne?

He retraced his steps through the bedroom and, still cautious, went up the stairs and through the two bedrooms and bath. When he was sure they were empty, he ran back down the stairs.

If he was reading the signs right, somebody had come in through the patio door and surprised Suzanne. There had been a struggle, witness the overturned chair. She might have fled to the bathroom. The dog had probably been barking and the intruder killed it. Then he must have gone, because he hadn't killed or snatched Suzanne. If he had, she couldn't have telephoned the office. Unless—jarring thought—she had called him before she found the intruder. He decided to operate on the assumption that she had called him after she found the intruder.

So she had called him and then she had gone—where? After the burglar? Or maybe she had been hurt in the struggle and had gone for medical attention. He didn't know who her doctor was, but the nearest emergency hospital was Houston General. If that was where she had gone, she would have been there such a short time that she wouldn't be on their records yet. Nevertheless he called the hospital. As he had expected, they had no record of her. He would drive to the hospital, but first he called a crime scene unit.

They rolled up fifteen minutes later. MacIver told them what he knew and what he surmised, and prepared to leave. "The dead dog, Sergeant, take it to the nearest vet. Ask him to hold it for burial instructions. I'm going over to Houston General and see if I can find Mrs. Hilbourne. I don't have a key to the house, so you're going to have to lock the front door from the inside and go out through the garage."

At the hospital, he parked at the emergency entrance and ran inside. A frizzy-haired woman behind the counter was carrying on a conversation with her co-worker and ignored him. "And then I told him that he'd just better watch his mouth—"

100

MacIver interrupted. "Has a Suzanne Hilbourne come in for treatment?"

The woman frowned at being interrupted, glanced at him, and turned her back. MacIver said, "Hilbourne," and spelled it.

The second woman said, "She's the one who just came in."

MacIver hadn't realized he was holding his breath until he gave a gusty sigh of relief.

Frizzy Hair said, "Was that her name? You sure?" She began to leaf through some records.

MacIver addressed the second woman. "Where is she now?"

"Go through those doors to the nurses' station. They can tell you where she is." He thanked her and started toward the doors. Frizzy Hair said to her companion, "You're right. That was her name."

The nurses were more helpful. "Mrs. Hilbourne? She just came in a few minutes ago. My, you got here fast. This way, Mr. Hilbourne."

MacIver didn't bother correcting her, which would only complicate things. Suzanne was in a small room, lying on a bed, dressed except for her shoes. She saw him and stretched out a hand. "How did you find me?"

"By guess and by gosh. Where are you hurt?"

She pointed to her stomach. It was grossly extended. She might have been in the last stages of pregnancy. MacIver said, "God, babe, what happened?"

She had gone by the house to pick up her mail and check her telephone calls. MacIver interrupted, "You shouldn't have gone by yourself. Why didn't you call me?"

"I did but you were out. I was going to put off going, then I thought that was silly. I wouldn't be there more than five minutes."

She had collected her mail at the door and was reading a postcard from a friend as she walked through the living room. "I was almost into the breakfast room when I realized that Ginnie hadn't come to meet me." She turned her head away suddenly and reached for a tissue.

MacIver patted her arm. "I found her. I'm sorry." What he didn't tell her was that he had been so afraid that it would be Suzanne's body he would find that his first reaction at finding the dog's was intense relief. When she had wiped her eyes and blown her nose, he said, "There was somebody in the kitchen."

"Crouched by the door into the garage. A young man. He was glaring at me! He looked furious! I didn't have time to say or do anything. He just lunged at me. He hit me in the stomach with his shoulder, and I fell. By the time I got up, he was gone. Out the front door."

She winced suddenly, and MacIver said, "Have they given you anything for the pain?"

"They don't want to give me anything till the doctor gets here." She drew a breath that looked as if it hurt her. "When I was sure he was gone, I called your beeper. Then my stomach began to swell. I called my doctor and he told me to go to the hospital. How did you know to come here?"

"I went to your house. The front door was unlocked so I went in. I looked around, decided you might have been hurt, and came to the nearest emergency hospital. Does it hurt you to talk?"

She said no, so he asked, "What did the assailant look like?"

"I'd guess he was in his twenties. He might have had red hair. I'm not sure. All I really remember is that glare."

"Blue eyes?"

"No, brown."

"Any idea of height?"

She shook her head. "He was crouched. Then he lunged."

"I don't suppose you had a chance to see if anything was missing from your house."

"I didn't even think about it. I went to the door to make sure he'd gone. Then I called you. That's when I noticed my stomach. It just ballooned all of a sudden. I went into the dressing room." She pressed her lips close together to keep them from quivering. Finally she said, "I didn't know one little dog could have so much blood."

MacIver took her hand and held it. "You drove yourself here?"

She nodded, and winced. So did MacIver. He hoped nothing had been ruptured in her stomach. He said, "That doctor should be here by now."

"I agree." She was quiet a moment. "Why would he do that? Ginnie was just a helpless little dog. She barked a lot, but she would never hurt anybody."

"I guess she bothered him. If he was trying to burglarize your house and she kept barking—" Then it occurred to MacIver that maybe the intruder hadn't intended to steal anything. Maybe he'd come to do exactly what he did. Killing the dog may have been Suzanne's punishment for working with the police. The crooks wouldn't have been happy when they discovered the boodle either. He wondered if they would make a second demand for money or did they want something else? He felt prickles on the back of his neck. They had terrorized her and made her suffer, but would that be enough?

14 Suzanne's doctor arrived and examined her. His diagnosis was better than MacIver could have hoped for.

"She has a small amount of internal bleeding—that's what's causing the abdominal distension—but that should clear up in a few days. I don't think there's any organ damage, and the bleeding isn't enough for me to recommend surgery. I'm going to keep her in the hospital overnight for observation, but I think she can go home tomorrow."

Good news. MacIver gave her a victory sign. "How long does she need to stay in bed?"

"She doesn't have to stay in bed, but she's probably not going to feel like being up much for a couple or three days."

When the doctor had gone, Suzanne said, "Whee, I can go tomorrow!" Then her face sobered. "The problem is where to go. I didn't mind staying with my friend Marge when I was only there in the evenings, but spending all day around her house is a different matter."

"I don't think you should go back home."

"I wouldn't think of it, but I can't bear the thought of going to a hotel."

"There might be something available in the Towers, a corporation suite that isn't being used."

"I know the building, but I've never been inside. Yes, that would be fine."

"I'll talk to the manager and get back to you."

Before leaving the hospital, MacIver called the office. Jarratt had called. He was supposed to pick up the boy this evening, but it looked like he'd be running late. There was nothing else among his messages that couldn't wait until the next day. He called Jarratt and didn't get an answer. He tried to call Rodriguez but the sergeant was still out, so he left a message about Suzanne. Because it was past six by this time, he decided to drive on out to Sharpstown.

Constance was there but not Jarratt. "He's gone to some big party. Didn't he tell you?"

"He left a call for me, but I couldn't get him back. Maybe I can pick him up tomorrow. How did he do in school this week?"

"About the same. His grades ranged from a hundred on an English paper to twenty on a social science test."

"Have you talked to the counselor again?"

"Just on the telephone. She's keeping track of his grades. She didn't say anything new. He's been doing a lot of sketching. Maybe you'd like to see what he's doing." The sketch pad was on the coffee table and she flipped it open.

The drawing, in pencil, was of some kind of monster, one-eyed, loose-lipped, with a drooping, pendulous nose and saliva dripping from the mouth. It looked like a comic strip nightmare. MacIver grimaced. "I think I saw him last week in the holding cell." She gave her that's-not-funny smirk, and turned another page to another monster. "Is that all he draws, monsters?" he asked.

"Yes. I mentioned it to the counselor. She thought it might be therapeutic, getting the inner monsters out and onto paper so they can't bother him."

"Just bother everybody else. The technique looks pretty good, though. He got the shadow just right under the wart on the nose."

"I think it's probably exceptionally good work for his age. Oh, there's one here I think you may be interested in." She turned several pages and held the pad so he could see. It took him a moment to realize that this monster looked like him. The nose was broader; the eyelids heavier and more sloping; the mouth wide open, twisted and angry, revealing gaping, broken teeth; and the hair stood on end over the head like a fright wig, but it was undeniably MacIver. Jarratt had even drawn his weapon in the lower right corner in fine detail. MacIver could feel Constance waiting for his reaction.

He forced enthusiasm into his voice. "He really got me, didn't he? Very well done. Maybe he can go in for portraits."

"Caricature anyway. It doesn't bother you?"

He thought she sounded faintly disappointed. "Why should it? He's done a good job. I'd like to have it. Do you think he'd mind?"

She looked doubtful. "I don't know. I guess it'll be all right."

MacIver tore out the sheet. "Tell him I'm going to put it up in my office. A lot of people will say he's captured the real me."

He didn't look at the drawing again until he had gotten home. Was that what he really looked like to his son: angry, shouting? The eyes were the worst, glinting furiously. He couldn't remember ever having looked at Jarratt that way. Still, it was hard to know how one person looked to another. He felt a deep sadness as he put the sketch away.

He called the building manager, explained that he had a friend who needed an apartment for only a few days, and asked if any of the corporate suites were available.

"We have one on five that I can let him use."

"Great. I'll pick up the key in the morning."

He hung up, and the phone rang. It was Rodriguez reporting that he'd covered the downtown hotels and jacked up the security people. He also wanted to know about Suzanne. MacIver told him what had happened. Rod said, "You think it was a warning?"

"More like a reprisal. But I think it went further than they intended. I hope that's all we hear from them."

"Okay, Loot. Talk to you Monday."

"Right. Get some rest over the weekend, Rod."

Jarratt called MacIver the next morning. "I'm sorry I didn't get hold of you yesterday. I called a couple of times, but you were out. You didn't mind me going to the party?"

"Of course not. Did you have a good time?"

"Yeah, it was okay. I can come over today if you want me to."

"Of course I want you to. I'm going to bring a friend home from the hospital, and I've got to do some things in the office." As he previewed the day, he realized that his schedule didn't leave much time for Jarratt. He added, "Damn, I'm sorry, son. I don't think I'll have to spend too long in the office, so we'll manage to do *something*. Maybe we could see a movie."

"Oh, sure, that'd be great." Jarratt's tone said he couldn't care less about a movie.

"If you've got something you'd rather do—"

Eagerness came into the boy's voice. "Some of the guys are driving down to the beach. Mom said I could go if it was okay with you."

MacIver had meant that Jarratt might have something in mind that the two of them could do together. On the other hand, he understood that it might be more appealing to Jarratt to go to the beach with his friends than to hang around while his father worked. He said, "That sounds like fun. Sure, son, go ahead. We can get together next weekend. We'll try to think of something special."

"Thanks, Dad." Jarratt sounded relieved. Then he said, "Uh, Dad, about that drawing—I'm sorry about that."

"No sweat, Jarratt. As I told your mother, a lot of people are going to say that's the real me."

"I couldn't believe she'd shown that to you. Jeez, I got no privacy around here. I'm going to put locks on everything."

"Don't blame your mother." Not too much anyway. "I think she was trying to tell me something."

"It isn't that you look like that. I just started drawing and it turned out, y'know?"

MacIver didn't but said he did. "The only thing that bothered me was the snaggle teeth. Grandma spent a lot of money on my teeth and she'd be pretty upset if she thought they looked like that."

Jarratt's laugh sounded relieved. "Anyway, it doesn't mean anything. It just happened."

"Okay, son. Glad to hear it."

MacIver wondered about that as he put down the phone. What was it Constance had said about getting the bad inner images out and on paper? Maybe it *was* healthy. Maybe he should try drawing Captain McNamee once in a while. He dialed Suzanne's room at the hospital.

Her voice sounded stronger this morning. "I can tell you're feeling better," he said.

"Much better, and the doctor's been here, and he says I can go home. Or somewhere."

"That's great. I talked to the building manager and he has a suite available. If you're ready to leave, I'll come and pick you up."

"That's too much trouble. I'll take a taxi."

"Forget it. I'll be there in twenty minutes."

Suzanne, her face only slightly drawn, was sitting in a wheelchair in the hospital lobby when he arrived. MacIver said, "You look a lot better than yesterday."

"I feel a lot better." She stood up slowly, gritting her teeth. In the car, she thanked MacIver for arranging for the suite. "Something I forgot to ask you, Tony. About Ginnie— what did you do with her?"

"I told the crew that examined the house to take the body to the nearest vet's."

"That's good. I'll take care of that later. And I called Marge. She's going to bring my clothes over to the high rise."

"What about your daughter?"

"I talked with her last night. She fussed at me for going back to the house. Oh, and she told me to tell you to get on the ball. Dallas is nice, but she wants to come home."

"Tell her I'm working on it as hard as I can."

Suzanne was enthusiastic about the suite. "Positively posh, and look at the view! Magnificent!"

She made out a grocery list, and MacIver did the shopping. They ate an early lunch of sandwiches and salad. Then Suzanne was ready for a rest.

MacIver was going to the office. "How about dinner at my place?"

"Sounds great."

"About five-thirty?"

"That's fine."

It turned out to be one of those days when he tried to make things happen but nothing did. The computer was down in the office so there was nothing new on the DARE cases. He caught up on his back paperwork and left early.

At five-thirty, he picked up Suzanne and the steaks he'd bought earlier in the day, and they rode the elevator to the fourteenth floor. Suzanne admired his apartment, which he explained wasn't his, petted Priscilla, and sat down on the couch as if she were trying not to bend. MacIver asked, "Can you have a drink?"

"The doctor didn't say not to."

"Good. Vodka collins?"

"Fine. Tony, I saw the cutest youngster today. I was walking up and down the hall to get my exercise, and he came out of one of the rooms. He went to the elevator, but I don't think he pushed the button. He just kept watching me, so when I got close, I said hello to him. He smiled—the sweetest smile, and it seemed to light up his whole face."

"I know the kid you mean. His name is Richard Pierce."

"I told him I was walking for exercise. He said I wouldn't get much if I didn't walk faster." MacIver laughed, and she added, "He didn't mean it in an impudent way. He was very serious."

"He lives here with his father. Apparently his mother is still back wherever they came from."

"Maybe that's why he was watching me. Maybe he's lonely for his mother."

"Could be. Whoops!" He jumped up. "I forgot to put the potatoes in to bake."

"What are we having?"

"Steak, baked potatoes, and broccoli au gratin."

"I didn't know you could cook."

"I can't, except for steak and hamburgers."

"And the broccoli?"

"Frozen."

As he put the potatoes in the oven, the phone rang. It was Clark Gilbert, an old friend and the head of security at an elegant Galleria-area hotel. "Tony, I think I've got your black-and-white team sitting in our bar."

15 Seven minutes later MacIver pulled up in front of the hotel. The valet parker, eyes shining with excitement, said, "Mr. Gilbert said to tell you he's on the sixteenth floor, 1625."

MacIver forced himself to walk, not run, through the sedate lobby. On the sixteenth floor he found Clark, along with two of his security officers, around the corner from Room 1625. A tall, lanky, fair-haired guy from Georgia, Gilbert said, "Man, what took you so long?" He was only half kidding. "If you hadn't made it in two minutes, I was going in by myself. Right after I called you, the lady took sick. The guys started helping her out. I tell you, Mac, it was all I could do not to step in and have a word with them. She's a resident of the hotel—name is Haines—and I was taking a hell of a risk with her safety, not to mention my job."

"How long have they been in there?"

"The white guy ten minutes. The black guy went down and registered for both of them for the night and got his bags out of the lobby. He took them into the room five minutes ago. I listened outside the door. Couldn't hear much, but I did hear one of them say 'Prop up the right leg.'"

MacIver considered for a moment. If they went in too soon, they might get no evidence. If they waited too long, the victim could be assaulted. "You have your passkey?"

"What do you think? I've got the camera, too."

MacIver had told him to get a camera with a flash and high-speed color film. "If we're lucky, we might catch 'em in the act," he'd said.

Clark unlocked the door. MacIver smashed it open and

sprang into the room, his .45 in front of him in both hands. The two men whirled to face him. He shouted, "Freeze, motherfuckers, or I'll blow your heads off!"

The black was crouched at the foot of the bed facing the victim, who was sprawled on the sheets. The blond man was pointing a video camera at the woman. All three were nude. The two men looked around wildly for someplace to run, then back at MacIver and the .45.

MacIver motioned the man off the bed. "Get over there with your friend." To the blond one, he said, "Put the camera on the table." They obeyed. The only sound in the room was their panicked breathing.

While MacIver read them their rights, Gilbert checked Mrs. Haines's pulse and covered her with a sheet. MacIver said, "Let's get these assholes dressed. Clark, check their clothes."

Gilbert went through them. "No weapons." He took out billfolds. "Roger Elliot Braden." He nodded toward the blond man. "And Richard Jefferson Hicks-Davis. That's Hicks-hyphen-Davis."

There was a small black mole on Braden's chin. MacIver remembered that Suzanne had mentioned it. For a moment rage engulfed him as he thought of these two with Suzanne, who'd had no one to help her. He forced the thought away. He said, "Okay, get your clothes on."

Clark called for a doctor and then for a blue and white. "Send it to the rear of the hotel to the security office."

Braden and Hicks dressed, and MacIver motioned them to lie on the floor. "On your faces. Hands behind you." When they were down, he holstered his weapon and handcuffed the men. Then he went to look at the victim. Her eyes were open, but obviously she had no awareness of what was going on around her. She was a pretty blond woman in her early fifties. "The doctor's on his way?" MacIver asked.

"Fifteen minutes." Gilbert glared at the still prostrate black-and-white team. "I'd like to have those two to myself for a few minutes. I think I just might be able to explain a few things to them."

"Wouldn't we all, but that's the quickest way I know to

111

spring 'em. Tell the doctor to do a blood test for narcotics on the lady. I'll send someone for the video equipment."

Clark tore his gaze away from the pair on the floor. "We have the glasses they used bagged for you, too. I told the barmaid to take care of them."

"Thanks. I'll pick them up after I get rid of these two." He nudged the white guy, the closer of the two, with his toe. "Okay, assholes, on your feet."

The blue and white was waiting by the time they got downstairs. MacIver gave the officers a rundown on the pair's offenses, then went back to the bar to pick up the bagged glasses. Once in the station wagon, he gave a shout of exultation. "Got 'em! Got those sons of bitches in the act. No way they can throw this one out of court." He sang, triumphantly, "La Donna e Mobile" from *Rigoletto*. The words weren't appropriate, but the music was.

A few minutes later he walked into Municipal Court. Immediately behind him was Silas Conover, the foremost criminal attorney in town. MacIver nodded. "Counselor."

"Lieutenant." Conover wore an ill-fitting gray suit, no tie, and white socks, but his rumpled appearance revealed nothing of his mind, which was sharp and deadly. MacIver hoped Conover was representing someone other than Braden and Hicks, but the lawyer ambled toward them. He spoke briefly to the pair and approached the judge. "I'm prepared to make bond for my clients immediately."

The judge eyed him levelly, then turned to the police officers who had brought in the pair. "Is this the only case for which they are suspected or charged?"

MacIver answered. "Nosir. They are suspects in two homicides that occurred out of the jurisdiction of this court. We request a bond that will insure they do not flee the country. We have evidence of their acquiring passports and being in possession of large amounts of currency." MacIver looked the judge squarely in the eye as he always did when he lied. "We also request an AIDS test on both of them."

The judge said, "I cannot order that they be tested for AIDS or any disease at this time. I can request that they voluntarily submit to an AIDS test."

Conover said, "No, they're not going to be tested unless they're indicted.

"Very well, Counselor." The judge addressed the top of his desk. "It is the finding of this Court that a bond of one million dollars cash *each* must be placed before this Court, or they are both remanded to the custody of these officers."

Conover went into his outraged protest act. "But Your Honor—"

The judge banged his gavel. "Next case!"

Outside the courtroom, one of the arresting officers rolled his eyes. "Shit, Loot, I thought a bolt of lightning was going to come down and strike all of us."

MacIver grinned. "I figured I could lie as well as the silver-tongued attorney."

Back in his office, he called Rodriguez and told him the news. "We've got to move fast now. We want a lineup soonest. Suzanne isn't in any condition to come in, but I can show photos to her. I don't suppose Craddock can get here either, but maybe Schultz can make it."

"But, Loot, we got plenty of time. They're not going to come up with two million in cash."

"Conover will have this bail reduced by noon tomorrow. He'll find some judge who'll do it. We were lucky tonight to get the judge we did. No, we won't have twenty-four hours."

He called Hermione first. The line was busy. He called Mrs. Craddock. She sounded sleepy when she answered.

"This is who? . . . Oh, Lieutenant MacIver. What time is it? . . . Tomorrow? No, there is simply no way. I've got seventy-five people arriving at two for a charity coffee. I'm truly sorry. Could I possibly do it the next day?"

MacIver said he didn't think so. "We'll only have them in custody a short time, but we'll take pictures and send them to your police department. You can look at them there."

"Yes, you do that. I'll make it a point to go look at them as soon as the police let me know they have them."

Next he called Suzanne. "We got 'em, lady. Caught 'em in the act. They're in jail on two million dollars bond."

"Tony, that's wonderful. You're sure it's them?"

He described the two. She said, "Yes, that sounds like them. You don't know what a relief this is."

"I think I do, at least a little bit."

After hanging up, he called Clark Gilbert at the hotel. The victimized woman had been given an injection to counteract the narcotic and had recovered consciousness within half an hour of the doctor's arrival. She had not been raped, and was grateful to the hotel staff for their quick intervention. A registered nurse was staying with her during the remainder of the night. Although she probably wasn't needed, neither the hotel management nor Mrs. Haines wanted to take any chances. The doctor had promised to have the analyses Mac-Iver had asked for sometime the next day.

He called Hermione again, and this time she answered. He told her about the arrests. She cried, "Whoopee, you got the bastards! You bet I'll come to a lineup. I'll be there with bells on."

16 MacIver had to look twice to recognize the tall, handsome redhead who walked into his office at 9 A.M. Sunday. Hermione Schultz in full regalia was as different from the swollen, disfigured woman in the hospital as a cruise ship is from a tanker. Her short red hair glowed. The left side of her face still showed a bruise, fading now to purplish yellow, but the puffiness that had swollen her face was gone, revealing good features, and she carried herself well. She wore a black pants suit, black heels, and a white blouse. MacIver stood to shake hands and found he had to look up to her.

"Hello again, Lieutenant. Congratulations on catching those mothers."

"We're not positive that it's them, Ms. Schultz. You'll have to tell us."

"That's what I'm here for."

As they went to the show-up room, MacIver explained the procedure. "There'll be twelve males, six black, six white. They'll take turns standing at the center of the room in the spotlight. Even if you recognize one of them, remain quiet."

"That's asking an awful lot of me. I'm not good at hiding my emotions."

He said firmly, "There can be no outbursts."

"Okay, okay. I'll stay cool."

"You'll be given two cards with six men's silhouettes on each. If you make a positive identification, check the corresponding number. If you make a tentative ID, put a question mark. A firm no, cross out the body."

"They won't be able to see me?"

"No. They'll look at what appears to them as a mirror. They can't see beyond it." He opened the door to the identification room, which held about twenty classroom desk chairs on either side of a center aisle. Jay Hudson, representing the district attorney's office, was already there. So was Silas Conover, puffy-eyed at this hour of Sunday morning but prepared to guard his clients' civil rights. Rodriguez came over to speak to Hermione, and she shook his hand vigorously. MacIver introduced the others, seated Ms. Schultz toward the back, and handed her the cards with the silhouettes. "Any questions before we begin?"

"Nope. Let's get on with it."

MacIver spoke through the intercom to the officer in the other room and told him to start the lineup.

Twelve men came into the room, six whites, six blacks, the two groups segregated. All wore jail whites stenciled in front and back "Property of the Houston Police Jail." Even in the jail garb, Braden and Hicks stood out like diamonds among pebbles. Their posture was more erect, their complexions clearer, and their hair more stylishly barbered. Hermione tensed and muttered, "Hello, you assholes." MacIver shook his head at her, but the remark delighted him. She had recognized her assailants. They had a witness.

The show-up began with the blacks. The officer told Number One to step forward. The man moved to a highlighted spot and faced the viewing room. At five-second intervals he was instructed to make a ninety-degree right turn so that he was viewed full-face, left profile, back, and right profile. When he again faced front, he stepped back and Number Two took center stage.

Hermione leaned close to MacIver and whispered, "You can stop the show. I've identified them."

MacIver looked at her card. She had checked Braden's and Hicks's numbers. Restraining a smile, he whispered back, "We need to go through the whole routine anyway. Legalities."

She settled back and glared through the glass. When Hicks stepped into the spotlight, her breathing speeded and became shallow. Her hands shook and she crossed and recrossed her legs. MacIver could sympathize with her. Again

116

he felt the red heat of rage as an image of the man and Suzanne flashed into his mind. He couldn't think about that. He made himself concentrate on Hermione's reactions. When Braden took the stage, she clasped her arms across her body and shrank into the chair.

Finally it was over. The twelve men filed out of the other room and Rodriguez turned on the lights. MacIver turned to Hermione. Her face had paled and sweat dampened her forehead. She was biting her lip to keep from crying. He dabbed sweat from his own upper lip, took the cards out of her hand, and turned to the others. "We have positive identifications of Numbers Three and Eight."

Hudson took the card, looked at it, and passed it to Conover. The lawyer gave it a cursory glance and handed it back. Hermione drew a long breath. "Anything else I can do to hang those bastards?"

Conover gave her an appraising look and turned to pick up his briefcase. MacIver guessed that the lawyer wasn't looking forward to a cross-examination of Ms. Schultz. He told Hermione, "We'll want you to make a written deposition downstairs."

While she gave the deposition, MacIver and Rod got coffee and waited in the hall. Rod was enjoying the moment. "She nailed them, didn't she? No tentatives, no 'I just can't be sures.'" The ends of his mustache were so long that they billowed gently with his breathing. MacIver found the movement disconcerting.

"She was ready to wind it up as soon as they walked into the room," MacIver said. "I think the reason she was so positive is because she first met these guys in a relaxed situation. She had plenty of time to see what they looked like. Usually witnesses are in danger. They're thinking about whether they're going to stay alive and not paying any attention to what the bad guys look like."

"If we don't get a conviction on this case, we never will. They were caught in the act and we have a positive identification."

"*And* we've made no technical errors. I don't think." MacIver knocked on wood. "I think Conover is going to spoil his no-loss record on this one. I don't see any way he can get these two off. Speaking of which—"

The lawyer passed them in the hall without a glance and went into the deposition room. MacIver fell into step behind him. He had no intentions of having his witness intimidated.

Hermione was reading the deposition she had dictated. Conover said, "Ms. Schultz, are you certain without the shadow of a doubt that you identified the correct men? I want you to remember that if you've made a mistake, innocent men may go to prison."

Hermione eyed him up and down. Then she picked up a pen, signed the deposition, and held it up for him to see. Conover turned on his heel and walked out of the room. She called after him, "Do me a favor. Tell 'em I'm the one who's sending them to the penitentiary."

Smiling to himself, MacIver caught up with Conover in the hall. "We've requested an interview with Braden and Hicks in about five minutes."

The attorney looked at his watch. "I don't want them questioned unless I'm present and I'm already late for an appointment. To see a judge, Lieutenant. I'm going to get that bail reduced."

"Yeah, I guess you'll probably do that, Counselor. Mind if we talk in front of them?"

Conover shrugged. He couldn't prevent that, and both MacIver and he knew it. MacIver turned to Rodriguez. "Sarge, have Braden and Hicks brought to one of the holding rooms."

When MacIver and Rodriguez walked into the room, the two prisoners were seated at the table, smirks on their faces. MacIver pulled up a chair on the opposite side of the table and turned to Rod, who also took a chair. Rod asked, "What do you think's going to happen, Loot, when these sweet things hit the penitentiary?"

MacIver glanced at the two men thoughtfully. "Braden is probably going to be sold for a carton of cigarettes as a punk for the courtyard. Hicks is a little tougher looking. He'll probably be sold for half a carton after he's had his ass whipped about five times."

Braden maintained his smirk and stared at the ceiling.

Hicks looked at his hands, long fingers spread palm down on the table.

MacIver went on. "Their muscles are pumped up from lifting weights, but I don't see any calluses on their hands and they've got no street battle scars around their eyes, so I'd say the tigers we're going to throw them in with will make them the object of sexual gratification within the first fifteen days. In three years their assholes are going to be so cultivated a watermelon could pass through."

"They're going to be in a minimum of twenty years. They'll be in real bad shape by then."

Hicks studied his fingernails intently. His smirk had disappeared, as had Braden's.

MacIver said, "They're real bad guys with middle-aged women who are knocked out, but they're going to find the roles reversed when they come up against the animals in the pen. They may not stay so pretty either. For that matter, they may not stay alive. People get killed in prison."

Rod's face was mournful. "I wouldn't want to face that, and I can take care of myself in the streets."

"Another thing these two have to worry about is the boss of this operation. What do you suppose he's thinking now?"

"I'd guess he's wondering how long these sweet things can stand up to life behind the wall before they spill their guts."

"You got it, Sarge, and I'll bet he's guessing it won't be long. If I were him, I think I'd find a way for them to disappear quietly before they roll over and become witnesses for the state. In fact, I think we're probably looking at a couple of walking dead men here."

Braden's glance crossed MacIver's briefly and slid back to the ceiling. Hicks was staring at his fingernails as though mesmerized. Rod said, "I think you're right. They've got themselves in a nasty situation."

"They've got an out, Sarge. All they've got to do is cooperate and turn state's evidence against crime figures in this city and they'd probably get probated sentences."

"Specifically, if I were one of these guys, how could I get out of this mess?" Rod continued.

Braden's eyes narrowed. Hicks worried a fingernail.

MacIver said, "Right this moment is the time to do it. You

would tell me, 'Lieutenant, I want to see you in private. I'm prepared to turn state's evidence. If you will take me before a judge and grant me immunity insuring that I don't go to prison, I will provide evidence that will lead to the conviction of those people I work for.' And, Sarge, we only need one of them. We don't need both. So the first one to tell me 'Lieutenant, I want to see you in private' is the one who doesn't go to the pen."

"You'd think they'd jump at the chance."

"I would in their place. Tell you what I'm going to do, Sarge. I'm going to give them one last chance. I'm going to wait awhile to let them think of what you and I talked about. If no one speaks up, it's their asses, literally. They will get what they deserve. Probably get AIDS, too, if they don't already have it." MacIver turned to face the two and stared at Braden's forehead.

After a moment, Braden's eyes blinked and he swallowed convulsively. Hicks leaped out of his chair and whirled to face the wall, standing with body rigid and hands doubled into fists.

"Time's up! Okay, guys, you lost your chance. I've got plenty to send you two to the pen anyway, but I want you to think about what the sergeant and I have said. After you've been in the joint awhile and had all you can take, give me a call." He shoved his card into Braden's hand and tossed another onto the table where Hicks had sat. "Take them to Booking, Sarge, and then let's get back to the office."

As soon as Rodriguez returned, MacIver said, "They're probably going to be released on bond. When they are, I want a technical surveillance team put on them. I want them covered like a blanket twenty-four hours a day."

A couple of hours later Rodriguez joined MacIver in his office. "Conover got the bail reduced like you said. One of his runners met Hicks and Braden."

MacIver nodded, and the radio crackled. "Suspects are getting into a Cadillac with almost totally blacked out windows and paper dealer's tags. No name given. They're pulling out. Heading for I-45."

MacIver asked, "Who's the trailing unit, do you know?"

"Sergeant Joe Dallas, but he's by himself. His partner called in sick."

"That's okay. Joe's a good man. He can handle it by himself. Tell him to be sure to get the number of the dealer's tags."

Rodriguez radioed the instruction and then joined MacIver, who was staring at the large map on the wall. MacIver pointed to the site. They waited. Rod paced impatiently. Then he saw Jarratt's drawing, and whooped. "Hey, Loot, that's you! That's damned good. Almost like a photograph."

"Right." MacIver glanced at the monster, and away. "My son drew it."

Rod stopped laughing. "Oh. Well—" The radio's crackling saved him from having to think of something to say.

"I have suspects northbound on Interstate 45, approaching I-10."

Rod acknowledged. "That's clear. Keep us advised."

They watched the map as the major thoroughfares were approached and passed. MacIver said, "They're heading for Houston Intercontinental Airport."

"You think they're going to forfeit bond?"

Before MacIver could answer, the radio sounded again. "Suspects leaving the freeway at the North Belt exit. They're making a U-turn . . . pulling up at Stouffer's. There's a helicopter in the lot."

MacIver said, "Uh-huh! Where's that radio number?" Captain Travis, commander of the helicopter division, had given him authority to use the captain's own radio number to divert the patrol Hughes 500 turboprop from its usual assigned mission if needed. MacIver keyed the mike and asked for the chopper. The reply came in a low, tense voice. "We have moving surveillance at this time, Priority One. Covering a one-point-four-million-dollar buy-walk to its source. Cannot divert."

MacIver said, "Oh hell. Wouldn't you know?" He'd thought he'd have the chopper sewn up.

Joe Dallas radioed, "Suspects getting into the helicopter."

"Tell him to get the number of the aircraft."

Rod relayed the message and Dallas read the number, adding, "They're taking off."

"Rod, have the Cadillac stopped ASAP."

Rod relayed the command, and Dallas replied, "It's taken off already. I couldn't keep both the car and the chopper in sight."

"Put out a general broadcast for the Caddie, and then let's find out who owns that chopper."

MacIver called the Federal Aviation Administration and read the helicopter's numbers. While he waited for an ID, he stared out the window that wasn't a window. At the moment he could see beyond the painted panes a helicopter lifting like a bumblebee into the sky, *whop whopping* its way to—where?

"Okay, Lieutenant, here's the information you wanted. That aircraft is owned by Al's Rent-a-Copter at Andrau Airpark. You want that number?"

MacIver copied the number, dialed it, and asked for the manager. A moment later a man's voice announced, "Donner."

Once he was convinced that he was talking to a police officer, the man was helpful. "Well, I'll tell you everything I can. It was just a routine charter. Nothing wrong, is there?"

MacIver ignored the question. "Who chartered the aircraft, Mr. Donner?"

"Let me get my records here. A man named Wolver T. Potworth. He called this morning, asked for a chopper big enough to carry four people, and he wanted one of our pilots. Said he was a real estate broker. Wanted to show some clients undeveloped land to the west of town, toward La Grange. I said we could handle that with no problem. Told him how much. He had a cashier's check over to us within the hour."

"Who brought it?"

"Young fellow in jeans and a T-shirt. I didn't get his name."

"What did—what's his name—Potworth look like?"

"I didn't see him. He wanted the pilot to pick him up at his office out by Hearthstone Country Club. Westside Realty. Said he could land on the golf course."

"You have a number for his company?"

"Yessir." Donner read the telephone number. "So Todd—

122

that's the pilot, Todd Graves—picked him up out there this afternoon at three. We assumed we'd get everybody there, but it turned out the two clients had to be picked up at Stouffer's over on I-45. We got them, oh, maybe ten minutes ago."

"Where exactly did they head?"

"Out I-10 toward Sealy and La Grange. Something wrong with these guys, is there?"

"We just want to keep tabs on them."

"I can radio my pilot. He'll tell me exactly where they are."

"No, that won't be necessary." MacIver didn't want to alert the passengers in the chopper to the fact that he was tracking them. "We'll find out later, and thanks for your cooperation."

He hung up and radioed two units to go to Andrau and wait for the helicopter. Then he leaned back in his chair. "Now, why do you suppose they're going out that way?"

"Maybe they're going to fly to Mexico."

"Maybe. Sarge, get hold of the sheriff's office in La Grange. Ask them to go out to the airport. If that chopper lands and our guys go off somewhere, request that they tail 'em. I don't want to lose those two."

Twenty minutes later, Donner, the helicopter owner, called. "That chopper you were asking me about?" He was shouting into the phone. "It's gone. Burned up out by Bellville!"

17

MacIver asked urgently, "What about the passengers?"

"They don't know yet. It's still burning. They can't get close. God, I don't know how this could have happened. Todd is an experienced pilot. He's flown that craft on a hundred charters. There's something wrong about all this. There's got to be more to this than just a crash with you callin' and askin' me questions. There's police cars out here, too."

"I sent them to wait for the chopper's return." MacIver hesitated, wondering how much he could tell Donner. "We were interested in the flight because the two passengers picked up at Stouffer's are felony suspects. That's all I can tell you at this time. How did you hear about the crash?"

A pilot on a Southwest Airlines flight from Dallas to Hobby Airport at Houston had seen the fireball made by the burning chopper and was flying low enough to identify the type of craft. He had radioed the tower at Hobby, who in turn had phoned the sheriff's office in Bellville. The sheriff had gone to the site while a deputy located the chopper's point of origin. Eventually they, like MacIver, had called Donner.

MacIver said, "Okay, Mr. Donner, I'll get back to you when I know more." He hung up and called the sheriff's office in Bellville. The sheriff and most of his staff were at the site two miles out of town. The man on duty in the office knew no more than Donner had told MacIver, who rang Rod and told him the news. "Notify La Grange that they don't need to watch for the helicopter. Then I think we better get up to Bellville and see what we can find out."

By now the patrol helicopter was available. MacIver requested permission to use it to fly to Austin County. The site wasn't hard to locate. They could see the smoke miles away. The Fox One pilot, Sergeant Ben Lowery, said, "One hell of a fire these babies make."

They landed in a field near the gravel pit where the chopper had gone down, and walked toward the cluster of people and vehicles collected beside the pit. Two ambulances were there and so many pickups that the road looked like a truck dealership. Flames still burned at several points in the wreckage. A cool breeze from the north competed with the heat from the aircraft.

Rod, Lowery, and MacIver headed for the knot of men closest to the pit who leaned on their cars well back from the wreckage, watching as the flames ebbed. MacIver picked out the sheriff by his badge.

"Evening, sir." He introduced himself and the other two. "We decided we better fly up and see what was happening here. We were tailing a couple of the men on that chopper."

"P. T. Gates." The sheriff put out a callused hand roughly the size of a baseball mitt. A tall man with a heavy middle that sagged over his western pants and belt, he took a spread-legged stance and eyed the three interlopers. "I guess you can stop following them now."

"Looks that way, if they were on board when it caught fire." MacIver turned to stare at the wreckage. The fire had spread well out from the aircraft where fuel had spilled.

The sheriff said, "If it crashed, they were on board. I wouldn't think anybody walked away from that."

MacIver agreed. "Is there any doubt that it crashed?"

"Some, maybe. The way it was sitting. Even through the fire, we could tell it was sittin' there right side up, not over on its nose or anything the way it might be if it crashed. We got photos and measurements of the initial scene. Damned interesting. Billy Carl, get those hulls."

One of the deputies went to his car and returned with a

handful of hulls. MacIver said, "They look like nine milli-
meters."

"That's what we thought. Bunch of 'em lyin' on the ground
down there 'bout thirty feet from the chopper. Two little trails
about six feet apart lyin' in kind of a curved pattern. Looked
like two people had shot a bunch of 'em all at once."

MacIver looked down into the gravel pit, imagining two
men with submachine guns firing from thirty feet at the
chopper. He said, "Any suspicious-looking car tracks?"

The sheriff smiled as though MacIver had asked the right
question. "Good set of fresh prints right back there." He
pointed to their right. "We got the area roped off before half
the county got here, and made plaster casts of them."

"Good work, sheriff."

"Yeah, well, we read a manual or two." Sheriff Gates
hitched up his belt. "What you want these men for, Lieutenant?"

MacIver told him. Gates said, "Been seein' something
about those cases on the computer. Nasty."

"They're nasty, all right. We want the man who's fielding
these people. That's why we're so interested in the two who
were on that chopper."

"Afraid you've lost 'em—" The sheriff stared down at the
mangled helicopter. "One way or the other."

The wreck was still smoking, but the fires were almost
out. One of the deputies trotted down the incline into the
gravel pit and circled the wreckage. Another made a move to
follow, and Gates called him back. "Let's take it easy, now.
We don't want to go in there trompin' around like a herd o'
cattle. Pete's been to them classes on how to investigate the
scene of a crime. Let's just leave it to him." He added,
"Hope you're agreeable to that, Lieutenant."

"Suits me." MacIver was itching to get down into the pit
and search for himself, but he was grateful that the whole
crew wouldn't be given free rein. Rod shifted uneasily, and
MacIver guessed that he wanted to be in on the search, too.

Pete took out a camera and began shooting pictures as he
worked his way closer and closer to the cockpit area. Mac-
Iver said to the sheriff, "Thirty-five millimeter?"

"Yep. Makes dandy little pitchers."

"I'd like copies of those shots, Sheriff."

"Happy to make you a set."

Pete picked up a twisted piece of metal and approached what had been the cockpit of the chopper. Gingerly he poked with the metal in the ashes and debris, bent closer, straightened, and called, "A body's here. Probably the pilot."

His name had been Todd, MacIver remembered, and he was a man who knew how to handle the aircraft. They waited while Pete moved methodically through the wreckage. "Here's another one." He circled back to their side of the rubble, poking and prodding.

The sheriff called, "What're you finding?"

"Can't tell for sure, but I think there's two bodies back in the passenger seats."

MacIver and Rod exchanged glances. When Pete had completed his examination of the area, the sheriff said, "Lieutenant, you and the sergeant might like to go down and look around before us country boys get into it."

MacIver jumped at the chance. "We appreciate that, Sheriff. Yeah, we'd like to have a quick look around."

The light was beginning to fade. MacIver and Rod separated and searched the area in a cross section. They found a few hulls, all nine millimeter, but the area was too dry and gravelly to show footprints, and there was nothing to indicate who had fired the guns. Last of all they looked at the wreckage. As Pete had said, there was a body in the cockpit and what might be the remains of two persons in the passenger area.

"Just the two," MacIver murmured. "But we know there were three passengers."

"Not when the fire started, I think," Rod replied.

When they had finished their search, they climbed back up the bank of the pit. MacIver said, "I'm afraid this is no crash, Sheriff Gates. I think it's a triple homicide. We'll work closely with you on this one. It's your case, but I think it's our crooks in the passenger area. The pilot was an innocent bystander." He shook hands. "Thanks for your courtesy. You've been a big help."

"Well, we don't get too many big-city police officers out

127

our way. Got to put our best foot forward, even when your crooks come out here to get themselves killed."

MacIver grinned. "Remember I owe you one."

"I may take you up on that one day. Never can tell when we'll need a little help."

MacIver handed him his card. "We'll be getting back now. I'd appreciate your keeping me informed on what you find out about that tire track." The sheriff nodded, and MacIver asked, "Who'll be doing your lab work?"

"We usually use the Department of Public Safety lab in Austin, but we want to work with you on your crooks, so we'll ship the remains on down to Houston. You've got an outstanding set of facilities, I hear."

"Good. Then I'll be getting back to you." MacIver started away, saw the band of reporters behind the imaginary line the deputy had drawn, and turned back. "I'm not going to make any statement to the media. I'll leave that up to you."

The sheriff gave them a curt nod and then called after them, "Nice meeting you, gentlemen."

When they lifted off, all three turned to look back at the wreckage. The smoke cloud was dispersing into streams and puffs. Beyond it the sun had set and the sky was a blaze of red. MacIver said, "Who do you think we've got down there?"

"Braden and Hicks and the pilot."

"So the guy who picked them up, who chartered the chopper, got off when they landed. Or else his body's there, too, and just hasn't turned up yet."

"We know somebody met them. Even if this Potworth did the killings, he had to have a vehicle to leave the scene in."

"And we can surmise that at least two people fired at the chopper, because of the position of the shell casings." MacIver stared into the sunset, part of his mind recording the glorious sweep of crimson across the western sky. "So they pick up Braden and Hicks at Stouffer's. Tell them they're flying them out to the country, where they'll hole up, or maybe they say they're going to connect with another aircraft. Anyway, they get there and Potworth gets out, giving them some excuse. One or two people from the car walk down to the gravel pit. They're hiding their Mach Tens or some other nine-millimeter sub-machine gun under their coats or something. When they get in position, they open fire, one at the pilot, the other at Braden and Hicks. Then they back up some and shoot the fuel tanks. And run like hell."

Rodriguez smoothed his mustache. "It could've worked that way."

"They couldn't risk the guys' turning state's evidence. They had to get rid of them."

"And the pilot was the innocent bystander, poor guy."

"Yeah." MacIver got out a scratch pad. "We're going to want dental records for Braden and Hicks, *and* the pilot, to make sure one of the bodies is his. We're going to have to make inquiries about the cashier's check that Potworth sent to the helicopter company. We'll want a copy of it to check the handwriting. We want to talk to the people at the realty office, find out if they knew Potworth."

Rod said, "I'll bet they didn't. He just used their name because it was a convenient place for the chopper to land."

"Yeah, but by giving Donner that number, he risked a callback, so he must have covered that some way." He finished writing. "Think of anything else?"

"Not until we get something on that tire track, Loot. Damn, I wish we knew what kind of vehicle they were driving. We could put out a statewide on the car."

"It's too late now anyway. They'll have been gone since about four. Three hours. They're probably back in Houston having a drink."

He turned to watch the sky. The red was fading to pink. "They should've listened to us. We *told* them they were in danger from their own people."

"At least they're not going to walk after five years in the pen."

"No, you're right. They're never going to walk."

18 The phone was ringing when MacIver unlocked the door of the apartment. Captain McNamee said, "I just got the news on television. That chopper up in Bellville—was it the one with those two guys on it?"

"Yessir." MacIver related what he knew.

"It's the Galveston drop all over again, MacIver. They outsmarted you again. Be in my office at eight in the morning."

MacIver said "Yessir" to a dead line.

He was brisk as he walked into McNamee's office the next day. He had decided that the best way to counter McNamee's suggestion that he take a vacation—if that was what his superior had in mind—was to be so involved in the case that it would be too much trouble to replace him.

He said, "The remains of three bodies were shipped from Bellville to Dr. Jack's morgue last night, but they haven't had time to do anything on them yet."

McNamee had a steaming cup of coffee on his desk. He didn't offer one to MacIver. "Who's the third?"

"Probably the pilot. I've called the real estate office that was Potworth's point of departure. They're not open yet."

"Why didn't we have a helicopter on surveillance yesterday?"

"I thought I had the patrol unit." MacIver explained the foul-up.

"Why wasn't the car they drove off in apprehended?"

MacIver explained about Sergeant Dallas being alone and being unable to cover both the chopper and the Cadillac.

The captain sipped his coffee. As though he hated to admit it, he said, "It looks like you did everything you could, then. Any idea why these men were killed?"

"My theory is that their boss didn't trust them. He was afraid they'd roll over and turn state's evidence against him."

"No leads to who their boss is?"

"No. Conover was defending them, but I don't know who retained him."

"And you won't find out."

"I'm going to follow up on this Potworth."

"That's a long shot."

"Yessir, but we're due for a break." The instant he said it, MacIver was sorry. It gave the captain the opportunity he wanted to lecture. "We make our own breaks, MacIver. It takes legwork, persistence, attention to detail, and follow-through. We don't wait for breaks to shower on us like manna from heaven."

"Nosir. That's why I'm going to follow up on every lead we've got. I'll check with the sheriff up in Bellville, too. He had a tire track that he thinks might be from the vehicle driven by the killer or killers."

"That won't help us catch 'em, but it may help us convict 'em. Remember this is the sheriff's case. Help him; don't direct him," McNamee said.

"Yessir."

"Anyway, I guess that will stop women being assaulted in Houston hotels." And get the chief off his neck. "Okay, keep me posted on what's happening."

Finally MacIver was out of the captain's office. *And* still in charge of the DARE investigation. There was a note that Mrs. Craddock had called the afternoon before, so he telephoned her in Minnesota.

"You told me to let you know if they called back, Lieutenant. They did. They want half a million on Tuesday. I told 'em fat chance."

"You've reported this to the police there."

"Yes. They say they're investigating."

MacIver told her to take care of herself, rang off, telephoned the real estate office again and this time got an answer. When he told the secretary who he was, she said,

"Police? Do you want to buy or sell a house, or is something wrong?"

"I don't want to buy or sell a house. I want to ask about a man called Wolver T. Potworth. Was he in your office yesterday?"

"Oh yes, a very nice man. He was Mr. Hanks's client."

"May I speak to Mr. Hanks?"

"He isn't in just now. I expect him within the next half hour."

"When he comes in, will you ask him to wait for me? I'm on my way out. Oh, and miss, did Potworth touch anything in the office, use the phone, have a cup of coffee?"

"Yes, he made some calls."

"Would you see that the phone he used isn't touched by anybody? We'll try to get fingerprints from it."

He called the crime lab and asked for a crew to fingerprint the telephone, then rang Rodriguez. "Let's go find out what we can about Potworth."

Bill Hanks was tall and thin with a wide grin. "Yessir, gentlemen. Have a seat. I understand you have some questions about Mr. Potworth."

"We'd like to know where to find him."

"He gave me a business card with an address in Dallas." After searching through a stack of papers on his desk, Hanks produced the card. "I guess you'll want to take this, so let me get a copy made." He rang for the secretary and handed the card to her. "Would you mind telling me what the problem is?"

"The helicopter he rented burned up in Bellville. Three people were killed, including two men suspected of robbery, assault, and extortion. If your Mr. Potworth is a legitimate businessman, we'd like to know what he was doing associating with people like that."

Hanks's face had fallen as MacIver talked. "He was too good to be true anyway, talking about million-dollar properties." His secretary returned with the card and copy; Hanks handed the card to MacIver. "Okay, what can I tell you?"

"What did he look like?"

"Close to six feet, light hair, nice-looking clothing, expensive shoes."

MacIver asked, "Did he wear a hat? Was there any evidence that he usually wore a hat, like a farmer or golfer would have?"

"No, he had a tan all the way across his forehead." Hanks ran his hands across his own forehead. "It went up past his widow's peak."

"You noticed a widow's peak."

"Yes, and blondish hair, beginning to gray."

"How was his hair cut?"

"About like mine, medium sideburns, short in back."

"Anything about the eyes?"

"Blue, I think. Maybe gray. I think he colors his eyebrows. They were darker than his hair."

"The ears?"

"Now that you mention it, I believe the man had a pierced ear, left side. Or it could have been a mole, maybe a sebaceous cyst."

"Do you have medical training, Mr. Hanks?"

"No, but my son had sebaceous cysts. We had a hell of a time getting rid of them. They leave a little pit, and that's what this looked like, but it might have been an earring hole that was partially grown together. Or a mole."

"Okay, you get all that, Rod?"

"I got it."

"Let's go to his teeth."

"I didn't notice anything about his teeth."

"Scars on his face?"

Hanks shook his head.

"The throat? Any sagging or turkey-skin look?"

"No, his jawline and neck were firm." Hanks ran a hand across his own dewlap. "He looked like a guy who takes care of his body. Walked easy, too. I'd guess he jogs or plays tennis or works out someplace regularly."

"Clothing."

"White shirt, button at the collar. Red-and-yellow tie, blue blazer."

"Class ring?"

"No, and no wedding band. Manicured fingernails though, I noticed that."

"Watch?"

"Gold Rolex."

"Good. You're an observant man. Let's go to the belt."

"I didn't see the belt. He wore his coat buttoned."

"How about the pants?"

"They were gray, I think. What I remember most is the razor-sharp creases front and back. They were obviously freshly pressed."

"Shoes."

"Tasseled alligator loafers. Close to four-hundred-dollar shoes."

"Black or brown."

"Natural state, brown."

MacIver stood, and thanked Hanks. "If you should happen to hear from Mr. Potworth, I'd appreciate your giving us a call."

"I'll do that."

Outside, Rod asked, "Did the description ring any bells, Loot?"

"It did, as a matter of fact, but it didn't ring loud enough. I have the feeling that something he said should remind me of somebody, but I can't think what or who. What about you?"

"Didn't remind me of anybody."

"Get a composite artist out here to put together a portrait of Potworth. Maybe that will give us something more to go on."

Back at the office, he called Donner, the helicopter owner, and got a detailed description of the teenager who had delivered the cashier's check. He'd probably never locate the youth, but he didn't want to overlook any possibilities.

At one o'clock, MacIver and Rod were scheduled to meet with Assistant District Attorney Charles Williams, an expert in the science of forensic evidence. When they entered the office, Williams was going over notes concerning the re-establishment of the base content of body fluids found inside Rita Davis's body. Williams was stocky, balding, and impatient. Halfway through MacIver's explanation of Dr. Jack's findings, he interrupted.

"I've just been looking over notes on that. It's good, hard

evidence and I think it will impress a jury. The D.A. and I have talked it over and we want to obtain a court order on Neimeyer. I'll draw up the necessary form—"

MacIver said, "Hold it, Mr. Williams. I'm not the primary case officer on this. My interest goes back to Ginger Falls's murder case eighteen years ago."

"That's fine. Who's the primary case officer on this?"

MacIver told him, and Williams said, "Okay. He can get in touch with me. We're going to go for a court order that will force Kurt Neimeyer to submit saliva, urine, and follicle samples for testing."

"Can you include his right-hand man in that? Either one of them could have done the killing."

"What's his name?"

"Joseph Piccolo." MacIver spelled it.

"Okay, we'll include Mr. Piccolo. By the way, do you know who Neimeyer's attorney is?"

"Silas Conover."

"That's right. You know what Conover's going to say when we ask for these samples? He's going to say stick it up your nose. He'll demand a hearing."

"But you *can* order the samples."

"Oh, sure. The hearing will just be a delaying tactic on Conover's part. We'll get the samples. The hardest part will be finding Neimeyer to present the order. Your best bet is to keep an eye on Neimeyer and Piccolo so we can find them when we want them."

"They're already on part-time surveillance."

"Better make it full-time." Williams was already on his feet, holding out his hand for a this-meeting-is-over hand-shake. "I'll get back to you when we have a court order."

Back at the office, MacIver told Captain McNamee what the assistant district attorney had advised. McNamee said, "MacIver, you've got enough to do with the drug-and-assault cases without taking on the Baron."

"We're working the drug-and-assault cases, Cap, Rod and I. We wouldn't be spending any of our own time on the Baron, but I'd like to get round-the-clock surveillance from CID."

"Okay, I'll call CID and see if we can get a priority commitment for a minimum of five working days, approximately sixteen hours a day, but I don't want you and Rodriguez slacking up on the drug-and-rob cases. That's *your* first priority."

"Yessir, Captain. No slacking."

Back in his office, MacIver brought his notes up to date, filed his reports, and phoned Suzanne. "How about a drink?"

"Your place or mine?"

"I'll come to yours. See you in thirty minutes."

Suzanne was wearing shorts, a T-shirt, and sandals. MacIver said, "Hey, lady, you're looking great."

"I think I'm almost back to normal. What's been happening with you?"

"Lots of things. Let me get a scotch and I'll tell you about it."

MacIver made their usual drinks and carried them to the sofa. Then he got the manila envelope with Braden's and Hicks's photos out of his briefcase. "You feel like looking at some photos?"

She eyed the envelope. "Are those . . ."

"Yes."

"I'm ready." She said it grimly.

He took the photos out of the envelope and handed them to her. She looked. The anticipation on her face vanished, replaced by revulsion. Her face and throat flushed scarlet. "That's Ken." She looked at the next photo. "Bob." She took a second look, shuddered convulsively, and handed them back. "I'm glad you've got them. I hope you put them away for the rest of their lives."

"You don't have to worry about them anymore."

"What if they get out of jail?"

"They got out of jail. That was their problem." He told her what had happened. "We're not a hundred percent sure that the bodies are theirs, but we're ninety-nine percent sure."

She stared at him, shadows passing behind her eyes. Finally she said, "I hope it's them. I suppose it's wrong to feel that way, but I can't help it. I hope they're dead."

"That's a normal reaction."

"Their own people killed them, you think. What monsters

they must be! But Tony, that means it's an organization. It wasn't just the two of them. So it could go on, the problems, I mean, even though they're dead."

"I'm afraid so. We've got to get the rest of the gang. We'll get them." He only hoped it would be before they caused any more misery.

19 He rang Rod the next morning. "I had a thought last night."

"Hey, Loot, that must have been exciting for you."

"Oh, hell, it was. If I could have gotten hold of it, I would have had it framed. Has it occurred to you that the only victims who had foreign objects introduced into their bodies were the ones in this area? None of the women east of New Orleans had a foreign object."

"Yeah, Loot, I guess that's right."

"It doesn't have anything to do with the team that's doing the job, because the New Orleans team was different. So it must have to do with the victims themselves. What makes Suzanne, Craddock, Elsing, and Schultz different from the other victims?"

"Well, the foreign object—"

"Besides that."

"They've all lived in Houston."

"Right. What else?" He answered himself, "We don't know, but I'm becoming more convinced that there's some link among those four women. Let's concentrate on them for a while. Let's do an in-depth study of each one of them and see if we can't find something they have in common."

"Okay, Loot."

"Let's get everything that's happened to them since they were in kindergarten. If that doesn't work, we'll go back to the cradle. Why don't you start with the Elsing family? I'll work on Suzanne."

When he had hung up, he called Suzanne. There was no

answer, so he rang Betsy Craddock's number in Minneapolis. The receiver was lifted, there was a slight pause, and then a man's voice said guardedly, "Craddock residence." MacIver asked to speak to Mrs. Craddock. The voice said sharply, "Who is this?"

MacIver gave his name without his rank, and added that he was calling from Houston. The tone changed. "Is this *Lieutenant* MacIver?"

"Yes. Who's this?"

"Lieutenant Erickson, Minneapolis Police Department. I was going to call you as soon as I got back to the station. Mrs. Craddock was killed this morning."

She had been shot at close range in the back of the head as she sat behind the steering wheel of her car in the driveway. A neighbor had heard the shot and seen a car driving away. She thought two people were in it and that it was a late-model Chrysler, medium size. She hadn't gotten the license number.

MacIver asked, "Anything to tie it in with the extortion attempt?"

"Yeah. They left the tapes in the backseat of the car."

"Arrogant assholes. But I'm glad you have the tapes."

"Yeah. They called her Sunday and demanded half a mil. They told her to meet them this morning at seven. The drop was to be at a downtown hotel. She told them she wasn't going to pay and she didn't. Not in money. They shot her at approximately eight-fifteen A.M. Her name was written with red spray paint on the door of the carport. Then a long X was painted across it. Under that there was the number two with a line in front of it."

MacIver jotted down a two and put a line in front of it. "Minus two."

"Yeah. You make anything out of that?"

"It might be two dead, Elsing and Craddock. Minus two."

"Crazy. I'll get tests run on the tapes. Let you know if I find anything."

"Good. I'd like to view one of them."

"Okay, I'll send one. Another thing, we're guessing the killers are from out of town. We've got the airport and bus station under surveillance, but we may be too late. The neighbor didn't call till eight-twenty-five."

"It took her ten minutes after the shot to find the body?"

"At first she thought it was just a car backfiring. Then she noticed that Craddock's car was still in the carport with the motor running, so she came over to investigate. Found the body. Called us. By the time I was notified, it was after nine. Two planes took off in that time frame, one to Chicago, one to Denver, ultimate destination Houston. We're working on the passenger lists now."

"I guess you're working on car rental agencies, too."

"Yeah, but we haven't come up with anything on that. We're backtracking on it, but I'm beginning to think they didn't rent a car."

"Okay. Listen, Erickson, I'm working on another angle down here." MacIver explained the similarities among the four cases. "I want every detail of Craddock's life that we can dig up."

"You may be on to something there. I've been puzzling over this homicide. Extortionists usually don't kill. It doesn't make sense. They're not going to get anything out of a corpse."

"These aren't ordinary extortionists." MacIver told him about Braden and Hicks. "I think we're working with somebody in organized crime. I don't mean Mafia, but a guy doesn't have to belong to the Mafia to have an organized operation. I think he knows this murder will be publicized and will act as a warning to any other victims who don't want to pay extortion."

"Well, it's a theory." Erickson sounded dubious. "And this will be publicized, that's for sure. We've had media all over the place. Have you thought of revenge?"

"I've thought of it. I haven't been able to tie it down."

"I'll talk to the victim's sister and see what I can find out. It would be a help to us if you could look into Craddock's background in Houston. See if you can find a motive there."

"Right. I'll see what we can round up."

MacIver hung up, called Rod, and told him what had happened. "Skip Elsing for the moment and get everything you can on Craddock's background. Talk to everybody who knew her. Find out any reason for somebody to want her dead. You'll have to get hold of her sister in Minneapolis to find out the names of her friends here. Anything else you think of, follow up on it."

Hanging up, MacIver twirled his chair around and stared out the window. He was tired of seeing just that one bird outside. Maybe he'd get another one painted in. Elsing and Craddock. Two homicides. Plus Suzanne had been attacked a second time. MacIver rubbed his chin for a few seconds. Then he went to the captain's office to tell him about Craddock.

McNamee said, "There's some reason she was killed besides not paying. I've never heard of an extortionist who killed, except one years ago and that was an accident."

"This was no accident."

"No, it sounds professional. Maybe she had some other problem up there. Any hint of that?"

"The police up there didn't mention anything else. She seemed civic-minded when I talked to her."

"She may have made enemies up there. Here, too. You know how women are." The captain made no pretense of being anything other than a male chauvinist; he was Number One on the female police officers' hit list and considered it an honored position. "It's either that or revenge. How many cases do we have now?"

"Seven. But foreign objects were introduced into the bodies of only four. The way I'm seeing it now, Cap, is that somebody got the bright idea of drugging and robbing women. And they decided to throw in some sex and go for extortion. But whoever organized it said, 'Hey, while I'm at it, I'm going to settle some old scores.' That's where the foreign objects come in. They've only been used on the four women who live in Houston, or used to live there."

"So what do those four have in common?"

"That's what we haven't been able to find out. And two of them are dead."

"Let's keep the other two alive. Go through their backgrounds. Find out everything about them. There's bound to be a common link."

MacIver returned to his office and called Suzanne. "How're you feeling, lady?"

"I'm fine, Tony."

"I want you to do something for me. I want you to list every school you ever went to, every church, every organization you ever belonged to from the Brownies on up. Look through your high school and college yearbooks to refresh your memory. List any special projects you were involved in."

"Wow, as Carol would say. How much time do I have for all this?"

"Start now. I don't know how long it will take."

"Tony, has something else happened?"

He didn't want to frighten her by telling her about Betsy Craddock's death. "Yes, we've decided there's got to be a common link among four of the victims, you included. I need your help in finding it. Another thing, I'm going to show you photos of three other victims." Police didn't usually show photos of one victim to another—it was considered an invasion of the victim's privacy—but he thought in this case circumstances called for it.

"All right, Lieutenant, sir. I'll begin this very instant."

MacIver hung up and called Hermione. The phone rang four times and was answered by a machine. "This is Hermione Schultz." She had an ebullient, youthful-sounding voice. "I can't come to the phone at this time because I am busy with the most fabulous diamond pendants and bracelets and rings—there is a cocktail ring you would kill for—and some fantastic lapis—leave your name and number, and I'll tell you more."

MacIver said, "I never kill for cocktail rings, but call me anyway." He started to give his name, and Hermione came onto the line. "Hi, Lieutenant. You would for this one, or your wife would. I was just being careful about who I talked to. Or is it 'whom'?"

"Probably." He told her the same thing he had told Suzanne, and she agreed to make the list. "I want to show you a couple of photos, too. By the way, have you had any demands or threats?"

"Why should I? You got the ones who did it."

142

"They were just part of an organization. I figure somebody will pick up where they left off. I don't want to alarm you, but other victims have received lewd photos along with threats to publish a videotape unless a specified amount of money is paid."

"These other women told you about them, huh?"

"First thing they did upon receipt. You can't work with extortionists, Ms. Schultz. You need the help of the police."

She said, "Um," noncommittally.

He pushed it. "So if you *do* hear from them, please let us know."

"Okay. 'Bye." She hung up.

He'd be willing to bet from her manner that she'd already had an extortion demand but didn't want to say so. Their threats must have frightened her. The phone rang.

"Lieutenant?" It was Hermione. "I *did* get some photos and a demand for money. It really scared me, because I thought with those bastards in jail it was all over and done with. The letter said if I contacted the police they'd do worse to me than they did before. . . ."

"I'm glad you called; I really am. Have they given you a deadline?"

"Not yet. They said they'd get back to me in a couple of days. I just got the photos this morning. Talk about porn!"

"Okay. When you hear from them again, let me know. We'll work out something." And this time, the police would win. "How much did they ask for?"

"Fifty thousand. It's more than I can afford. I'm going to have to put off paying some bills, but—"

"Maybe not. We're going to try to save it for you. I'd like to come out and pick up those photos. Will you be there in half an hour?"

"I'm not going anywhere."

"Okay. See you then."

He assembled a set of photos of the three victims. Then, searching through the files, he found photos of two more women, both middle-aged, one white, one black. A cover sheet identified the photos only by numbers one through five. He put the package in an envelope and headed for Ms. Schultz's house.

Hermione, in a long, flowing, hot pink caftan, studied each of the photos carefully, and shook her head over each. "I can't place them. It's like having a word on the tip of your tongue. They look vaguely familiar but—all I can say definitely is that, if I ever knew them, they weren't close friends."

MacIver took the photos back. "Well, if anything comes to you, or if you think of anything that might help you to remember, don't hesitate to give me a call and I'll come back over with them."

"Could you leave them with me? Maybe if I keep looking at them it will jog my memory."

"Sorry, I can't do that. If you look at the photos long enough, you may begin to believe you know them even if you don't." He returned the photos to his briefcase. "What about the ones the extortionists sent?"

"I hid them away in the depths of the bedroom. I didn't want anybody to find them." She left the room and returned with a manila envelope, similar to the one Suzanne's photos had been in. The address was typed, and MacIver made a mental note to have the type on the two labels compared. "Those should steam up your lab, Lieutenant."

"That happens every once in a while in the crime lab. Thanks, and be sure and let me know when you hear from them again."

MacIver stopped for lunch and then took the Schultz photos to the crime lab. They had also gotten the report on the prints from the telephone at the real estate office. All the prints had been identified as belonging to people who worked in the office, which was disappointing but not surprising. If Potworth was the professional MacIver suspected, he wouldn't have been careless enough to leave prints behind.

Next he called the district attorney's office to find out if the court order on the Baron and Pico had been issued.

Williams was out, but his secretary said, "I can give you that information, Lieutenant. The judge has issued, but the proper filing of the papers has not been submitted. We'll have them in a matter of hours."

"Could I ask a favor?"

"Sure, Lieutenant."

"As soon as the judge signs, would you notify homicide unit one-four-six? That's my radio signal that the package is ready. I'll come over personally and pick it up."

"I'll be glad to, if it's during office time. If not, I'll call you in the morning."

Next he called CID to set up a meeting with the surveillance team. The dispatch sergeant took his call.

"We had to pull them off, Loot. We have a little foreign counterintelligence activity with the Bureau. They jerked your guys by priority."

"Why the hell didn't somebody let me know?"

"I couldn't say, sir."

"Let me talk to your lieutenant."

The lieutenant was defensive, but agreed that CID should not have yanked the surveillance team without notifying Homicide to give them a chance to substitute a team.

"Where were they when your guys dropped them?"

"Hold on." The lieutenant returned to the phone a minute later. "Neimeyer and Piccolo were at the Racquet Club on Memorial Drive about an hour and a half ago. They were dressed in tennis attire but headed for the dining room."

"What are they driving?"

"A beige Mercedes sedan."

MacIver called the lieutenant on the homicide desk to ask for some sergeants to form a surveillance team. Nobody was available. It looked like the surveillance team was going to be MacIver and Rodriguez.

"Is Rod in the office?"

"No, he called. He's on his way in."

"Tell him to meet me at the Racquet Club. I'll be in the front parking lot."

20

There were three beige Mercedes in the club parking lot. Since MacIver didn't know Neimeyer's license number, he parked where he could keep all three in sight.

Rodriguez arrived a few minutes later, parked his official vehicle to one side, and got into the station wagon with MacIver. "Do we know they're still here?"

"I'm not certain. I didn't want to go into the club or around to the tennis courts. I haven't seen the Baron in fifteen years, but he'll recognize me. I'm just hoping one of those cars is his."

"I hope so, too, and I hope he comes out and gets in it pretty soon, because it's hot as hell out here."

It was after two now, the hottest part of the afternoon. MacIver had taken off his coat and rolled his shirtsleeves above his wrists, but he was drenched with sweat. "I can't keep the motor and air-conditioning running. The engine would overheat."

Both tennis players and diners were exiting the club in droves, the former because it was too hot to play and the latter because they'd finished lunch. MacIver watched car after car pull out of the lot. One of the beige Mercedes left, then another. That left just one. Rod said, "I'm beginning to feel kind of exposed, Loot."

"Yeah, our cover keeps driving away. Whoops! Here they come."

MacIver remembered what the Baron looked like but he had wondered if he would recognize Pico—he hadn't seen the man in fifteen years. However, the instant he saw the figure beside the Baron, there was no doubt. He could have picked Neimeyer's sidekick out of a throng.

Carrying tennis rackets and bags, the two headed for the remaining beige Mercedes.

MacIver slid down in the seat and turned his head toward Rod. He told the sergeant, "Just act natural. He doesn't know you."

"He sure knows you though, Loot."

"Not the back of my head."

"Then how come he's heading for our car?"

MacIver looked around. While Pico, with rackets and bags, continued walking toward the Mercedes, Neimeyer had changed direction and was stalking toward them, his jaw set. His blond hair had some gray at the temples and there were lines in his face that hadn't been there the last time MacIver saw him, but he still had his looks.

MacIver said, "You keep an eye on Pico."

Neimeyer reached the car and leaned down to look in the window. "You want a follicle sample, MacIver?" He yanked a hair out of the crown of his head and threw it in the open window. "There! Test that! You want a saliva sample?" He leaned closer and spit in MacIver's face. "Test that! Now—" His voice rose to a shout. "You two-for-a-nickel cops—"

MacIver wiped his face with his sleeve and started out of the car. The door slammed hard in his face. Neimeyer had stepped back and kicked it shut. He leaned in the window as Rod jumped out of the car. "I said, you two-for-a-nickel cops get out of here. This is private property. Unless you're a member of the club—"

MacIver jammed his shoulder into the car door, shoving it open. As Neimeyer fell back, MacIver swung the door as wide as it would go. It caught the Baron dead center. He stumbled backward and sat down hard on the asphalt surface.

Rod called, "Loot, we've got a security guard."

The guard was running down the front steps of the club, his weapon drawn. He shouted, "Hold it right there!"

Neimeyer scrambled to his feet. He yelled, "He assaulted me! Watch him. He's got a gun."

147

A group of young women carrying gift boxes, apparently coming from a bridal shower at the club, had paused a few yards away to watch. At sight of the guard, they scattered.

He ran up, panting. "What's going on here?"

Rod, at the front of the car, and MacIver kept their hands in front of them and slightly raised. "Hold it, Officer. We're HPD Homicide!"

The guard looked from MacIver to Rod. "Let's see some identification."

"I'm going to pull my coat back," MacIver told him. "You will note that I have a gold badge on my belt. You will note that on the other side I've got a forty-five automatic. I'm showing you the badge; then I'm going to show *him* the gun. And you put yours up. I'm taking this man into custody."

Neimeyer snorted. "I'm the one that's assaulted and you're taking *me* into custody? You got a warrant?" He turned and motioned the Mercedes forward.

MacIver eyed the security guard, who was looking uncertain but still held his gun. "You're both officers?"

"We're both officers."

The guard holstered his weapon, and MacIver started after Neimeyer, who was climbing into the passenger seat of the Mercedes.

Grabbing the open car door with his right hand, MacIver grasped Neimeyer's shoulder with his left. "Come out of there."

Neimeyer shouted, "Drive, dammit!"

The Mercedes leaped forward, leaving MacIver with the choice of turning it loose or being dragged. He turned it loose and flung himself back from the car.

Rod was running toward MacIver's car. "Never mind!" MacIver hauled himself up. "We'd never catch 'em in the wagon."

The young ladies had rehuddled and were whispering among themselves, sending dark glances at MacIver and Rod. The security guard walked toward them. "Sir, I'm going to have to make a report on all this."

"Rod, you talk to him." Ignoring the onlookers, MacIver

dusted off his pants, got into the car, and turned on the air-conditioning.

Then he got out of the car again and began to search the seat. Rod came up behind him. "What's the matter?"

"I can't find that damned hair."

"Never mind, Loot. You've still got the saliva sample."

21 Back at the office, MacIver and Rod reported to the on-duty deputy chief about the confrontation. "The order asking the Baron for follicle and bodily fluid samples hasn't even gone out yet, but he sure as hell knew about it."

"Leak in the D.A.'s office," the chief said. "Some lawyer heard about it and alerted Neimeyer's lawyer."

"That's Conover," MacIver said. "I suppose he'll be getting hold of Internal Affairs. Maybe we should go to them first."

The chief thought about it. "No, hold off. Let's wait and see what happens."

When Captain McNamee heard about the ruckus, he said, "I told you that you didn't have time to spend on that old case, and you said you weren't going to."

"Yessir, but CID had pulled off the surveillance teams, and Homicide didn't have anybody to send."

"So you decided to do it yourself. Wrong decision, Mac-Iver."

"Yessir."

The captain glared at them for several seconds and turned away in seeming disgust. "Get on back to work. All we can do is wait and see what happens."

Every time the phone rang for the remainder of the afternoon, MacIver expected to hear that the incident was being investigated by Internal Affairs. When the word still hadn't come by five, he began to feel slightly optimistic. Maybe Conover had advised the Baron to let the matter drop.

*   *   *

At the Towers, he stopped off on five to show Suzanne the photos of the other victims before going to his own apartment.

"Good afternoon." She kissed him. "I've worked myself up to the present in my list of schools, clubs, jobs, et cetera. It's all pretty boring. Can I get you a drink?"

"No, I'm going swimming before I get too comfortable. I wanted you to look at these photos." He handed her a set.

She looked at Hermione's photo. "These are other women who have been attacked?"

"Some of them. You probably knew them some time ago, because one of them hasn't lived in Houston for ten years."

She shook her head at the photos of Hermione and Lurinda Elsing, but hesitated over Betsy Craddock's. "She looks familiar—but I can't place her. It may just be that she has a sort of typical look—blond, Germanic." She studied the photo a moment longer. "No. Sorry, Tony. I don't recognize her."

"Thanks for looking." He took the photos. "I want to see your list later, but right now I need a swim."

He stayed in the water half an hour. Instead of having his usual poolside drink, he headed back upstairs, planning to call Suzanne and look over her list. He ambled down the hall, yawning. Then his mouth snapped shut. The matchbook at the top of the door was missing.

He stood still, possibilities racing through his mind. Somebody from the building might have come in to check the electricity or plumbing. Or there might have been an intruder and the intruder might still be inside. Cautiously he tested the doorknob. It was unlocked. He got his .45 out of his towel bag, set the bag down, and pushed the door open a fraction of an inch. It was dark inside. He slid through the opening and flattened himself against the wall while his eyes adjusted to the dimness.

He had, as usual, left the east draperies open, and the lights from the city kept the room from total blackness. He picked out the recliner and the television, and the thought

151

crossed his mind that he was probably behaving like a damned fool. On the other hand, he'd be a worse fool to walk into a trap. At the tail end of the thought, he heard something. It sounded like the squeak of a rubber-soled shoe on tile, and it came from the direction of the kitchen.

MacIver switched the .45 to his left hand and eased forward toward the recliner, feeling in the dark for the remote control for the television. When he found it, he retreated to the wall again. He could make out the right side of the counter and cabinets in the kitchen. There was no sign of a person. He turned the television volume up on the remote control and then pressed the button to turn on the set.

The result was startling even to MacIver, who expected it. Lights flashed and sound blared. MacIver watched the kitchen, half anticipating that the intruder would shoot at the TV screen before realizing what it was. As luck would have it, he had tuned in to a cop show in the middle of a shootout, but the guns on the screen were the only ones firing. MacIver switched to a nonreceiving channel, so the screen would stay lit without sound, and edged toward the kitchen.

A figure was silhouetted against the south window; it looked like a man crouching. Lights from the Galleria formed a pink-and-purple backdrop and showed that his right arm was raised. It was no wonder that he hadn't fired at the television; he held a knife in his uplifted hand.

MacIver dropped the remote control, flipped the .45 from his left hand to his right, and aimed at the spot where the man's heart should be. Whoever had taught this thief his trade hadn't taught him well. You didn't come to a gunfight with a knife. He shouted, "Drop the knife or I'll blow your fucking head off!" The figure swiveled. MacIver raised the sight another three inches and squeezed off a round. There was a deafening boom.

The flare from the barrel lighted his opponent for a moment and he cried out. He flung himself to the side as Richard, the boy from the fifth floor, raced for the door. Grabbing the child by the leg, he threw him down. "I'm not going to hurt you," he said reassuringly, but he kept a tight hold on Richard as he jumped up and turned on the light. Then he looked the boy over for injuries.

"Thank God, you're all right." Once he knew the child was unhurt, MacIver, shaken at the near call, took refuge in anger. "What the hell are you doing here? God, I almost killed you!"

The youngster stuttered, "I-I-I." He could not get past the word.

MacIver shoved his weapon into his robe pocket. Still rattled, he brushed a hand across the boy's head. The bullet had come close to giving Richard a new part in his hair. MacIver hesitated a moment, deciding what he was going to do. What he should do was call Internal Affairs and the shooting team, but he hated to put Richard through a formal investigation. Instead, he grasped the boy by the arm. "All right, young man, we're going to see your father."

Richard tried to pull away. "He's not home."

"Then we'll wait for him." MacIver pushed the boy through the doorway, locked the door, and reinserted the matchbook. "What were you doing in my apartment?"

Richard had stopped pulling away from him. "Are you going to arrest me?"

"Maybe. That's what I usually do to burglars."

"I thought you would." There was a degree of satisfaction in Richard's voice. He seemed to have recovered from his initial fright.

"You want me to arrest you?"

"I guess you have to. I shouldn't have come in when you weren't home."

"How'd you get in?"

The youngster reached into his pocket with his free hand and drew out a key that MacIver recognized as a master. MacIver pushed the elevator button. "Where'd you get that?"

"In that room behind the bellman's desk."

"You stole it."

Richard's gaze dropped. "Yessir."

"Why? What did you want in my apartment?"

"Nothing. I was just looking around."

"You were going to take something?"

MacIver could see the boy's struggle between telling the truth and a lie. Finally he said, "Yes."

The elevator arrived, they stepped on and MacIver pushed the button for five. "You wouldn't have gotten much. Not much there worth stealing."

"I could've taken the television."

"What would you have done with it?"

"Sold it to somebody."

"Wouldn't your father have wondered where you got a strange TV set?"

"I'd have hidden it someplace. Downstairs in one of the storage rooms."

MacIver asked, "Were you going to stab me?"

"No! I wouldn't do that. When you came in and didn't turn on the light, I thought you must be a burglar. I was scared."

"How'd you happen to have one of my knives?"

"I'd gone into the kitchen. I was kinda hungry and I was looking in your refrigerator." He added anxiously, "I hope you don't mind."

"That's just a minor offense." He saw that the boy didn't understand and added, "Never mind."

"There's not much in there, in your refrigerator."

"I wasn't expecting guests. You didn't find the knife in the refrigerator."

"No, it was just lying on the table. When you came in and all that, I grabbed it. I thought I might have to fight somebody."

The elevator opened on five and they got off. MacIver asked, "Where's your father tonight?"

"He had to go out."

"Where's your apartment?"

"Down here." Richard told him the number. "Do you have to tell my father?"

Normally, MacIver would have insisted upon telling a parent about such an incident, but this time something stopped him. He said, "If you promise never to do anything like this again—"

"I promise. Scout's honor."

"Okay, I won't tell him this time."

"Thanks."

"It's okay. Oh, I'd better have that key." Richard handed it over and unlocked his own door. "Lock the door from the inside."

"I will. Thanks again."

When MacIver heard the lock turn, he continued down the hall to Suzanne's room and rang the bell. He still wore his robe and thongs, and his swimsuit was only partially dried. When she opened the door, he said, "If you'll forgive the way I'm dressed, I'll let you give me a scotch and soda."

"What a privilege, Lieutenant. How could I turn down such an honor?"

"Go ahead and laugh. You don't realize I just found a burglar in my apartment."

"You're not serious."

"I am. Do you mind if I help myself to a drink? What about you?"

"No, I'm drinking lemonade."

He brought his drink over to a chair near the couch where she sat. "I like your dress."

It was a long, purple Mexican dress, heavily embroidered at the neck and hem, with slits in the sides. "Thanks. It's good for my stomach. Now, about the burglar . . ."

MacIver explained what had happened from the missing matchbook until he switched on the light. "And there was young Richard, eyes the size of saucers and pale as a sheet."

"Richard from next door?"

MacIver nodded. "I imagine I was pale myself. It's a wonder I didn't kill him."

"That's frightening. What was he doing there?"

"He said he was going to steal something."

"I can't believe that. He seems like such a nice boy."

"He snitched a master key from the custodial staff. That's how he got in."

"That's just—kids do things like that. If he was going to rob someone, why would he pick a police officer's apartment?"

"I don't know. Maybe he was looking for the cat. Who

knows what goes through kids' minds? I imagine he gets bored hanging around here all day. Idle hands and all that."

Suzanne sipped her lemonade. "I saw his father today. He's not very sociable."

"No, he seems to keep to himself."

"The odd thing was—Richard was so friendly the other day. Today he wouldn't even look at me."

"Probably his father has told him not to talk to strangers, so he didn't want to let on that he knew you."

"Maybe. Are you going to tell his father about this?"

MacIver frowned. "I suppose I should, but I told Richard I wouldn't, if he promised not to do it anymore."

"Good."

"Why do you say that?"

"I don't know. I think maybe he's too harsh with the boy."

MacIver laughed. "How long did you spend with the two of them?"

"About thirty seconds, while we waited for the elevator."

"Time enough for an in-depth analysis."

"I know it sounds illogical, but you do pick up something from people, even in a short time. It would have been normal, since we live in the same building on the same floor, to at least say hello. I did, as a matter of fact. Mr. Pierce turned his head about a quarter of an inch and gave a barely perceptible nod."

"Maybe he's shy," MacIver suggested.

"Maybe he's weird."

"He may be nervous about people finding out Richard isn't in school."

"That's another thing: why isn't he? What kind of parent keeps a child out of school even for a month?"

"It happens more often than you'd think, usually with transients."

Suzanne furrowed her brow. "I suppose he could prefer to teach the child himself."

"That's possible." MacIver had finished his drink. "I wanted to look over your list, but I'm beat. Let me take it with me and I'll look it over tomorrow."

She got it for him, four pages handwritten. "If I think of anything else, I'll call you."

At the door, he leaned down and kissed her. "See, you tomorrow."

Back in his apartment, MacIver examined the bullet hole in the cabinet door. He'd have a hard time explaining that to the maintenance men. Inside the cabinet the slug had struck the jar of peanut butter and lodged in the pressed wood behind it. Peanut butter oozed over everything. MacIver left the bullet where it was and cleaned up the mess. He had just finished when the phone rang.

"MacIver, this is McNamee." MacIver felt his stomach tighten. Here it came. "Concerning that incident at the Racquet Club—Internal Affairs is conducting an investigation. You'll be relieved of duty pending outcome of the investigation. Be in my office first thing in the morning—*on time!*"

"Got it, Cap. See you then."

At 6:30 the next morning, MacIver walked into the parking garage. It was quiet and still shadowy. His footsteps echoed hollowly on the concrete. He got into the wagon, strapped on his seat belt, pumped the gas pedal twice, and turned the ignition key. Nothing happened. That surprised him. The motor usually caught immediately. He shouldn't need a new battery. He turned the key again. The motor came alive, throbbing faintly. He listened to it a moment, his gaze fixed in front of him. Then he saw the marks on the hood.

The wagon was coated with dust, as usual, from the oyster shell parking lot at headquarters. He had filled the tank and washed the car three days before. The hood shouldn't have been touched since then, yet there were smudges and smears at the front. Sudden realization spurred MacIver into action.

He released the seat belt and let it slide gently into place, then opened the door. He left the motor running. Moving as if on the edge of a precipice, he eased out of the seat and set one foot on the concrete, then the other. He slid around the door quickly. Then he ran like hell, heading for the hallway, the telephone, and the bomb squad, in that order.

22 He tried to keep the concrete stanchions between himself and the wagon as he ran. If there was a bomb, it might be on a time delay or a time fuse and could be removed for evidence before it detonated. Just as that thought came to mind, MacIver was hurled against the wall by the blast. The heat and sound came a split second later.

He found himself looking up at a man whose mouth was moving but he wasn't saying anything. MacIver said loudly, "A bomb just went off in my car."

The man's mouth moved some more. MacIver shouted impatiently, "Call the police!" Then it dawned on him that the man was talking normally; it was his own hearing that was at fault. The man disappeared, and MacIver moved first one arm, then the other, his legs, his head. All his parts seemed to be in working order.

Sometime later a bomb technician was standing over him. "You all right, Lieutenant?"

MacIver nodded. The technician's voice seemed to come from far away. It went on. "We're probably looking at sixty percent pure DuPont dynamite per stick, about six sticks, and an electronic fusing device."

"Overkill. They didn't need that much." MacIver hauled himself to his feet. That was the last thing he remembered when he woke up in the hospital.

Dr. Scarswell was standing over him with a cheerful look. "The human body was not made to withstand a blast of dynamite. Don't they tell you cops that, Anthony?"

"They've mentioned it. How am I?"

"Severe concussion. Some loss of hearing, probably temporary. You'll be okay."

"Good." He closed his eyes.

The next time he woke, Suzanne was beside him. She said, "You're going to be fine. Everything's all right. I want you to get well fast. You're a very important person to me." She kissed him on the cheek and then the lips. He wanted to put his arms around her, but he was too weary.

When he woke again, Jarratt was sitting beside the bed, his young face solemn. Surprised and pleased, MacIver said, "Hi, son."

"Hi, Dad. How you feeling?"

"Okay."

"Good. Look, I brought you something." He held up a drawing. MacIver squinted to see it. It wasn't a monster this time but a normal-looking person with MacIver's mouth and eyes and hairline. MacIver said, meaning it, "That's very good, Jarratt. I like it."

"You can take down that other thing. I don't want people seeing it. You can put this up instead—if you want to."

"I'd like that. Thanks." MacIver reached for the boy's hand. "Listen, I've been hard on you lately. I'm sorry."

"It wasn't you; it was me. I was being a real shitass. I'm not going to do that anymore."

"I want us to see each other more, do some things together."

Jarratt's eyes brightened. "Okay."

"Since you're interested in art, maybe we can go to some museums, that sort of thing." Jarratt's face fell. MacIver felt that his did, too. He added, "Or whatever," and closed his eyes. Maybe he'd just go to sleep.

After a moment Jarratt said tentatively, "Dad? We used to go fishing."

That woke MacIver up. "Would you like to do that?"

"Yeah, that would be great. Mom takes me to museums and stuff, but I'd like to go fishing a lot."

"You're on. As soon as I'm up and out of here."

"Great. Can we get a boat and everything?"

"We'll get a boat and everything." He closed his eyes again. He didn't know when Jarratt left.

The next time he woke, a woman was rolling up the head of his bed and a tray was in front of him. "What time is it?"

"Breakfast time. Why else you think I bring you breakfast? It's seven in the A.M."

"What day?"

"Thursday."

He'd lost 24 hours. He shifted to adjust to the angle of the bed, and groaned. His whole body ached and one of his ears had a ringing like a distant carillon. "Where am I? I mean, what hospital?"

"Houston General. And you better eat that breakfast fast 'cause they're going to come take you for tests just any minute."

Three balloons were tied to the foot of his bed. "Where'd those come from?"

"A lady brought 'em yesterday."

"What'd she look like?"

"She was wearing a green suit and she had kind of reddish hair."

He wondered how Suzanne had managed to get balloons. Then he remembered her visit, or had it been a dream? And Jarratt—had that been a dream, too? He said, "Do you see anything like a drawing around here, about so big?"

"Naw, I don' see no drawing."

"What's that paper rolled up on the chest of drawers?"

"This?" She picked it up and unrolled it. "Yeah, I guess that's a drawing. It looks kinda like *you*."

"It is me. My son did that."

"My, that's good. He must be an artist." She handed him the drawing, and MacIver examined it. Jarratt had done a good job. "Yeah, he's working at it."

"You better eat your breakfast now."

"Right." MacIver took the tops off the plates of food. Oatmeal, runny; scrambled eggs, congealed; bacon, greasy; toast, room temp; fruit salad, canned. The coffee was good and the cream was real.

While he ate, he puzzled over the bombing. Had it been done by the same person who had fired at him? He'd have to find out if Odetts was back in town, although he'd never heard of Lenny using dynamite. That made two attempts on his life in less than two weeks. He was going to have to call a halt to this before the third time came around.

When he had finished breakfast, he called Suzanne. "Thanks for the balloons. Was I awake when you brought them?"

"You're welcome. Yes, more or less." First step affirmative. Before he could proceed to the second step, she asked, "How are you this morning?"

"Stronger than a wet noodle. How are *you*?"

"I'm fine. A nurse told me you had a concussion and possible hearing damage."

"I don't know about the hearing yet. My left ear sounds like Sunday morning on church row. I'm supposed to go for tests in a little while. Oh shit, here they are now." An orderly had entered with a wheelchair.

She said quickly, "Call me when you come back."

"Right." He replaced the receiver and sat up. His head whirled.

The orderly said, "Hey, man, not so fast. Just take it easy now."

When the tests were finished, and he'd taken a short nap, he telephoned Suzanne. She said, "I'll be over in a little while. Stay where you are."

"I don't think I've got any choice."

She arrived in half an hour, and MacIver forgot the ringing in his ears and the ache in his head. She wore a beige skirt and a green shirt that made the flecks in her eyes greener and her hair redder, but it was the look in her eyes that made him smile. He held out his hand. "Hi. I'm glad you're here."

She came to the side of the bed, took his hand, and leaned over to kiss his cheek. "What did the tests show?"

"I'm hearing better all the time. I've got to wait for the doctor for the final report. Thanks again for the balloons." He wanted to tell her that when she came in the room brightened, that everything became all right with him, that nothing was important at this moment except the two of them here together, but he didn't say any of those things because he would have felt foolish expressing such thoughts. Instead he squeezed her hand. "You look great."

"You look pretty good yourself. A lot better than yesterday."

He patted the side of the bed. "Sit here."

She eased onto the bed. He could feel the warmth of her through the silk blouse, and she smelled good. He put his arm around her waist. "I remember your visit." Her eyebrows went up. "Or was I just dreaming?"

"I couldn't say, Lieutenant. What do you remember, or what did you dream?"

"Did you kiss me or was I just dreaming and wished you would?"

Her smile deepened. "You'll never know, will you?"

"Maybe I will. It seemed to me you leaned over." He drew her down.

"Did I kiss your cheek like this?"

"Um-hum. Then you—"

She moved her lips to his and murmured, "Was it like this?"

"Um." After several seconds, he said, "I think it was. Or maybe it was like this."

After the second kiss, she sat up. "Wow, you've made a miraculous recovery. No sick man could kiss that way."

"I have inspiration." Her skirt had slid up, and he stroked her leg, explored the silky inner thigh above her stocking, then drew back. "We're going to have to continue this later. My control is slipping."

She laughed, gave him one more quick kiss, and slid off the bed. "Fine thing, MacIver. I have to take advantage of you in the hospital before you know I'm alive."

"I knew you were alive all right, but—"

A nurse came in and grinned. "Am I interrupting something?"

MacIver said "Yes," and Suzanne said "And not a moment too soon." She moved over to the single chair. When the nurse had gone, she said, "Do you know who put the bomb in your car?"

"I don't have any idea. I've been wracking my brain, and I can't think of anybody who would want to kill me."

"Remember the questions you asked me? What about your wife?"

162

"She doesn't like me, but she wouldn't try to kill me. If I were dead, she'd lose the child support."

"Be serious, Tony. You have life insurance, don't you?"

"Yes, I hadn't thought of that. But no, as a matter of fact, Constance wouldn't try to kill me. Nor would Jarratt."

"A former girlfriend?"

MacIver shook his head and wished he hadn't. The ache was accelerating into a pound. "No serious attachments."

"You've got to have made some enemies in your career."

"A few. Most of them are behind bars. I've been all through this, Suzanne. I can't think of anybody who has a reason to want me dead."

"It's so scary to have people out there doing things to you and you don't know why."

"You understand about that, don't you?"

She nodded. "But I feel safe at the high rise. It's different with you."

"Maybe." He closed his eyes.

"You need to rest so I'm going to stop talking to you, but I want to ask you one thing first. If I suspected a parent was abusing his child, whom should I contact?"

MacIver opened his eyes. "You're thinking about Richard?"

"Yes."

"What makes you think so?"

"I'll talk to you about it later. Just tell me whom to call."

"The juvenile division at HPD."

"Thank you. Go to sleep now."

When he woke, Dr. Scarswell was in the room and Suzanne was gone. "The tests came out all right. We didn't find any blood in the spinal tap. How's your hearing?"

MacIver listened a moment. "I've got some ringing in the left ear, but the right ear is okay."

"You could hear both high and low octaves with the right ear on the hearing tests. That ringing will probably go away in a couple of days."

"Good. When can I leave?"

"In a couple of days."

"I can't stay here two days. I feel great."

"That's why you're staying. You'd be out running all over

town and that's not the way to let the body heal. You can stand a little rest, Tony. Just lean back and take it easy for a while. Do you want a tranquilizer?"

MacIver growled, "No, I'll just lie here and meditate on patience."

As soon as the doctor was gone, he called Rodriguez. "What's going on?"

"Hey, Loot, how you feeling?"

"Okay. Did those tapes come in from Florida?"

"Yesterday afternoon. Minnesota, too."

"Have you looked at them?"

"Not yet."

"I'd like to see them. I wonder if you could get a technician to bring a VCR and hook it into a TV here."

The sergeant wasn't sure it could be done, but he'd talk to a tech and call back. Suzanne arrived along with MacIver's lunch tray. He said, "Now what's this about Richard?"

"I think his father abuses him."

"Do you have any evidence?"

"Not unless you count gut feeling."

"You can on a personal basis, but it doesn't look good on a report. Have you seen bruises, broken bones, anything like that?"

"No, but I saw his father holding him yesterday evening, gripping his arm so hard that I'm sure he has bruises today. I was walking in the hall. Richard and his father got off the elevator. They didn't see me at first. Pierce was holding him and talking in the most hateful, threatening tone. He said, 'And you know what you're going to—' Then he saw me, and stopped. Richard looked at me, just for an instant, but there was the most pleading, pitiful look on his face. I wanted to scoop him up and take him away from that man.

"And I had seen Richard earlier in the day, when I went out to get my car. He was bright and talkative. He asked me if I had a little boy. I said no, I had a litte girl, but she was older than he. Then I asked him when his mother was going to join his father and him. His face tightened up. He said, 'I don't know,' and ran away."

MacIver sighed. "That's not much to go on."

"I know it isn't, but if you'd seen the way he looked at me—Tony, I couldn't just not do anything."

"Well, call the juvenile division—"

"I did, while you were asleep."

"You don't waste time, do you? What did they say?"

"That they'd send somebody out to investigate. I don't know what that means."

"That means they'll ask the neighbors if they've noticed any signs of child abuse. They'll probably talk to the building manager and the maid. Then, if they have enough to go on, they'll talk to Pierce and the boy."

"I think Richard is too afraid of his father to tell the truth."

"That's one of the problems in child abuse cases."

"Maybe I shouldn't have called them."

"You said yourself you had to do something."

"I thought I did, yes. Do you think I was just being a busybody?"

"I think you're a tender-hearted person who probably brought your child up very differently from what you're seeing."

"That's true. I just hope I haven't caused Richard more problems." She leaned down and kissed him on the cheek. "You look as if you could use a nap."

"I think I could."

MacIver awoke two hours later when Rodriquez walked in with a VCR. "Afternoon, Loot. Thought maybe you'd like to go to the movies."

23 Rod played the Craddock tape first. It started with a blond woman, probably in her mid-fifties, leaving a brick house. She wore what looked like a silk dress and her hair was carefully coiffed. She turned and walked toward the carport, unlocked and got into a Lincoln Continental. MacIver said, "I'll bet that's the same car and carport she was killed in."

The scene ended as the car began to move. In the next scene, she was in bed with Hicks. Rod said, "It gives you a funny feeling watching this, knowing that both of them are dead now. Braden, too."

They watched a few more minutes, and MacIver said, "At least seeing those guys in action keeps me from feeling sorry for them."

The door opened suddenly. A nurse entered and caught a glimpse of the screen before Rod could turn off the machine. She snapped on the light and stared at them. "I've seen some weird things in hospitals, but this is the first time I've seen anybody playing dirty movies."

With just enough pomposity in his voice to make her doubt his word, MacIver said, "We're Houston police officers, Nurse. We're not watching for fun. This is official evidence."

She said, "I'll just bet it is," and wrapped a pressure cuff around his arm.

MacIver was disappointed in the tapes. "You'd think that on at least one of the tapes they'd have made a mistake and shown part of a face, or a tattoo, or something distinctive. I guess if they made any mistakes in the filming, they edited them out."

"Yessir. Well, the ones east of the Mississippi did have the same mode of operation as Braden and Hicks. I guess that could indicate that they'd had the same instructions," Rod suggested.

"Probably," MacIver agreed. "Although there are only so many positions and so many camera angles." MacIver's headache was picking up. "Did you time them?"

"All fifteen minutes."

They looked at each other, at the wall, at the ceiling. MacIver said, "The opening on Mrs. Craddock's film must have been shot some weeks ago. She wasn't wearing even a jacket and I think it's been chilly up there for—" He broke off. "The ones from Miami didn't have an intro. They opened up on the bed scenes."

"That's right! Craddock's did and Suzanne's did, but not Miami."

Excitement quickened MacIver's speech. "Suzanne and Craddock were targeted, picked specifically and in advance. The intros show that. The Miami women weren't. That makes two things Suzanne and Craddock have in common, the intros and the foreign objects. Anything else?"

"Both are white females, affluent—"

"Craddock used to be from Houston. I've already shown Craddock's picture to Suzanne, but maybe if she saw the video—" MacIver picked up the phone and dialed Suzanne's number. When she answered, he asked, "Could you come over to the hospital and look at a videotape I've got here?"

"You have a VCR in the hospital?"

"Yes, thanks to Rod."

"Is this a tape from one of the victims?"

"Yes. It has an intro the way your tape does."

"I'll be there in half an hour."

The tape was rewound and ready when Suzanne arrived. Rod closed the door, turned off the light, and turned on the tape. They watched as Betsy Craddock came out of her house and walked down the sidewalk. The moment before the scene was to change, Rod pushed the Stop button.

Suzanne said, "She looks familiar, but it may be because I saw her photo."

"The hairstyle could have changed, and she's older than when you would have known her. Run it by again, Rod."

They watched a second time in silence. When Rod turned off the tape, Suzanne said, "I'm sorry, but I just can't place her."

"Okay, don't push it. If you did know her in the past, it will come back to you eventually. Have you heard anything from the juvenile division?"

"Not yet."

After Suzanne and Rod left, MacIver considered calling his doctor. He had thought earlier that he would try to talk Scarswell into releasing him today. Now he thought he would take a nap instead. Maybe that would stop the pounding in his head.

He woke the next morning with only a dull ache in his head and a faint ringing in his left ear. Nobody was present to tell him not to, so he took a shower.

It was still too early to call the office, so he called Suzanne.

"Good morning. I think I'm back among the living today. How are you?"

"I managed to squeeze into slacks this morning. The swelling is almost gone."

"I'm glad to hear that. I'm leaving the hospital today."

"The doctor has released you?"

"No, I've released me."

"Don't push it, Tony."

"No, I won't, but I want to get out of here. Did the juvenile people ever show up?"

"Yes, they came late in the afternoon. They talked to me. Then they were going to talk to some other people. I don't think they were impressed with what I told them—except that they were interested that Richard wasn't in school. That got their attention."

"Then maybe you did some good, after all."

"I hope so. Are you coming home?"

"No, I'm going to Central and turn in my badge and gun the way I was supposed to three days ago."

168

The doctor wasn't enthusiastic about releasing him, but agreed upon the condition that he would get plenty of rest and would return for an examination in two days. MacIver checked out of the hospital and called a patrol car to take him to Central.

Captain McNamee said, "You don't look too good, Mac."

"You should've seen me yesterday."

"This is a good time for you to get some rest, since you're relieved of all official duties anyway."

"Yessir. Do you know how long the IAD investigation will take?"

"Shouldn't take more than a few days. By the way, Louisiana finally released the Elsing body. The funeral's scheduled for three days hence."

MacIver thought about Roscoe Elsing. "I'd like to go, if it's all right with you."

"Good idea. There's a chance that the couple who killed her will show up. Get hold of the woman who roomed with Elsing in New Orleans and have her watching the crowd. No, tell Rod to do that. If you're not reinstated by that time, you can go in an unofficial capacity."

"Yessir. How's my bombing case coming?"

"We're asking questions. Not getting any answers. The garage is trying to put your wagon back together, but I don't think it's going to work." MacIver hoped it wouldn't. The captain went on, "It's worse than Humpty Dumpty. Twenty cars were damaged one way or another in that parking garage. There was in excess of four sticks of dynamite."

"I didn't have time to count 'em. They were moving a little fast when they went by me."

When he came out of the captain's office, Rod was waiting for him in the hall. "Hey, Loot, you got out."

"Yeah, I got time off for good behavior, but I have to report to my parole officer in two days."

"You're not going to leave me out on a limb with these DARE cases, are you?"

"No. I can't work on them officially, but I can unofficially. Come on into my office and catch me up on things."

"We have a new one from Baltimore."

"Sounds like they're working north. How many is that in all. Eleven?"

"Twelve. All with the same MO, except for this last one, which involved a lone male."

"That's going to be a copycat. Has Hermione gotten instructions for the drop yet?"

"No, they haven't come in. Maybe they won't now with Braden and Hicks dead."

"They won't let a perfectly good extortion tape go to waste. One of the teams will pick up on it. What's happening with the order for the Baron's fluids and follicle tests?"

"The order came through but they can't find Neimeyer or Pico to serve it."

"Shit! That's why CID was supposed to be on surveillance."

"They've been too busy helping the feds."

"He probably left the country."

"I'm still interviewing Mrs. Craddock's friends. Nothing's come up so far that puts her with the other three women. In fact, I've got an interview in twenty minutes. I better cut out."

"Okay, I'm probably going home in a couple of hours. I'll talk to you tomorrow."

MacIver continued to review notes on the DARE cases. The three bodies in the helicopter had been positively identified by dental records as Braden, Hicks, and the pilot. All had been shot multiple times with Mack Tens and once each in the head with a nine-millimeter automatic pistol. They were making damned certain that the three men were dead, MacIver thought.

No prints or other identifying marks had been found on photos or envelopes on any of the victims.

The last report, a rather plaintive one, came from the crime lab. The fingerprints found on the phone booths still were being processed; it was probably going to take a long time.

MacIver took down Jarratt's old drawing and put up the new one. As soon as he could squeeze out the time, he was going to arrange that fishing trip. He started out the door to get a cup of coffee, and the phone rang.

"Tony, this is Suzanne." She was almost whispering. "Richard is in my apartment. His father was going to move, and he ran in here and hid. I've locked the door, but—"

"Does Pierce know he's there?"

"I don't think so, but he may figure it out."

"Keep the door locked. Don't talk to him. I'll be there in fifteen minutes."

MacIver was on the elevator going down before he realized he didn't have a vehicle. The captain wouldn't lend him one either, since he was officially off duty. He could get a rookie to take him home in a patrol car, but that was a nuisance. He rubbed his chin a moment, and the elevator came to a stop. What the hell, the garage didn't know he was off duty. He hurried over to see what they had available.

The car he was assigned turned out to be a red Jaguar, probably confiscated from some drug dealer who'd been riding high long enough to buy himself the car of his dreams. MacIver liked it, too; it was like a toy after the wagon. He pushed it up to ninety on Memorial Drive, trying to make up for lost time. He arrived at the Towers only three minutes later than he had promised.

The fifth floor hall was empty. Pierce's door was closed, as was Suzanne's. MacIver rang the bell and identified himself. Suzanne opened the door only wide enough to let him through.

"Thank God you're here. Pierce came to the door and rang about five minutes ago. At least, I guess it was him. I didn't answer."

"Good. Where's Richard?"

"In the bedroom."

"What happened exactly?"

"I had been walking in the hall. I was going to come back inside. I opened my door just as Richard came out of his apartment. He saw the open door and just bolted in here like—I don't know—like a little wild animal. He said, 'Don't tell him where I am. Don't let him in.' I locked the door and then looked around for him. He'd disappeared. I found him crouching in the corner behind the chair in the bedroom, and the look on his face—Tony, I wanted to cry."

"Have you talked to him?"

"Not much. He's too frightened. All he said was that 'he' was taking him away again. I just told him everything would be all right and that you were on your way."

"Okay, I'll talk to him."

Richard was no longer crouched on the floor, but he huddled against the bed as far as he could get from the front door. MacIver said, "Hello, son." Richard was trembling. "There's nothing to be frightened of. You told Mrs. Hilbourne your father was moving?"

Richard nodded. "He didn't like it because people were asking questions about us. He said they were going to put me in jail."

"Nobody's going to put you in jail. Isn't he good to you?" Richard shook his head.

"Does he spank you or beat you?"

"Not much." He ducked his head. "He does other things."

MacIver was beginning to get a sick feeling in the pit of his stomach. "Do you want to tell me about those things?"

Richard shook his head.

MacIver said, as much to Suzanne as to Richard, "I'm going to call the juvenile division. I don't know the exact procedure for dealing with juveniles, what rights the state has in this situation. It could just be a family squabble. I don't know if I have probable cause at this time to keep a father from his—"

Richard shouted, "He's not my father! My father lives in Wisconsin. He stole me. He grabbed me and shoved me in his car." He broke into a torrent of weeping.

24 Juvenile officers were at the apartment within an hour. By that time Richard had talked to his real parents, in Beloit, Wisconsin. The conversation between mother and son had been a tearful one, and was reenacted five minutes later when Richard's father called from his office. After talking a few minutes, Richard turned to MacIver. "He wants to talk to you."

MacIver reassured the father, Dick Smollett, that Richard was in good physical condition, and explained what the lieutenant in the juvenile division had told him. Juvenile officers, as well as MacIver, would try to verify as much as possible of Richard's story before taking Pierce into custody. Richard himself would be taken by juvenile officers to Child Protective Services, where he would be held until his parents arrived.

"I'll be on the next plane. Let me have that phone number. I'll call you back as soon as I know exactly when I arrive. I can't tell you how much this means to me and my family, Lieutenant—" His voice broke.

MacIver said they'd wait to hear from him, hung up, and told Richard, "Your father will be here tonight."

The boy was almost jumping up and down with excitement. Suzanne asked, "What about Pierce? Hadn't you better arrest him?"

"We need to get some more facts before we arrest him, but I do want to make sure he doesn't drive away." MacIver called the security guard downstairs and identified himself as a police officer. "We have a little problem with Pierce on the fifth floor. Are you familiar with his car?"

The security guard said he was, and MacIver told him, "Keep an eye on it for the next few minutes. If he tries driving away, stop him. I'll explain later."

The juvenile officers had questioned Suzanne and MacIver, and were talking with Richard when the phone rang. It was the security guard. "I have Pierce with me, Lieutenant. He was on his way out of here."

"Okay, hold on." He relayed the message to the juvenile officers. They told him they had enough information to warrant an arrest.

MacIver told the security guard to telephone for patrolmen to arrest the man. Not only was his headache coming back, but he didn't want even to lay eyes on Pierce.

Richard's father phoned back to say that he would get into town shortly after nine o'clock. The juvenile people gave him the number of Child Services. "He'll be waiting for you, Mr. Smollett."

When everyone had gone, MacIver said, "You did a good deed today, lady."

"I wish they had let Richard stay with me."

"He'll be all right." MacIver yawned. "Let's go across the street and get some lunch. Then I'm going to take a nap." His head was starting to ache again. "I've got to get that car back to the garage, too."

"Can't you do that tomorrow?"

"No, I'd better do it today. I don't want IAD to have another mark against me."

"I'll follow you and drive you home."

"I was hoping you'd say that."

When MacIver woke from his nap it was dark outside. His watch showed 7:45. He got up and showered, dressed in jeans and a sport shirt, and called Suzanne. "You still feel like going downtown with me?"

"Ready and waiting. I'll meet you in the parking garage."

The Houston skyline disappeared as they entered Memorial Park headed for downtown. MacIver was driving in the left-hand lane next to the median behind Suzanne's blue Pontiac. At Picnic, she caught an amber light and went on through. The light changed to red and MacIver stopped.

174

A black BMW pulled around the bus on MacIver's right, did a butterfly stop—just long enough to make sure no cars were coming from north or south—ran the red light, and swerved toward the left to approach Suzanne's car. It was trying to draw level with Suzanne's Pontiac, MacIver realized. A man's arm appeared outside the left rear window.

The Jaguar's tires screamed as MacIver ran the red light and raced to close the distance between himself and the two vehicles. Something glinted, and he saw that the man in the BMW held a long-barreled weapon. It was aimed at Suzanne.

She had slowed, probably to give MacIver time to catch up. The BMW put on its brakes.

MacIver caught up with them, braked abruptly, and drove the Jaguar into the left rear of the BMW. There was the sickening crunch of metal against metal, and his body jerked hard against the seat belt. At the same time, he heard the staccato blast of a machine gun.

He rammed the BMW a second time. The Jaguar swiveled to the right, rocked, and righted itself.

Glass was flying from Suzanne's car and the right door swung open. She had accelerated, but the BMW was back on track and drawing close to the Pontiac.

MacIver stepped on the gas and maneuvered the Jaguar between the two cars in front of him. The powerful sports car was able to wedge itself between the two vehicles, forcing them apart. He saw the Pontiac jump the median. The next instant his windshield blew out. Momentarily blinded, he stomped on the brakes, felt the car slide. Then he crashed into something.

He managed to stop the car and stumble out. He was on the median. The Pontiac, behind him, had jumped across it into oncoming traffic and overturned.

"Suzanne!" He wasn't sure whether he spoke aloud or if the scream was inside his head. A form tumbled out of the driver's side of the car. Waving frantically to stop approaching vehicles, he ran to the car. Suzanne lay still on the pavement. He dropped down beside her, reaching for a pulse. She shook his hand away. "The next time, get a taxi to take you downtown!"

Two hours later they reached Suzanne's apartment. They had gone to Twelve Oaks for examination. Doctors had confirmed that, amazingly, they were suffering nothing worse than cuts and bruises. The Jaguar and Pontiac were totaled. The BMW got away.

Suzanne set her purse down and turned to face him. "I'm tired of it, Tony. I'm damned tired of being a target. I'm tired of being hurt. I'm tired of not being able to go outside this apartment without wondering if somebody's going to try to kill me." Her lips quivered. "And I want my daughter to come home!"

"I know." MacIver took her in his arms and held her as closely as he could. Both of them had cuts on their arms and faces. "It's going to stop."

"When?" She was sobbing now.

"Soon. Something in this case has got to give. I think it's going to be soon."

MacIver crawled out of bed the next morning and spent ten minutes in the shower, letting hot water loosen up the muscles in his aching body. By the time he had a cup of coffee, he decided he'd probably live.

It was Saturday, and officially he was suspended, but unofficially there were things he needed to do so he went to the office. He called Odetts's brother-in-law at work. The man said he'd heard nothing of Leonard. On the off chance that Odetts's sister knew something she wasn't telling her husband, he called her home but got no answer.

Rod came in with two cups of coffee, and MacIver did a double take. "What happened to your mustache?"

The drooping ends were gone. The sides were now trimmed in a curved Fu Manchu look. Rod looked sheepish. "I haven't told anybody else, Loot, but Rosa got mad at me on a date. See, I was dead tired when we got back to her house, and I went to sleep on the couch. So she got out her scissors and cut off the ends of my mustache while I was asleep."

"Notice any loss of strength?"

He grinned. "No, nothing like that." He fingered the

mustache. "I trimmed it up best I could, but I guess it looks kinda funny."

"Well, it's different."

"Maybe I'll shave it off."

"I thought Rosa was the one who wanted you to grow it in the first place."

"She was. That's what I told her. She said, yes, but I was snoring and the mustache ends kept blowing in and out and they were making her crazy so she cut 'em off. I said nothing could make her crazy; she was already that way."

"You-all still friends?"

"I didn't call her last night. I'm gonna let her worry a little."

"Sarge, the Elsing funeral is Monday."

"Yessir."

"Elsing's assailants may attend. Get hold of Mrs. Robb. She's the only one who would recognize them. Work out some hand signals with her to identify them."

"Okay, Loot, but I'd think they'd be afraid to show themselves around Mrs. Robb."

"Never can tell. They may be arrogant enough to think they can get away with it."

"Gotcha. Say, I been noticing your new drawing." He went to the sketch and studied it. "Your son do this, too?"

MacIver felt a little swell of pride. "Yeah, he brought it to me in the hospital. Said he didn't want people seeing the other one."

"No kidding. Well, this one's good, but I'd have to say the other one looks more like you."

"Get out of here."

Rod left, grinning.

MacIver made a written report on the incident the evening before with the BMW. He mentioned that the Jaguar had come from the police garage, but did not emphasize the fact that he was officially off duty when he took it. Maybe nobody would think of that.

Dr. Scarswell's office called to remind him that he was to see the doctor Monday. Could he make it about two? MacIver said he could.

Shortly before lunch, the captain called him. "Got something here ought to please you. Internal Affairs has found Kurt Neimeyer's complaint via his attorney Silas Conover to be superficial and malicious. No charges will be filed against Lieutenant Anthony MacIver."

"Hey, that's good news, Cap."

"I thought you'd like it."

"I'm going to need a car."

"Cripes, MacIver, you go through vehicles like a guy with hay fever goes through Kleenex. Pick something that it won't matter when it gets totaled."

"Yessir. And thanks, Cap."

The first car he saw in the garage was a black Porsche. Twelve thousand miles on the odometer. He guessed that wasn't what the captain had in mind. There was a beat-up pickup, but MacIver figured its engine was as decrepit as its body. He examined a six-year-old Chevrolet with a hundred and ten thousand miles on the odometer. Nobody would care if it got totaled, but he wasn't sure it would get him home. The Jaguar had spoiled him. No doubt about it. He gave in to temptation and told the garage attendant he'd take the Porsche.

When he reached the office Monday, Rodriguez followed him through the door. "The artist finally got that composite drawing of Potworth." He dropped it onto the desk.

MacIver looked at it, took a second look, and said softly, "By Jesus, do you know who that is? It's Joseph Piccolo, the Baron's right-hand man."

25 "I should have recognized him from the verbal description." MacIver and Rodriguez studied a photo of Piccolo taken from the files. "I told you it rang a bell, but I couldn't come up with a face. Look, there's the mark on the left ear. It's a tiny scar. Hairline—widow's peak. The shoes—dammit, that should have tipped me immediately. Pico's known for having a penchant for shoes made out of skin, alligator, snake, ostrich—you name it, he's got a pair of shoes or boots made out of it."

"So the black-and-white team worked for the Baron?"

"Sure. They'd probably worked for him in one of the health clubs. That's why they were in such good physical condition. He probably recruits all the teams from his health clubs. There again, I should have seen it. I thought the teams might come from college campuses, but I didn't think of health clubs.

"The MO is the same, too. The Baron's been victimizing women for more than twenty years. He just decided to go after some who weren't prostitutes."

"But why did he target Suzanne and Craddock?"

"I haven't figured that out yet, but there must be some connection." MacIver picked up the photo of Pico. "Put together a set of photos and show it to that real estate agent. If he picks Pico's mug, we're in business."

"Okay, Loot, but what about the funeral?"

"The funeral!" MacIver slapped his forehead. "I'd forgotten about the funeral. Okay, it's after nine now. You'll have to talk to the real estate man after the funeral. We should leave here in about fifteen minutes."

*   *   *

The church, on Elgin Street, was a white clapboard building with gray trim and a steeple. There was no parking lot, and the nearby curbs were already jammed with cars when Mac-Iver and Rodriguez arrived. The sergeant finally found a vacant spot three blocks away, and they joined the mourners approaching the church.

Most of the older people were black, but there was a smattering of Hispanics and whites in their thirties and forties, probably Mrs. Elsing's pupils in the 1960s, when integration first went into effect. The sun was bright, but the temperature was a few degrees cooler than usual, a hint that the summer heat couldn't hold on forever.

MacIver asked, "What kind of signals did you work out with Mrs. Robb?"

"If she sees the couple, she's going to rub the top of her nose. Then, as soon as she can, she's going to go stand behind them and adjust her hat."

"Nice and simple. That's good."

They reached the door of the church and stepped inside. Gray-gloved ushers in dark business suits took them down the center aisle to the first available seats, two rows from the back; the church was nearly full. By craning, MacIver could see Mr. Elsing in the front row with a young woman on one side of him and a young man on the other. Mrs. Robb was sitting in the back row, on the center aisle, where she could keep an eye on everybody.

The organist ended "Rock of Ages," began "In the Garden." The choir, in ivory robes with royal blue albs, filed in from the back, followed by the song leader, also in robes, and the minister, in a dark suit, blue vest, and collar, and with a medallion of a fish on a chain around his neck.

Everyone stood to sing the hymn. The people to MacIver's right had taken the only hymn book at that end of the pew. To his surprise, he remembered some of the words. When he ran out of words, he hummed. A four- or five-year-old girl to his right, hair elaborately braided, stared at him wide-eyed and openmouthed every time he began to hum. He winked at her, and she shrank against her mother's side.

The hymn ended, the minister stood and made a few introductory remarks. There was already some sniffling and nose blowing among the congregation. He continued. "Many friends of our dear, departed sister asked to speak here today, so many that we couldn't accommodate all of them. I, along with some of the deacons, have tried to select speakers who we think will give a representative view of sister Lurinda's life."

The first speaker was a high school boy who had been a student of Mrs. Elsing. MacIver was impressed with both the boy's description of the teacher's expertise and his presentation. Next, an Hispanic youth, another former student, now a professional baseball player, told of the values Mrs. Elsing had taught him that had been important to his career.

Two speakers followed with similar tributes. Mrs. Robb kept looking around the sanctuary, but she hadn't rubbed the top of her nose so it looked like the assailants hadn't shown up. MacIver was disappointed but not surprised.

The last speaker was the local constable, the chief law enforcement official in the area. He praised Mrs. Elsing's civic duties. ". . . never did she turn down the call to duty. Over the years—I went back and counted so I could tell you exactly—she served on a total of eighteen juries, a couple of appellate, a couple of corporation courts, but primarily at the district level in various civil and criminal trials."

MacIver didn't hear the rest of the eulogy. The thing that linked the four women—why not?—might be a jury, one of the few places where rich River Oaks, poor Third Ward, and small business enterprise might meet. And where it was possible to make a serious enemy. He whispered to Rod, "Did you check out whether any of the women were on a jury together?"

Rod looked thunderstruck. "Nosir, we never thought of that."

"Okay, I want to get to the courthouse. Mrs. Robb hasn't turned up anything. Probably won't, but we'll get one of your men to speak with her afterward. You'll come with me." He wondered if it would be unforgivably rude to leave early and decided it would be. "We'll go as soon as the service is over."

He listened with impatience to the minister's closing remarks. Finally the choir stood; the congregation followed suit and they began "Nearer My God to Thee." The tyke on MacIver's right, apparently disturbed at her neighbor's intermittent humming, picked the hymnal out of her mother's hands and handed it to MacIver. He thanked her, and winked again. She smiled and ducked her head.

As soon as the benediction ended, MacIver and Rod left, headed for the courthouse.

Inside the building, they went to Public Records and identified themselves. A pretty brunette helped them, smiling brilliantly at Rodriguez. "My brother is Chico Mireles. You probably know him."

She said it with such pride that MacIver wondered what deeds of derring-do Mireles had claimed to his family. Fortunately, MacIver did know him slightly. "Yes, ma'am. Fine officer. We're trying to find a link between several women, and we think it's possible they may have sat on the same jury. Where can I check on that?"

"Aisle six, book seven. Book seven has been transcribed to microfiche. If you do not know how to use a microfiche, one of the clerks will be happy to assist you." She gave Rodriguez another dazzling smile. "I will tell my brother I met you."

They reached aisle six, were handed a little tag with the number ten on it, and told to wait until their number was called. The number currently being processed was seven. MacIver said to Rod, "You stay here. If our number is called, give them the names of the victims and ask if they ever served on a jury together. I'm going to call Suzanne."

He found a pay phone in the lobby and called Suzanne's apartment. Nobody answered. He hung up and redialed. Still no answer.

By the time he returned, they were working on number eight. Finally ten was called, and both officers came to their feet. MacIver began, "We have—"

The clerk asked, "What can I do for you?"

"We have the names of several women who we think sat on a jury together—in any combination. Can you track that down?"

She looked at the names. "It will take a while."

MacIver said, "We'll wait."

They returned to their seats, and Rodriguez said, "I think I'll try to find some coffee. You want any, Loot?"

"Sure. And two packets of sugar."

Rodriguez returned in ten minutes with the coffee and a broad smile on his face. MacIver asked, "What's up?"

"Nothing."

"Then why are you grinning like that?"

Rodriguez answered obliquely, "I think I'll shave my mustache off this afternoon."

"How come?"

"I was just talking to Delores Mireles, the one who has a brother on the force?"

"You didn't waste much time, did you?"

He shrugged. "Anyway, she said she didn't much like mustaches."

"I suppose she also said she'd go to dinner with you tonight, but you told her you'd be working."

Rodriguez's benign look vanished. "I'm not working tonight."

"You may be. We may be putting together a case." He added, "Here we go," as the clerk returned.

She said, "Craddock's name was misspelled, but three of the others were clearly on Docket Number w8756-56, which means they were on the 186th District Court jury. The final verdict was guilty by unanimous agreement. Confinement in TDC, that's the Texas Department of Corrections, later confinement in Huntsville and subsequent confinement in Ramsey Prison, unit number one, for a period of fifteen years. Subject was released on probation—pardon me, parole—after serving seven years and two months." She looked up and smiled. "Anything else?"

"Yes, the subject's name."

"Oh, didn't I say that? Kurt Herman Neimeyer, a.k.a. the Baron."

MacIver slapped his fist into his other palm. "We've got the son of a bitch!"

The clerk said, "What?"

"Nothing, ma'am. Could I get a copy of that?"

"Yes. That will be three dollars. No checks. Cash only."

On the way to the office, MacIver said, "That asshole. To think he's the one behind all this. It was revenge, after all."

"He waited a long time for revenge. That trial was fifteen years ago."

"I guess he was just working up to it. That was three years after Rita Davis was killed. I was the arresting officer. The Baron was charged with aggravated promotion of prostitution. We almost lost the case because he tried to get rid of all the hookers involved, and they were our only witnesses. We found two of 'em buried in a shallow grave in New Mexico, but we never could prove he was guilty of murder."

"Funny to think we've been tracking him on an old case, and he turns out to be Mr. Big on the current one."

"The leopard doesn't change his spots. I just wish I'd seen the connection sooner."

They reached Central One and went straight to Captain McNamee's office. MacIver showed him the jury list with the names of four of their victims. "And I was the arresting officer, Cap. I figure he's also the one behind the two attempts on my life."

"Revenge just because somebody was on a jury?"

"I've been recalling that case, Cap. His lawyer made the damnedest plea to the jury I've ever heard. He asked them to find Neimeyer not guilty because the defendant was young and handsome, and if he was sent to prison he'd be badly abused by the other inmates. And that happened, as a matter of fact. He was raped several times, I heard. I guess that could make a man want revenge."

"But what about the men on the jury? Why just the women?"

"I don't know. Maybe he's doing something to the men we don't know about."

"You'd better follow up on that. Contact the entire jury panel and find out if anything's happening with the men. It looks like you've got the key to these crimes here, Mac, but this is like a lot of cases: you've got a pretty good idea who's behind the crime but you still have to prove it. Prove Neimeyer had anything to do with Braden and Hicks. Prove that he's had anything to do with the black couple.

184

Prove that he's connected to all these cases all over the country. I think the hardest part of this case is before you."

"Rod's going to show Pico's photo to the real estate agent."

"That will put Pico on the scene, not the Baron."

"Any suggestions, Cap?"

"Don't get frustrated and impatient and make mistakes. Don't violate any departmental policies, any of the general orders, the SOP of the division. And most of all, do not violate the rules of criminal procedure in attempting to make the case rapidly. If you do, we'll lose him."

"Okay, Cap."

"Besides showing Pico's photo to the real estate agent, what do you plan to do?"

"First I'm going to eat lunch. Then I'm going over to Special Crimes at the district attorney's office to find out the evidence we'll need in order to get an indictment. Then we'll start putting together that kind of evidence. Oh, I've got to see my doctor this afternoon to get a release so I can return to full duty."

"Okay, you guys go and get some lunch. I'll see you later."

MacIver reached the doctor's office at two, as scheduled. The nurse with the chirrupy voice said, "I saw you drive up, Lieutenant. That's a snazzy car you're driving."

MacIver grinned and said, "I'm enjoying it."

Scarswell did a quick examination and pronounced him in good shape. "With your constitution, Anthony, you'll live to be a hundred—if you manage to stay away from bombs."

MacIver was still thinking about that when he left the office and Leonard Odetts stepped out of the shrubbery. The muzzle of his sawed-off twelve-gauge shotgun touched MacIver's temple.

26 Odetts looked as scraggly as ever, although he'd picked up a tan, and his hair, sunbleached, was blond instead of bayou mud color. He wore a sport shirt with its short sleeves rolled up above his biceps, blue jeans, and cowboy boots. The barrel of the .870 pump shotgun was as big as a cannon, but what chilled MacIver's blood was the shine of manic excitement in Odetts's eyes. The felon had killed at least twice. MacIver was afraid Odetts had learned to enjoy it.

He said, "I been waiting for you, Loot."

"Yeah, I see."

"We're going to take a ride, you and me."

"Sure, Len."

Odetts sidled back on the sidewalk. "Walk past me to the parking lot. Try anything and I'll blow your goddam head off right here."

"I won't try anything." MacIver moved slowly and fluidly without sudden starts or stops, the way he'd move around a coiled rattlesnake.

The minute between the doctor's door and the parking lot went by too quickly. Nobody drove into the lot. Nobody came out the door. MacIver could have been alone in the world with only Odetts as a companion.

"Go to the Trans Am. Passenger side." Odetts's voice sounded choked. He was breathing shallowly.

MacIver recognized the Trans Am, which was parked headed out for a quick getaway. The trunk lid had a triangular dent.

"Open the door easy." Odetts reached inside MacIver's

coat and pulled out his service revolver. "Give me your handcuffs."

"Look, Leonard, you don't want to cuff me. Somebody will see and report you."

The shotgun barrel jabbed against his head. "Give me the cuffs. Easy—easy when you reach."

"Okay. They're inside my belt in the back. I'm going to have to reach all the way around."

"Do it slow."

MacIver did it slow. He brought the cuffs out and passed them to Odetts.

"Get in the car. Put your arm around the center post."

"This isn't necessary. I'll come quietly without all this."

"Yeah, I know how quietly you'd come. You'd wait till I was on the freeway—" MacIver decided he couldn't risk further argument. He put his right arm through the open back window, around the doorpost, and back in through the open front window. Odetts said, "Get your arm farther around, goddamit." He held the shotgun with his right hand and fumbled the cuff onto MacIver's wrist with the left. "Get that other hand up, goddamit." He was almost panting now, and MacIver, afraid that the man's frustration would set him off, wriggled his wrist into the cuff. Odetts snapped it shut. "There, MacIver! Gotcha!" He ran around the car and got into the driver's seat. "Now you're gonna have your last ride."

MacIver was turned almost with his back to Odetts because of the angle of his arm around the doorpost. Hot air blew into the car, whipping his hair. He looked over his shoulder at the driver. "I don't understand this, Leonard. You've got no reason to kill me."

"I got a bunch of reasons, a whole bunch." Odetts laughed loudly. "Yessir, I got fifty thousand reasons."

"You're being paid?"

"You got it."

"Who by?"

Odetts grinned at him. "You don't know?"

"You tell me."

"Guess."

MacIver had a sense of the craziness of the situation, having to play a childish game to learn the name of his would-be killer, but he was more concerned with strategy, whether it would be better to mention the Baron or pretend he had no knowledge. He couldn't see an advantage either way, so he said, "I guess it's the Baron."

"Right the first time. You get the prize. Great prize you're gonna get." Odetts chortled at his own humor. "I got a Polaroid in the back. Got to get a picture of you to show Neimeyer you're dead."

MacIver had a fleeting image of himself, eyes open and staring, blood reddening his shirt, or would Odetts shoot him in the head? Wouldn't be much to take a picture of if he did, not with the cannon Odetts was carrying. "Why does the Baron want to kill me?"

"He hates your guts. Didn't you know that?"

"Because I was the arresting officer when he went to the pen?"

"I don't know. He didn't say."

"Why did you try to kill me that evening on Drexel?"

"How'd you know that was me?"

"I recognized the Trans Am just now. Was that for the Baron, too?"

"Yeah, but he didn't pay me since I missed. I was surprised when he called and gave me a second chance."

Big of him. "Were you the one put the bomb in my car?"

Odetts glanced at him in surprise. "Not me. I don't know nothing about no bomb. How'd you get out of it? What went wrong?"

Nothing had gone wrong, at least not as wrong as it could have. He was still alive, at any rate. For the time being. "I saw some prints that made me suspicious and got out of the vehicle before it blew. How did you and the Baron get together?"

"He got hold of me right after I was released and put it to me." He added almost apologetically. "I needed the money. My lawyer was on me about paying him, and my wife was broke."

"What about the other night?"

"That was a helluva thing for you to do, to ram our car! If

there'd been somebody in the next lane, we could've been killed."

"But there wasn't. The Baron told you to kill Mrs. Hilbourne?"

"Is that her name? He just showed her to me in the parking garage that evening."

So the Baron knew that Suzanne was staying at the Towers. That meant she wasn't safe there any longer, and he wasn't in any position to tell her. "Did he say why he wanted her killed?"

"Just said this would settle an old score."

That was the trial, MacIver guessed. They were on the freeway by now. The traffic around them made such a roar with the window down that it was almost impossible to talk. MacIver concentrated on watching the vehicles they passed, willing the drivers to see his arm around the post, to look farther and see the handcuffs. They passed one car after another, but as far as MacIver could tell, nobody even looked at the car, let alone saw his arm out the window. He turned his head toward Odetts and shouted, "Where we going?"

"Just a ways out here, little place I know."

MacIver was sweating, and ideas flashed through his mind like neon lights going on and off. He saw himself shifting and kicking Odetts, and fast after that, he saw the car careening, smashing into other vehicles. Bad idea. He imagined himself screaming out the window. It wouldn't do any good. Nobody would hear him because their windows were up and the air-conditioning on. There was nothing he could do in the car. He'd have to wait until he was out, till Odetts took off the cuffs—if he did. Maybe he'd shoot MacIver where he sat. MacIver told himself that wasn't likely. It would mess up the inside of his car too much. No, Odetts would take him out of the car before killing him, but MacIver didn't know if that would make things any better. Leonard had been arrested so many times that he knew procedure as well as MacIver. He would know the safe way to get MacIver out of the car and keep him immobilized. Shit, the more he thought, the worse his future looked. Then it occurred to him that this was the third attempt on his life. Third time lucky.

Odetts continued over Loop 610 but moved to the far left lane. They were going out 290, then. Lots of empty land out that way, lots of trees and brush, and oversized ditches with enough water in them to hide a body. That was the area where the body of the postwoman had been hidden years ago.

A blue and white appeared across the median, going in the opposite direction. MacIver gazed at it longingly. The patrolman never looked his way. You could never find a cop when you needed one.

How long would it be till he was missed? He was supposed to go to the D.A.'s office this afternoon and then meet with Rod for a planning session, but if he didn't show up, the sergeant would probably assume he was just doing something else. He wouldn't become alarmed until morning, when MacIver didn't turn up at the office. By that time MacIver could be long dead.

His only chance, it looked like, was to talk Odetts out of it, and he didn't give himself much hope there. Odetts *wanted* to kill him. He wanted the glory of it. He wanted to show MacIver once and for all that he was a big man.

They left 290 past Jack Rabbit Road and took a curving, bumpy road north and east. MacIver's arms were numb. The wind was stinging his eyes and kicking off his allergies. He sneezed three times and wished he could blow his nose.

Finally Odetts slowed, turned onto a dirt track leading into a field, and brought the car to a halt. "This is it, Mac-Iver. Nice, secluded place. Anybody hears a shot out here, they think somebody's shootin' rabbits."

"I've been giving this some thought, Len."

Odetts gave a high, excited giggle. "I just bet you have."

"I want to tell you a little story."

"I've heard your stories before."

"I think this one will be worth your time."

Odetts got out, grabbed the shotgun, and came around the car. MacIver said, "I want to tell you what happens to people who work for the Baron. What was the first thing you learned on the street about witnesses to a crime?" He kept his voice low and calm, and spoke deliberately, almost slowly. He wanted to bring Odetts down from his emotional high, get rid of his excitement, make him think.

Odetts looked blank at the question, and MacIver said, "Why did you kill that woman and her kid in the convenience store?"

Odetts frowned and then grinned. "Doesn't matter what I say now, does it?"

"Makes no difference. Why did you kill them?"

"So they couldn't identify me."

"No witnesses, right?"

"Yeah, sure. I learned that before I was out of grade school."

"Okay. Who's going to be a witness if you kill me?"

Odetts made a show of looking around the field. "I don't see nobody."

"Except you. You're going to be the witness, Len."

"That's different."

"Not to the Baron it isn't. Because you could involve him. He won't like that. He takes people out for that." MacIver had Odetts's attention now. "This is the story I wanted to tell you. We arrested two guys last Saturday night that I'm almost certain were working for the Baron. They were bonded out the next day at three P.M. At five o'clock they were both dead. Riddled with machine gun bullets and their bodies burned. How do you think he's going to feel about being involved in the murder of a police officer?"

"You're making all that up."

"I'm not making it up. You heard about that helicopter crash out by Bellville?"

"Yeah."

"Those were the guys I was talking about."

Some of Odetts's excitement had vanished. He looked across the car, frowning. "I'll collect my money and get out of town."

"He'll find you. He's got connections all over the country. Listen, Len, I can tell you how to get the fifty thousand dollars and not risk your life."

"Sure, you're going to pay me not to shoot you."

"I'm going to pay you to testify against the Baron."

Len rubbed his nose and sniffed. "That would get me dead for sure."

"No, it wouldn't. We'd give you police protection."

"I know a lot of people in the graveyard that were supposed to get police protection."

"He'll kill you, Leonard. I promise you. Now, you can have the money *and* go free if you do what I tell you. All you have to do is put down the gun and take off these handcuffs—"

"No, goddamit. You're tryin' to trick me. One reason I took this job is to show you what I could do. You know how you've always treated me, MacIver?"

"I treated you all right."

"You treated me like I was shit. You treated me like I was a two-bit hood, and I was for a while, but I'm not anymore. I've pulled some pretty good jobs. That store hijacking, I did everything right. I don't know how the hell you nailed me for that unless it was that motherfuckin' brother-in-law of mine."

"Okay, you did everything right."

"But when you arrested me, you acted just like you always did. I was still shit warmed over. I bet you don't treat the Baron like that."

"Yeah, I do. He's nothing but a pimp and a murderer."

"No, you respect him. Yeah, that's what I mean. You don't give me any respect."

Again MacIver felt a sense of the ridiculous. He was about to be killed because this sociopath wanted his respect. He wanted a pat on the head and Daddy to tell him he'd done good. Well, if that's what it took . . . "I never looked at it that way before, Len. I guess you're right. I guess you have learned to do your job well. You're a true professional."

Odetts thrust his shoulders back and held his head higher. "That's right. I am."

"You've gotten smarter, too. You know when a person is telling you the truth, and I'm telling you the truth about the Baron."

Odetts sagged again. "Well, I believe you. You never lied to me that I know of. But I said I'd kill you, Loot, and I guess I'm going to have to do it."

"No, you don't have to do it." But Odetts lifted the shotgun and MacIver looked down the black barrel. Another set of images flashed through his mind. He could see the pellets blasting out, crashing into his chest, his throat. At this range it would almost cut him in two. He forced his glance up to meet Odetts's, and felt a jolt as though he had run into a steel wall. In the second's interval that had passed, Odetts had made up his mind. His jaw was set. There was death in his eyes.

"Wait a minute." MacIver's voice came out in a croak. "Just listen to—" His voice was drowned out by the boom of a bullhorn. "Put down the gun. We've got you covered."

27

MacIver was as shocked as Odetts. He twisted in the seat to look for the source of the command. Odetts didn't look around. He screeched "Shit!" and jammed the shotgun against MacIver's forehead. The bullhorn blast came again. "This is Sergeant Noskrent with SWAT. My sniper has you in his sights. If you do not drop the weapon, you will die."

Odetts screamed, "I'll take him with me!"

MacIver said quickly, "Let me talk to them."

"Keep still."

"They're going to kill you, Leonard. There isn't time to argue." He shouted, "Hold your fire! This is Lieutenant MacIver. Hold your fire!"

The bullhorn blared. "We can't risk your life, sir."

"Give me two minutes."

After a hesitation, the bullhorn responded. "Two minutes. We are covering the suspect. Rose, notify command we have an officer-hostage situation here."

MacIver said, "They can drop you any instant. Don't try to shoot or you're dead."

"Not before I kill you."

"Yes, before. You've seen it on television. The sniper is watching your hand. If your finger starts to tighten on the trigger, he'll shoot. His bullet will hit you in the medulla oblongata. You'll die instantly, and there'll be no reflexive action so that you could shoot."

Odetts blinked. Sweat was dripping from his forehead and across his face. MacIver said, "Listen fast now. Take my deal. I'll give you the fifty thousand. Have I ever lied to

194

you? You remember the time I wanted information on that hijacking in Bellaire? I knew you were involved, but I promised that if you met me and gave me the name of the guy who did the shooting, you'd walk. You met me and you walked, remember?"

"Yeah, I walked but—"

"You'll get your money. I promise you that. You'll have the money and you'll be free. You put down the gun and you'll have it all. You don't put down the gun, you're a dead man."

Odetts blinked again. His shirt was wet with sweat, and the sour odor of body juices and fear emanated from him. MacIver pressed. "The SWAT snipers are accurate at two hundred yards and they're a lot closer than that. Leonard, put down the weapon."

"They'll kill me if I put it down."

"No, they won't. Leonard, the clock is ticking. You know the command they give? 'Let the man die.' In about thirty seconds they're going to give that command, and I promise you, you'll die. If you put down the gun, they won't shoot. Do what I tell you. Now!"

Odetts had begun to shake. "Okay. Tell them I'm putting it down."

MacIver shouted, "He's going to drop the weapon!"

A second passed. Odetts said, "You're sure they won't shoot?"

"Positive. They won't shoot. You're safe if you drop it."

Odetts exclaimed, "Goddamit to hell!" and dropped the weapon.

There had been only three of them—the sergeant, one officer, and the sniper—but they had been sufficient. The nurse at the doctor's office had been looking out the window when Odetts forced MacIver into the Trans Am. She knew it was the wrong car, and when she saw Odetts handcuff MacIver's arm around the car's center post, she called the police. Dispatch immediately notified SWAT. Patrol units located them on the freeway and Fox had picked them up by the time they reached 290. The roar of the wind in the car had covered the sound of the helicopter.

Sergenat Noskrent said, "Trouble was, everybody was out

of pocket. We three were all that showed up and we didn't have a negotiator. At least we had Pinky here. He would have blown the guy's head off like that." He snapped his fingers.

Odetts, leaning against the front of the Trans Am and trying to look nonchalant without success, twitched at the sound.

MacIver said, "You did just fine, all three of you. You saved my life, that's for sure." He turned to Leonard, who was still pasty and shaking, and asked, "Got your camera ready?"

"Yeah. Sure. It's in the car."

"Get it out. Let's take a practice shot."

Odetts's face turned hopeful. "You mean we really have a deal on Neimeyer?"

"I told you I'd never lied to you. Yes, we have a deal."

MacIver posed at the side of the car and Odetts took a picture. The camera worked the way it should. By that time an officer had returned with a bottle of catsup.

MacIver lay on the ground beside the car and closed his eyes while the sergeant poured catsup liberally over his chest and neck. There went another coat, MacIver thought. The cleaners would never get out all that catsup. The sergeant said, "Keep your eyes closed a minute, Loot. We're going to kick a little dirt over you to make it look real."

The three SWAT officers chuckled and chortled like children at a picnic as they kicked dirt and gravel over his face. MacIver sneezed. "Enough with the dirt. Let's get the goddam picture."

"Okay, open your eyes." MacIver opened them and stared fixedly as a dead man at the sky. He heard the whirr of the Polaroid. Odetts said, "Wait a minute. Let me get one closer up." Another whirr. "Okay, that ought to do it."

MacIver sat up and spat dirt out of his mouth. "Anybody got a towel?"

He didn't get clean until they reached the motel on the Katy Freeway. Rod met him there and the SWAT men took their leave. Rod said, "You look awful and you smell worse, Loot."

"Yeah, well, I don't feel too hot either. Get us something

to drink while I shower. I want a big glass of iced tea first and then a scotch and soda."

He was able to clean his body, but he had to put back on the catsup-and-dirt-covered clothes, which made him feel dirty again. He chugalugged the iced tea, and told Odetts, "Okay. You're going to call the Baron. Tell him you've got pictures of me dead. If he wants more proof, tell him you've got my identification and my service revolver."

Rodriguez said, "He wouldn't call it a service revolver."

MacIver took the weapon out of its holster. "What would you call this, Len?"

"I'd call it a piece."

"Okay. Say that, then. How're you feeling?"

"I'm feeling okay." Odetts had taken a turn in the bathroom after MacIver showered and he'd been much calmer since. MacIver guessed he'd either had a toot or a downer.

MacIver said, "No, I don't mean that. I mean, how would you be feeling if you'd killed me?"

Odetts thought a moment. "You want the truth?"

"Yeah."

"I think I'd be feeling pretty good. If the SWAT guys hadn't shown up, I mean."

"Okay, act that way. You want to do a practice run?"

"No, I'd rather just go on and do it."

"Okay. Tape ready, Sarge? You're on, Len."

Odetts dialed and asked for Mr. Neimeyer. A moment later they heard the Baron's rumbling voice. "Yeah?"

Odetts suddenly turned manic. "I've done it! I've done it! The son of a bitch is dead! I finally got him!"

The Baron said, "Calm down, will you? How'd he take it?"

"Right in the heart. Knocked him backwards about six feet."

"Was he scared?"

"Sure." Odetts glanced at MacIver. "He tried to talk me out of it."

"Was he on his knees?"

Odetts looked a question at MacIver. MacIver nodded, but Odetts said, "No, I gave it to him standing up."

"You got pictures?"

"Two."

197

"Any other proof?"

"His ID and his piece that he always wore at his waist. Is that enough?"

"Put everything in a sack. Meet me at the warehouse." That was the one that MacIver passed so frequently. The Baron said, "Make it in exactly two hours." The connection was broken.

Odetts wiped his face and grinned at MacIver. "Okay, huh?"

"You did very well, Lennie. I think you missed your calling. You should have been an actor. Now, I want you to be wearing a wire when you go in." Anticipating an argument, he added, "For two reasons. First it's to assure us, Lennie, that you're not telling us one thing and the Baron another. Second, it'll keep us advised on the progress of the payoff so we'll know when to come in."

Odetts shrugged. "That's okay with me. You can put it in my cowboy boot and run it up my back."

"No, I'm not going to run it up your back. That's where the Baron would expect to find it. I'm just going to run it up to your knee."

"Whatever. I *do* get to keep the money?"

"Yeah, Lennie, you get to keep the money."

Two hours later, Odetts crossed the oyster shell parking lot to the front door of the Texiana, Inc. warehouse. A transmitter was in his right boot with a flex antenna running up the inside of his leg. MacIver and Rodriguez were in an eight-cylinder Mustang Interceptor a block away. Three other units, also at a distance of approximately a block, ringed the warehouse. One of these contained Captain McNamee, who had announced he was going along on this operation to make sure nothing got screwed up. MacIver expected part of the reason was that he wanted to be on hand when they finally nailed the Baron.

The car radio was set on frequency 111.1 FM. MacIver listened to the crunch of Odetts's boots in the oyster shell. The footsteps changed sound as he reached the concrete porch. A door opened. Although he was expecting it, MacIver tensed when he heard the Baron's guttural voice. "Turn around, Odetts."

"What for? I'm not holding." Odetts's voice was higher than the Baron's, and there was an edge of excitement.

The Baron growled, "I can't take a chance at this stage." In the short silence that followed, MacIver imagined the Baron running a hand over Odetts's back and across his waist, and he smiled grimly to himself. Neimeyer wouldn't find the wire that way.

Odetts said, "Is that you over there, Pico?"

"Hi, Lennie."

"How you doin'?" Two sets of footsteps moved across the concrete floor. Paper rustled. Odetts said, "Here's what you need. Here's his ID." A billfold splatted onto wood. "Here's his gun." MacIver flinched as his forty-five struck the desk. That was no way to treat a weapon.

The Baron said, "Let me have the photographs."

Paper rustled again as they were taken out of the envelope. The mike was silent for several seconds. Finally the Baron spoke, his voice gloating. "I've waited a long time to see that motherfucker wasted. I just wish I'd been there."

"I did like you said," Odetts said eagerly. "Once I had him, I told him you were the one ordered it."

"What'd he say?"

"He asked how come you wanted to kill him? I said I didn't know."

"He knew, though. He knew, all right, son of a bitch. If I could've done it personally, MacIver, I'd've made you crawl first."

In the car, MacIver went rigid at hearing himself addressed. Then he realized the Baron must be speaking to the photos. A drawer opened. The Baron said, "Here's your money."

Odetts asked, "How much is in here?"

"Fifty thousand, as agreed."

Odetts giggled. "I'd've done it for half the price."

The Baron said, "And I'd've paid twice as much."

There was silence for a moment, and MacIver could imagine the tight smiles the two were exchanging. Then the Baron said, "I want you to count that. You can spread it out here on the desk."

"It's okay. I trust you."

MacIver thought that was the most laughable statement he'd heard all day. The Baron insisted. "Count it. I could've made a mistake of a thousand or so."

Paper rustled again. Odetts apparently was spreading the money out on the desk. The police radio cracked and captain McNamee said, "I've got eight-ten. At eight-twelve we go in. Respond." All units responded. Rod started the car.

The next instant a blast thundered through the transmitter, making the radio vibrate. It was followed a second later by a thud. MacIver yelled, "Aw, shit! They did Lennie. Go go go!"

Rod had already shifted into gear and the car squealed away from the curb. As they roared around the block, MacIver said, "Don't stop when we get there. Just drive on in."

"Gotcha!"

The car was doing thirty when it hit the doors. The wood and sheet metal splintered and gave way as the car exploded into the warehouse. MacIver, the nine-millimeter automatic he'd borrowed in his right hand, threw up his left arm for protection. The inside of the warehouse was dim. Rod had the headlights on, but one of them had been knocked out when the car hit the door. The car motor had died, and MacIver heard a voice screaming, "I don't have a gun! Don't shoot! I'm giving up!"

Then where the hell was the weapon that had blasted Odetts? MacIver, eyes adjusting to the dimness, dived out of the car and took a marksman's stance, holding the nine with both hands. The Baron was halfway across the warehouse, his hands up. Pico was at the back, his hands empty and aimed at the ceiling. He was the one who had called out. MacIver shouted, "Don't move, either of you, or I'll blow your goddamned heads off! Rod, check 'em out."

The Baron was staring at MacIver as though seeing a ghost. MacIver walked toward him, rapidly closing the distance between them and stopping only when their noses were almost touching. He glared at the Baron for several seconds. Then he said, "Anything you want to talk about?"

The Baron's mouth snapped closed. He looked toward the front of the room. "Odetts was wired! Fucking Odetts was wired."

200

MacIver said, "You got it."

The captain and several detectives had arrived. One officer called from the back, "I got the shotgun! He almost hit me with it when he slung it through the window. I was trying to make entry."

As Rod finished searching and handcuffing both men, MacIver holstered his gun and looked around for Odetts. The body lay in front of the desk. He walked over, looked at what remained, and swore, both with anger and regret. The captain joined him, and grimaced. "His own mother wouldn't be able to identify him."

"Nosir. I didn't think the Baron would make his move so fast."

"No, I thought they'd take him off the premises before trying to kill him. Don't feel guilty about it, Mac. Remember that three hours ago, he almost killed *you*."

"For the second time in ten days, no, I don't feel guilty." He had done what he had to do to get the Baron, and Odetts wasn't much of a loss to society. Still, Leonard had in a way been under MacIver's protection and MacIver had failed to keep him alive, and he felt bad about that.

McNamee said, "You almost gave me a heart attack when I heard you go through that door."

MacIver looked at the captain in surprise. He hadn't known his superior cared. The captain added, "I didn't know which vehicle you were driving. Thank goodness it was the high-mileage one. We can't afford to lose any of the good vehicles."

28 MacIver was eager to tell Suzanne the news, but he wanted to do it in person. He telephoned from the office. "I'm going to be busy here two or three hours, but I would consider it a privilege to take you out to dinner after that, if you feel like going."

"I'd love to if you think we can get to a restaurant and back without getting shot at, or blown up, or run down by a truck."

"I think we can manage. See you later."

It was well after dark when he finished his paperwork. He went home, showered again, and put on clean clothes.

Suzanne was wearing a dark green dress when she opened the door. He stepped inside, closed the door, and kissed her. "Um, you smell good."

"What's going on, Tony? What are you so happy about?"

"Do I look happy?"

"You look as if you'd just eaten a box of Godiva chocolates."

"I didn't, but I could stand a drink. I'll make it. Anything for you?"

"I'll have a glass of wine."

When he had made the drinks, he sat down on the couch and smiled at her. "Remember my asking if you had an enemy?"

"You've discovered one?"

"I asked if you'd ever hurt anybody, or could have been perceived to hurt anybody."

"And I said no."

"The problem was, I didn't ask the right question. Did you ever send anybody to jail?"

"No. Oh, you mean—Kurt Neimeyer? But that was years ago."

"Fifteen. He's got the memory of an elephant and the disposition of a rattlesnake."

"You don't mean he's been behind all this. I can't believe that. Fifteen years ago! Are you positive?"

"We arrested him this afternoon—"

She clasped her hands. "Thank God!"

"And we've got the evidence to put him away. Do you remember that jury, Suzanne? There were four women."

"The three you asked me about?"

He nodded. She stared at her wineglass. "There was a black woman. I do remember that. And a blond-haired woman, older. Mrs. Craddock! That's where I knew her, of course."

"And Hermione Schultz. You're the four he went after. And me. Why he picked only the women—if he did—I don't know."

"I do. That's the one thing that stands out clearly in my mind. The blond woman, Mrs. Craddock, told us, we four women, that we were going to have to stick together on this jury because the men would be somewhat inclined to see Neimeyer in a more sympathetic light. They might not approve of pimping, but they wouldn't consider it as reprehensible as we did. And she was right. If the four of us hadn't held out for a conviction, I don't think they would have found him guilty."

"He must have learned about that some way. And that might explain the time delay. He might only have found out about it recently."

"So he decided to get even." She shuddered, and then suddenly she sat up straight. "So it's over. It's not hanging over us anymore. It *is* over, isn't it? They're not going to turn him loose the way they did those other two?"

"He'll probably get out on bond," MacIver admitted. "But he'd be crazy to try anything then. I think we can relax. Not only relax but celebrate." He finished his drink. "Where would you like to go for dinner?"

29 The district attorney's office acted rapidly on the Neimeyer case and so did the 2045th District Court grand jury. Within hours after they were arrested, Kurt Herman Neimeyer and Joseph Salvatore Piccolo were indicted for the murder of Leonard Odetts. The judge set bond for one million in cash, and the pair, unable to produce it, were alternately sulking and ranting in the county jail.

The day after the indictment, Neimeyer's attorneys, headed by Silas Conover, found a judge who would reduce the bail to ten million in real property. Conover made calls to a long list of Neimeyer's acquaintances around the country and finally was able to satisfy the bond demand. The Baron and Pico left jail in the back of Conover's Mercedes.

MacIver heard the bad, but not unexpected, news that afternoon, and wondered if the Baron would put out another contract on him. Or maybe he already had.

Captain McNamee also had heard of Neimeyer's release. "It was inevitable, but we've got the indictment. He'll stand trial. We've done our part. The rest is up to the courts."

"Yessir." MacIver still wasn't happy about it.

"It's a waste of time to worry about what the courts are going to do."

"Yessir, I know." MacIver changed the subject. "I went out to the Baron's health studio and interviewed the people who had worked with Braden and Hicks while they were still employed there. Every one of them said they thought it was next to impossible that either of the guys had a venereal disease. Both men were fanatics about their health. They

204

didn't do drugs and they were *very* careful about their sexual partners."

"That's good news for the victims, the remaining ones, that is. Mac, I want to congratulate you on your handling of this case."

MacIver was surprised. "Thank you, Cap."

"I knew you could get it settled if you had the proper motivation. You really thought I was about to send you on a vacation, didn't you?"

"Yessir, I did." MacIver looked at the captain. McNamee smiled broadly. So did MacIver. He *still* believed it. It was hard to bullshit an old bullshitter.

Back in his office, he leaned back and stared out the window. He could see blue sky, but there was still a cloud and he didn't know why. Everything in his life was looking up. He'd arrested the Baron and solved the DARE cases, the captain was off his back, he was on better terms with his son, and Suzanne was safe and well. She was scheduled to meet him in about an hour in his apartment for dinner. Even the summer heat had finally broken. A cool front had moved in during the night and dropped the morning temperature to seventy-two degrees. So why wasn't he dancing with joy? Anticlimax, maybe. The letdown that came after an absorbing case. Whatever, there still definitely was a dark cloud hovering outside his window. He scowled at it and stood up. He had to drive out to Sharpstown and pick up the cat.

Neither Constance nor Jarratt was at home so he used his key to get in. Constance had left a large note on the kitchen table for Jarratt. "Be home by 2. Probably. Don't wait up. Love ya, Mom." She must be out for a big night. He waited for the familiar pinch of jealousy. It didn't come. He probed again. Nothing. He didn't care. He really didn't care. Maybe it was because of Suzanne, he thought, or maybe time had gotten around to healing this particular wound. "Anyway," he told Priscilla, "it's a good nonfeeling." He opened her carrier. "Time to move out."

In the parking garage, Priscilla began to show nervousness as soon as he transferred her to the paper sack. He whispered, "I've got news for you. I'm going to move to a ground-level apartment that accepts cats. I'll start looking

205

this weekend." He hadn't realized he'd made up his mind until this moment. Immediately he felt relief. High-rise living wasn't for him. He added, "You're the first to know. The point is, you're not going to have to make this ride many more times, so cool it."

Priscilla's meow sounded worried. They had reached the garage elevator. MacIver punched the button and the doors opened. The elevator was empty. He stepped on. Holding the sack with one hand, he punched the button for his floor. The doors began to close. Suddenly they were caught, held, forced open, and MacIver looked into the face of the Baron. Piccolo was at his side, holding a thirty-eight with a silencer pointed at MacIver's forehead.

Neimeyer said, "Don't go for your gun or you'll die now."

Pico motioned with his head toward the right. "Get over there."

MacIver moved sideways to the corner of the elevator. His forty-five nestled against his waist, back right side. He couldn't even make a move for it with the cat in his arms.

The two men stepped onto the elevator, Pico first. The gunman was a pro and taking no chances of MacIver's seizing his weapon. He held the thirty-eight close to his right hip and had his left arm fully extended toward MacIver, keeping him at a distance. The Baron released the doors. They closed and the elevator began to move up.

The Baron said, "Hell, you'd already punched the button. Well, you're going to live a little longer than I intended, shithead."

Priscilla shifted uneasily, and automatically MacIver tightened his hold. The Baron said, "We're going up and we're coming back down to the garage. Anybody gets on, if you make any hint that anything's wrong, they'll die along with you."

Buying a heartbeat, MacIver said the first thing that came into his mind. "Does this mean we're no longer friends?"

The Baron's eyes were deadly. "I've been planning to kill you for fifteen years. I used to plan how I'd do it when I was inside. Sometimes I think it was the only thing that kept me going."

"And the women?"

"Those bitches held out for conviction! I would have gotten off if it hadn't been for them. I just found that out a few months ago. Guy who'd been on the jury told Pico about it. So I decided to make them suffer a little."

"More than a little," MacIver said. "You killed two of them."

"The first one was an accident. The other—" He shrugged. "She was stubborn."

Priscilla gave a plaintive moan. The Baron said, "What the hell is that?"

"My cat. She doesn't like elevators."

"I don't like cats."

Priscilla began to thrash. Pico said, "Stand still!" The cat gave a convulsive leap toward the top of the sack. Neimeyer said, "Quit shifting around, MacIver."

"I can't help it. She's hard to hold."

"Then drop it."

"I'm going to have to. I can't hold her." As MacIver spoke, he gripped Priscilla's hind legs with his left hand, released his hold on the top of the sack, and shoved the cat upward. As she began clawing toward the surface, he whirled and jammed her full into Pico's face. All twenty claws were out and attempting to purchase a hold.

Pico's weapon went off, the shot crashing into the top of the elevator door. MacIver already had turned toward the Baron, who was reaching for his weapon. MacIver kicked with his right foot, catching the Baron in the groin. Off balance, MacIver fell backward, at the same time and in one motion drawing his automatic, snapping off the safety and bringing it around to shoot Pico.

Priscilla, using Pico's face as a launching pad, had sprung to the wall, richocheted off, and, apparently identifying the gunman as the cause of her woes, sprung onto his right shoulder, clawing and wailing as if demented. MacIver shot from the floor, aiming low to miss the cat. The bullet caught Pico in the middle body and he crumpled. As he fell, the cat leaped back to the carpeted wall and clung there, fur bristling and flying. The sound of the forty-five automatic thundered and reverberated in the confined space.

The Baron, in spite of his pain, had cleared his three-eighty Llama. He screamed, "You motherfu—" He never finished the epithet. MacIver shot him through his open mouth. The back of his head seemed to mushroom and then explode, splattering over the elevator wall and ceiling. He went down like a log, shot through the medulla.

Pico, bloody foam bubbling from his lips, was trying to raise his gun. MacIver rose to a crouch and leaned over the gunman. With his automatic an inch from Pico's forehead, he squeezed the trigger. The gunman's body lurched and went limp.

MacIver backed up, punched the Stop/Hold button, and holstered his gun. Two men had died between the fifth and the fourteenth floors.

EPILOGUE

Once he had stopped the elevator, MacIver mentally reviewed the procedure manual. He had to do things right now, follow procedure by the book, or he'd sure as hell wind up with an indictment against him. Priscilla was clinging to the carpeted side of the elevator close to the ceiling. He stepped across the Baron's body, plucked her off the wall, and held her tight against his chest.

"You did good, Pris. Calm down now. You did good." Her heart was thudding even harder than his, and her claws clutched his coat. He couldn't let her go because she would run around the elevator and he could be accused of allowing her to destroy evidence. Nor could he let her out of the elevator because he had to keep the crime scene sealed until reliable witnesses showed up. He stroked her. "Calm down, baby. That's it."

Holding her with one arm, he opened the emergency telephone compartment and rang the doorman downstairs.

"Rogers, this is Lieutenant MacIver. I'm on the elevator at the fourteenth floor. I've got an emergency here. I'll explain to you later. What I need you to do is patch me through to police headquarters. Can you manage that on your switchboard?"

"Yessir, I can do that."

Seconds later, the night commander came on the phone. "Captain Brightwell."

Priscilla was beginning to squirm, and MacIver tightened his hold on her as he identified himself. "Sir, I've been involved in a shooting. Will you please make a recording of my incoming call?"

"Certainly. Okay, you're on tape."

"I'm on elevator number two at the Towers." He gave the address. "I was assaulted by two men. We had a shootout. I think they're both dead." If they weren't, he'd been shooting blanks. "I've stopped the elevator and all evidence is intact."

Now for the important part. "Sir, I request a Homicide shooting team and an Internal Affairs shooting team and a supervisor of my rank or higher to be present at initial interviews. I also request that a representative of the Houston Police Officers Association legal counsel be present during all interviews with me."

Brightwell said, "Do you think that's necessary under these circumstances?"

"Captain, if I could, I'd get Jesus Christ to come down and be present to witness that I did this right."

A long twelve minutes later, Rogers rang the elevator. "Police in the garage, Lieutenant."

MacIver thanked him and took the elevator down.

Two hours later MacIver's part in the investigation of the scene was ended and he was free to go upstairs. He collected the cat from Rogers, who had found a cardboard carton to put her in, and took elevator one upstairs.

Suzanne had offered to prepare dinner in his apartment that evening so he rang the bell to signal that he was home, then unlocked the door, and walked in. He didn't want her to see him the way he was now, blood and splattered body parts all over his clothing, in his hair, scratch marks on his neck. Priscilla hadn't wanted to be held twelve minutes.

Suzanne had started toward the door, but when she saw him she stopped. "What happened? Are you all right?"

"I'm all right." He set the carton down, opened it, and Priscilla leaped out. "Would you give my little buddy here some food?"

"Yes, but—"

He didn't hear the rest of what she said. He supposed she'd get angry with him—Constance always did when he came home like this—but he needed desperately to cleanse everything about himself—his body, his mind, even his taste buds. He put ice and four fingers of scotch in a glass and headed for the bedroom, shedding apparel as he went. First the forty-five, watch, and signet ring. Shoes off, dropped as he stepped out of them. Tie and coat went on the floor. He didn't bother with buttons, but ripped the shirt open and peeled it off. Pants off. Still wearing socks and shorts, he grabbed up a long Italian cigar, bit off the end, and stuck the cigar in his mouth. It was only to chew on. It was the strongest thing he knew of besides garlic. He turned on the stereo, selected *Carmen,* and turned the volume to screamers level. As the music blasted through the room, he turned on the shower full blast, stepped into the Jacuzzi, leaned back in the tub and tra-laed with the music.

He had been in the tub ten minutes when the volume of the opera faded abruptly. Suzanne appeared at the door. She wore the long Mexican dress that looked as if it would peel off like a sheath, and carried a tray of crackers and cheese. "I thought you might like some food to go with that scotch."

He appreciated the gesture but he wasn't hungry. He motioned to the end of the tub. "Thanks, babe. Just set it there."

Keeping her eyes averted, she carried the tray to the tub and put it down. "Do you come home very often like that?"

"Not very often, and God willing, not again anytime soon." He thought he should tell her about the Baron and Pico, but he couldn't bear to bring back the images just now. Tomorrow, when he was rested.

She said, "I won't ask what happened."

"Thanks. I'll tell you, but not now."

She stood. "Well, I'll turn your music back up."

He stretched out a hand toward her. "You're not mad at me?"

She smiled and took his hand. "You always did have trouble with your prepositions, MacIver. I'm not mad *at* you; I'm mad *about* you."

"Lady, why don't you take off that pretty dress and come have a bath?"